Dario Lisiero

Castor and Pollux

ISBN 978-0-578-01942-0

Introduction

This story, set in modern times, transcends geographical and chronological barriers. It could have happened during the first Chinese dynasty or Charlemagne's conquests. It might likely occur with cosmetic variations in 2500 or 3000.

Time and space are not its defining characteristics. They happen to be there because of its earthly composition, spicing up what is already flaming hot by essence.

Its vital component, deeply ingrained in human nature, opens up a world of possibilities in the vast field of social behavior.

What is this mysterious and explosive detonator, abundantly researched and analyzed by psychologists, and yet vastly unknown like the dark side of a distant moon?

Its name is seduction, commonly associated with sexuality. However, its tentacles, far-reaching like the wrath of God, expand from the mineral to the vegetable and animal kingdoms.

This all-embracing reality is primarily a defense mechanism. Where predatorial actions constitute basic manifestations of life, seduction, attraction and camouflage are survival instruments compensating for any lack of size and strength.

Undoubtedly, the most basic instinct in nature is survival. The power of seduction turns out to be its best secret weapon.

Mother Nature, in her infinite wisdom, has endowed every creature on the planet with this cunning ability to stack up against overwhelming odds.

Instinctively and unconsciously, in the presence of danger, the survival instinct will put in motion the power of seduction, with an incredible display of forms, colors and smells that will neutralize the exposure and vulnerability.

In particular instances, it will step up its action, passing from a simple defensive posture to an offensive act of conquest and assimilation.

Seduction can be more successful than aggression and more lethal than pure violence.

In humans, seduction is commonly associated with bad intentions and devious conduct, while in animals similar connotations are obviously absent.

To what extent are free will and clear determination responsible for the guilty feelings arising from a behavioral response induced by seduction?

More to the point, is man always and everywhere in total control of his actions and therefore solely responsible for their outcome?

In jurisprudence there is an exculpatory mechanism called "for reason of insanity" that justifies heinous actions like murder.

Could seduction and deception, as primary unconscious processes of survival, become mitigating factors of otherwise inculpatory conduct?

Can man divest himself of the influence of basic instincts and proclaim himself the conqueror of nature? Some psychological and religious currents might induce you to believe so, but the truth is science and religion are far from a comprehensive understanding of human nature and its innermost drives.

In light of these sketchy considerations, one thing appears sure. Even in the most unselfish human decision, there is always a trace of seduction, deception or camouflage.

Self-interest and survival are in fact primary components of human nature and nobody can ever suppress them without at the same time destroying the essence of nature.

People can find impressive and startling descriptions of human actions, but their interpretation and evaluation will be more often than not subject to errors because of their awesome complexity.

The instinct for survival and procreation, with seduction as its secret weapon, is like an Ariadne's thread that gives meaning and keeps this unbelievable story together.

Kimiko Ishida's forbidden love, Castor and Pollux's undisclosed paternity, Fresco's and Nemoto's relentless investigations, underground racist movements and local criminal organizations, religious prelates in a frantic run to ecclesiastical stardom and potential unsettling scandals, are just some of the twists and turns of the present yarn, an unbelievable maze of raw passions, heroic acts and tragic decisions.

Human nature seems inexhaustible in its volcanic activity of spewing new magma of astonishing feats and debasing monstrosities.

The only thing left for the reader is to follow the intricate corridors of this labyrinth and surrender to their alluring attractiveness.

To live is to deceive and to deceive is to live.

Chapter 1

*"Men are so simple and so inclined to obey immediate needs that a **deceiver** will never lack victims for his **deceptions**."* – Niccolò Machiavelli

The murder scene was something resembling a horror movie. Nothing was left to the imagination and everything to fear, shock and consternation.

Detective Fresco, a veteran in the Pittsburgh Police Division, during his twenty years as chief investigator, had never encountered a bloody murder with similar characteristics, the most gruesome ever.

Even weeks after the fact, when trying to recollect the event, a cold shiver ran up his spine and a feeling of impotence gripped his soul.

What had happened in that modest student building on Lincoln Street probably nobody would ever know.

Before being sucked into the tragedy, Ken Fresco secured the crime scene with the clear intent of avoiding any contamination. How many times in the past had he and his colleagues lost a conviction because of the defense impugning their careless procedure in handling the initial investigation?

It would not happen this time under his watchful eyes. On the contrary, every move would be executed by the book. Immediately after that, his team took pictures of every single square inch of that room and from every possible angle.

Subsequently, the medical examiner was called in for the preliminary examination of the disfigured body.

While the adrenaline rush of the first minutes had simmered down and the detectives wrapped up their tedious proceedings, the examiner, Jack Stockdale, arrived.

His demeanor and disheveled appearance clearly conveyed a sense of annoyance and irritation ready to erupt at any moment.

He was not happy to have been dragged out of bed at six in the morning, and to make matters worse, to substitute for a fellow that loved partying more than his duties.

As soon as Jack distractedly observed the bloody scene, his self-absorption went out the window and a more professional attitude transpired from his body language.

He listened to the few disconnected pieces of information given by Ken. A student had informed the police of the tragic happening around five-thirty a.m., discovered by pure chance since a trail of blood led to the half-open door of the victim's room. As soon as he looked inside a scream of horror echoed ominously among the walls of that deserted corridor.

Terrified, he rushed away with only one thing in his mind's eye – the horrific image of a dead body with a crushed skull and blood splattered all over. He dialed 911. Almost unable to speak or utter a full sentence, he asked for help.

The timely arrival of Ken Fresco, with his investigative team, put an end to the eerie silence and the student complex became the focal point of onlookers and bystanders.

Ken immediately cordoned off the place, keeping the small crowd at bay, impatient for news. With his shoes protected by a transparent plastic cover, he entered the room, insufficiently illuminated by the pale luminescence coming from outside.

The moment he switched on the light, the indistinct objects came to life revealing their true colors and size. Unfortunately, what followed was extremely unpleasant for our detective.

The veteran of many crime investigations, with clinical eyes and a desensitized heart, was unprepared for what jumped out at him in that stuffy, smelly place.

The disorder was an added value to the horrendous sight. A young male of medium stature with a crushed skull, mutilated limbs and a brutally bashed torso, lay lifeless in a pool of blood.

The face, whose ethnic features had disappeared under the rabid fury of the killer, could not offer any identification clue.

The left eye, popped out of the socket, dangled down as if from a Halloween mask. The front teeth missing, the nose smashed in and no sign of one ear.

From a large crack in the front of the face, a gelatinous substance had emerged, covering what was left of the right eye and cheek. Some fragments of skin and blood-soaked hair stuck to the walls. These gave the impression of a futuristic painting where red and white were the only colors.

Who could make sense out of that horror? Ken Fresco, sick to his stomach, was waiting for the coroner's arrival. Meanwhile he mechanically evaluated a series of possibilities.

Was he dealing with a bizarre ritual sacrifice by a group of Satanists, choosing a random victim? Alternatively, was it a calculated and premeditated act of revenge for some serious insult or provocation?

Was it a crime of passion or ethnic cleansing? Who was responsible, a criminal organization or a single individual with no ties to organized crime?

Unaware of the confused murmurings around him, he was greeted by the medical examiner, Jack Stockdale. Being well acquainted, they addressed each other on a first-name basis.

"Hi, Ken, how can I be of service?"

"The usual," answered the detective, "Give me a preliminary report, including possible cause of death, probable weapon, and approximate time of passing."

Untouched by the gruesome reality, Jack, assisted by a young internist, moved closer to the corpse. Intensively observing that disfigured body and measuring its temperature, he came up with some unimpressive findings.

A powerful blow to the skull with a round, possibly wooden, instrument was the cause of death, which occurred within the previous ninety minutes or so. The killer or killers seemed determined to erase any distinguishing feature, brutalizing their intended victim beyond recognition. A complete report would be forthcoming from the coroner's office after the formal examination.

At the medical examiner's indication, the corpse was bagged and transferred to the morgue. Detective Ken Fresco and his men were left with an impossible task ahead.

No murder is perfect. No crime scene is mute. No hard-core criminal is immune to notoriety. The bug of fame will bite into his fertile imagination. Somehow, he will leave his personal signature, in a way that will eventually separate his actions from any other real or presumed competitor.

Time, patience and intuition, combined with good police work, would pay off in the end. No rush to conclusions, no sloppy investigations, no instant gratification could be part of Ken's frame of mind.

He would conduct himself in the most professional manner. A well-deserved reputation and an irreprehensible career could not be jeopardized by an impulsive or reckless move.

Any crime scene has a back-story. This should come to light slowly under a relentless pursuit of the truth and painstaking attention to detail.

Apart from the murder scene, marked by brutality and blood, Ken had no knowledge of the victim.

Who was the poor soul crying out for justice in his muted condition? The still-absorbed detective did not have to wait long for that piece of information. The manager of those apartments, at the news of a murder in his complex, arrived in a state of shock. Stumbling over his words, he gave the name of the tenant, his age, and nationality.

He was a twenty-four-year-old Japanese man, on a student visa, taking post-graduate courses on Immunology at Pittsburgh University. His name was Castoru Ishida.

When the manager inquired about his brother, Detective Fresco was taken by surprise. It was true there were two beds in the room, but he would never have thought of a sibling sharing the same flat. That was certainly an unexpected twist in a murder mystery, so atypical and bizarre at the same time.

Where was the brother? Was he the assassin, leaving the incriminating scene after massacring his brother?

Speculations were rampant and immediately the brother came under suspicion. His absence, that early in the morning, increased the odds of his involvement. That was the first credible clue worth following. The investigation was taking off on a positive note, at least in Ken's perception.

This preliminary framework had a sudden jolt, of considerable magnitude, when, out of nowhere, Castoru's brother showed up in a jogging suit, sweating and breathing heavily.

The commotion, in addition to the police presence at the door of his room, startled him. He forced himself through the cordoned-off area, but he was stopped forcefully by a police officer.

In good English, but with a strong accent, the youngster, panting for breath, said, "I live here; can I get into my room and change?"

"This is a murder scene," answered the officer, "nobody is allowed in."

Ken Fresco, who had listened to the short exchange, asked, "Who are you?"

The young man, slowly perceiving the implications of that police presence, looked positively shocked. With his mind somewhere else, he replied, "My name is Polluxe Ishida, and my brother is in there."

In a softened tone of voice, Ken grabbed his left arm and pulled him closer. After leaning over him in a confidential way, he whispered something in his ear. No discernible reaction showed in Polluxe's face and posture.

Everything seemed instantly frozen and petrified in that vibrant, exuberant student. Ken, observing every slight movement and body language, was totally put off by that lack of reaction. Either Polluxe was a great actor or he was really shaken to the core by the dire news.

Assuming a pretended air of concern, the veteran detective politely asked the young man to follow him to the police station.

"Am I a suspect?" asked Polluxe with imploring eyes. "Just a person of interest, with a great knowledge of the victim," was the answer.

"Can I see my brother?" implored the sibling, finally letting his emotions surface. He tried to fight them back, but a few tears welled up in his eyes.

"This is not the right moment. It would be extremely painful for you. It is better to remember your brother as he was. After the coroner has done his job, we shall accompany you to the morgue for the proper identification. Meanwhile, at the police station, we need to ask you some pertinent questions."

Without taking a quick peek at his brother and without being able to change, he reluctantly followed the detective into the official car.

At the police headquarters, he sat in a small cubicle, staring into space. The wait before the interrogation seemed an eternity. Every move, every sound, was perceived in a different light. His heart was sinking into the depths of despair. Alone, far away from his country and family, he felt his small world had collapsed. Overwhelming feelings of impotence darkened the reduced space of his perception. It was a frightening sensation, never experienced before.

Finally, the lead detective, Ken Fresco, stepped into the cubicle and, looking calm and relaxed, addressed the shaky, young student.

"You are free to answer my questions. If you require a lawyer, it will be provided at no cost to you. All your statements will be recorded and could be used against you in a court of law. Do you understand me?"

"Yes," Polluxe responded in a trembling voice, "I don't have anything to hide and I don't need a lawyer."

"Then let us proceed," said Fresco, "Can I have your full name?"

"Polluxe Kento Ishida."

"Nationality and date of birth."

"I am Japanese and I was born in Kyoto, June 8, 1984."

"Your parents' names."

"My mother's name is Kimiko Ishida and my father's name is Hiro Kimura."

"Do you have brothers and sisters?"

"Only one brother. His name is Castoru Seizo Ishida. He was born in Kyoto, June 8, 1984."

"Are you twins?"

"Yes."

It is not easy to describe Ken's huge surprise at this revelation. Superseding his impulses of incredulity, as if nothing abnormal had been said, he continued with his interrogation.

"At what time did you leave your apartment this morning?"

"I left around four-thirty a.m."

"When you left, did you notice anything unusual around you?"

"No, everything was normal."

"Did you see anybody in the proximity of the students' complex?"

"Nobody that caught my attention, even though I heard some muffled voices coming from somewhere. I did not pay any attention and went straight to the nearby park. Following the jogging trail I started my morning exercise."

"Can anybody corroborate what you just said?"

"You mean did anybody see me?"

"Yes."

"Every morning I meet a middle-aged couple. Today we exchanged greetings and went our separate ways."

"Can you describe them?"

"Sure!" said Polluxe. He gave a summary description and added, "You can meet them in the park around five a.m."

"I will do that," said the detective. After a pensive pause, he asked, "Did you hear or see anything else while jogging?"

Polluxe frowned with concentration, trying to recollect. Nothing came to mind. However, unexpectedly he came up with something that left Ken not knowing what to think or say.

"I just remember hearing a very peculiar noise, unidentifiable at first. After a while, the screeching sound turned familiar. It was an owl hooting nearby. However, the most unusual thing happened next. That crepuscular bird of prey followed me, as if it wanted to deliver a personal message."

"What are you suggesting?" asked Ken Fresco.

With an impenetrable facial expression, the student elaborated on his last statement. "It is widely known that owls have fascinated people from time immemorial. To some cultures, they are symbols of wisdom, while to others they are harbingers of doom and death."

Struck by a supersensory flash of inspiration, Ken insisted, "Are you saying the owl, in its twilight activity, forewarned you of your brother's impending death?"

"That appears to be the significance of such an ominous occurrence. Twins are special creatures that communicate on a superior level. United at birth, they will not separate in death."

Ken remained mesmerized by that stoic philosophical posture, so engrained in the oriental, and particularly the Japanese, culture.

Shrugging off his sudden pensiveness, Ken went back to his previous matter-of-fact posture. "Do you recall anything else that might be pertinent to this investigation?"

"No!" answered the detached young man. Overwhelmed by fatality, he sat staring into space. His delicate, sensitive nature had been frozen. Finally, the harsh reality was taking hold of him. Nobody should carry so heavy a burden alone, let alone somebody of that age.

The detective, perceiving the slow psychological inversion in that poor soul, in a soothing voice said, "This is all for now. If something relevant comes to mind, please let me know. I will assign a detective that will provide you with new accommodation. Later on, he will take you to the morgue for the official identification of your brother. After we break the news to your family, you will be able to talk to your mom and dad."

Having said that, Ken escorted Polluxe out of the cubicle and assigned him a young woman detective.

Returning to his desk, Fresco had some serious thinking to do.

In the first place, he had to verify the alibi, comparing the time of death established by the medical examiner and the encounter of Polluxe with the middle-aged couple on the jogging trail. For this, he had to wait until the following morning.

In the second place, there was something that bothered him, which he could not reconcile with his notion of ethnicity.

Polluxe did not even blink when he affirmed that his parents were Japanese. However, his looks were more Caucasian than Asian. How could that be possible?

He was not an expert in genetics, but a sure anomaly was present in that scared youngster.

After the coroner's complete examination of the twin brother, in which he would certainly establish the race, that mystery could receive a solution.

Utterly intrigued by this first puzzle, with an air of dissatisfaction Ken left his office and went for a cup of coffee. A few sips were enough to convince him the idea was bad. The coffee tasted disgusting, it was stale and lukewarm.

Back at his desk and with half his usual concentration, Ken flipped through the crime scene photos in a concealed attempt to kill some time. Clearly, it was a routine impulse deprived of any clear objective.

All of a sudden, he observed something unusual in one of the pictures. On the wall behind Castoru's bed, a sign seemed depicted, but whether intentionally or by chance, he could not determine.

It looked like a letter of the alphabet, a capital X. It could be interpreted also as a St. Andrew's cross (or Crux decussata, X-cross, saltire cross). Was that the killer's signature, or just a freak accident produced by the splattering of blood?

Ken Fresco, who during his long investigative career had encountered numerous bizarre findings, would not discount anything. He would let the experts in blood-splattered walls decide the relevance of the alleged symbol. Whether it was a solid clue and a viable interpretational key was not in his hands. He had to wait.

A phone call diverted his attention away from the pictures. The medical examiner was on line two, telling him he had completed the autopsy report. He was forwarding it to him in an e-mail attachment.

Ken rushed to his computer and after a few clicks the document was under his inquisitive eyes. Useless to say, Castoru's ethnicity was unmistakably Asian. The time of death was approximately five-thirty a.m. The fractured skull contained a minute wood splinter and some unidentified fibers. No other relevant elements emerged from the medical examination. However, the ones brought to light were sufficient to transform Ken's initial mood.

Polluxe, escorted by the caring detective Mary Rosenthal, was not very talkative. To her questions, he simply answered "yes" or "no," without volunteering any further information. He was assigned a new apartment in the same student complex, after collecting his belongings from the crime scene.

Back at the police station, Polluxe assisted Ken in getting in touch with his parents. In spite of the awkward time (the wee hours in Japan) and the heavy accent of the translator, the detective broke the news to the mother.

A long silence ensued during which Ken remained immobile. Believing his basic duty was over, he handed the phone to Polluxe.

As soon as the young boy heard his mother's voice, he burst into tears. It was the final much-needed catharsis, through which the internal suffering broke out with some uncontrolled vehemence.

The conversation, halted and interrupted several times, did not last very long. The therapeutic effect of hearing a familiar voice could not erase the overwhelming sense of guilt for not having protected his twin brother.

The phone was back in Ken's hand, while Polluxe furtively dried his eyes. He gave the impression of wanting to disappear from the face of the earth.

The time had come for the proper identification of his brother's corpse. If he broke down at the sound of his mother's voice, what would happen at the sight of his slain twin? Since they were born, their lives had been inseparable. He had always been his big brother, his protector and defender. In spite of their differences, they complemented each other in a way incomprehensible to outsiders.

At the morgue, the smell of chemicals, the pervasive odor of detergents and the suffuse light created a surreal atmosphere. The presence of dead bodies added drama to the already surcharged environment.

The medical examiner in his hospital-like attire accompanied our visitors, Polluxe and Mary Rosenthal, to the refrigerated area. Looking into the eyes of his visitors, he asked, "Are you ready?" Mary held the shaky boy's right hand, waiting for an answer.

Polluxe hesitated for a moment. At the coroner's insistence, he voiced out of necessity a meager "yes." Then the man, who seemed in a hurry, slid the corpse out of the refrigerated receptacle, uncovered the face and asked, "Is this your brother?"

Shaky on his feet and stressed by the unusual ordeal of that unfortunate day, Polluxe wanted to hug his brother and resuscitate him with his breath of life. Was it possible to bring him back? How much he wished for a miracle in that very instant. However, none would ever materialize. Everything was real. His brother was gone for good. An arctic chill went up his spinal cord and a suffocating sensation took hold of him. Before losing his mind and his consciousness, he kissed that inanimate body and with a frail voice said, "Yes, this is my brother."

He kept staring at Castoru, unwilling to let him go. Finally, the coroner pushed the brother back into that gelid place.

"When the investigation is over," the coroner explained, "the body will be flown back to your family in Japan."

Polluxe raised his hand in a farewell gesture and slowly, silently, almost afraid of disturbing his brother's eternal sleep, walked away. All had been so prosaic, ordinary and unremarkable that he felt extremely dissatisfied.

Unfortunately, the circumstances, the place and the company were not conducive to a deeply heartfelt ceremonial encounter like the ones performed in his homeland on similar occasions. The absence of fuming incense, the total lack of flickering candlelight, the non-existence of weeping relatives, prayers or chants made those few empty instants more solitary and deprived of meaning.

Polluxe never felt so out of place, so insignificant and powerless. Everything seemed to conspire against him. He needed superhuman strength to face the immediate future.

His tranquil life had an abrupt end that fatal day, marking him with an ugly scar, that of a suspect. His small but comfortable world had crashed down with unimaginable fury. His reserved, almost stoic attitude, so embedded in his national character, was ready to burst out, uncovering a volcano of emotions never before experienced.

Would anybody be able to come to his rescue before he was swallowed up by a magma of burning lava?

Mary Rosenthal, the accompanying detective, the only one who could have helped him, was not there to reassure or comfort the poor lad, in spite of what her feminine instinct told her. Deep down she was certain the boy was above suspicion, that his feelings were genuine and he should be treated with great consideration. Nobody would convince her otherwise. It was the classic case of bad things happening to good people.

Contrary to her instincts, she maintained a professional poise. The lessons at the Academy told her not to become emotionally involved with the case. In that particular instance, it was not easy at all.

Back at the police station, Ken Fresco noticed the perplexed expression on Mary's face. To her detriment, she was like on open book, unable to hide her true feelings.

Ken wasted no time with perfunctory questions or unsubstantiated comments. He reminded her that a detective's basic mission was to collect evidence, explore motives and opportunities, and find the murder weapon. Nothing should be assumed and everything verified.

For Mary, this came like a slap in the face and an unwarranted criticism. However, Ken, with his penetrating look and almost jovial mood, patted her gently on the back and whispered, "Take the boy back to his new apartment and go home. Tomorrow will be a brand-new day."

Indeed, the following morning was a totally new day, rich with surprises and stumbling blocks. The middle-aged couple unequivocally confirmed Polluxe's alibi. Not only was the time of their rendezvous in the park perfect, they also lavished the detective with a considerable amount of unsolicited details.

The young jogger was wearing a baseball cap with the L.A. Dodgers logo and a Seattle Mariners jersey with the number fifty-one on the back. That appeared quite odd to the couple. Any true fan would never simultaneously show allegiance to two rival teams. However, the most astonishing piece of recollection was the extemporaneous hooting of an owl. They had jogged in that park for years, and that was the first time the peculiar sound of such a bird reached their ears. They suspected an impending storm was brewing not far away, displacing animals and birds into unfamiliar territories. Nevertheless, no storms, or strange weather patterns, were ever recorded for that region in that period.

They brought up some other details, like the foreign accent and mannerism in greeting, which would make the jogger unmistakable.

Unfortunately, along with this abundance of information corroborating Polluxe's alibi came some serious damaging testimony and a potentially explosive finding.

A student, residing next door to the twins – the one who alerted the police of the crime scene – in his interrogation told Ken Fresco the brothers had a heated argument the night before that went on for quite a while. He was tempted to knock on the door and tell them to keep it down, but instead chose to raise the volume of his television.

Since they were arguing in Japanese, he could not grasp anything, except for one name that surfaced now and then. That name was Susan.

Slowly, the investigation was unearthing disturbing details that could cast a shadow on Polluxe's credibility.

Then, to make matters worse, a bloody murder weapon, a baseball bat, was found under a pile of dead leaves in the park. The bat belonged to Polluxe.

Confronted with these serious allegations by Ken, the student did not look startled or shaken, on the contrary impassive, almost stoic, he presented his version of the facts.

The night before the murder, he had argued rather forcefully with his brother, as he had on previous occasions. The argument was over the allowance money received monthly by his parents. Castoru was overspending, trying to impress his girlfriend, Susan, leaving him high and dry. Susan, extremely attractive, but selfish and greedy, would not hesitate to take advantage of his weak character, imposing her whims on him.

Polluxe made every effort to open his brother's eyes, and to reason with him. However, Castoru, completely infatuated as he was, would not listen to his brother; moreover, he accused him of misperception and jealousy.

That ongoing battle irritated him in the extreme. However, it would have been totally out of character to kill his brother over that disagreement. He loved his sibling deeply and could never imagine hurting him, let alone killing him.

Concerning the second allegation, he did not even know his bat was missing. He had always kept it under his bed and could not even remember the last time he had used it.

Polluxe wanted to clarify another detail, related to his mismatched attire. He wore a Dodgers' cap in honor of Hideo Nomo and a Mariners' jersey with Ichiro Suzuki's number. As a baseball fan, those were his two greatest Japanese sports heroes.

No sooner had he concluded with his explanations than Ken's phone started ringing.

Another detective, Charlie Wilson, had come across an eyewitness that swore he had seen somebody resembling Polluxe fleeing the crime scene at ten minutes past five.

This new discovery left Fresco rather disconcerted. Even the alleged airtight alibi of the middle-aged couple greeting him in the park seemed on shaky ground.

From the look on Ken's face Polluxe understood his position was worsening. What looked up to that point an easy ride, was transforming itself into a bumpy one.

Sensing the difficulty of the moment, the young lad stared at the detective, waiting for a comment, which never came. Instead, Ken gave an unequivocal order to detain him for seventy-two hours, time necessary to carry out some additional investigations.

Polluxe experienced the world caving in, and the distinction between fair and unfair, wrong and right, totally blurred and fell away.

The sudden reversal of fortune, so often read about in novels and watched in movies, had become his lot. The difference was that this was not fiction; it pertained to his real life.

An excruciating pain, unimaginable a few days or even a few hours before, started eating away his self-confidence and respectability, plunging him into a sea of annihilation.

The only person that seemed sympathetic toward him was Detective Mary.

She maintained, throughout the whole ordeal, the clear conviction that Polluxe was innocent. No proof, however smashing it would turn out to be, would ever convince her otherwise.

She suggested a polygraph test, to which the student was submitted almost immediately. To her dismay, the test was inconclusive. To the question, "Did you hate your brother?" he answered "no" and the test revealed that was a lie.

Doubts, suspicions, accusations were piling up with no end in sight. He needed a super-lawyer to get him out of that strangling entanglement.

Was the murder weapon and a powerful motive enough for the prosecution to prove beyond reasonable doubt that Polluxe was guilty?

Alternatively, would the defense discredit the prosecution's strategy, demolishing their evidence in light of the middle-aged couple's testimony?

At this point, nobody was confident of succeeding in a court of law. Too much was at stake and any rush to judgment could be highly detrimental.

A long cooling period was in order.

However, the problem with these tactics was too familiar. If a timeout could be beneficial to the investigation, the passing of hours and days would cool off clues and the trail, converting that hot case into a cold one.

Nobody was more aware of that ineluctable possibility than Ken Fresco was. In his long career as a detective, he had seen too many excellent opportunities fade away in a mist of bureaucratic delays and partisan obstructionism.

A delicate balancing act was required for a successful outcome. This was not a subject taught at the Police Academy and very few could claim such a gift. Unfortunately, for various reasons Fresco, Rosenthal, Wilson and the rest of the gang were not among them.

Their eagerness and hard work to solve the case were admirable, but their skills and judgment at times were lacking, making them vulnerable to setbacks and mistakes. Far from being a dream team or an unbeatable bunch of sleuths, like the ones portrayed on *CSI*, they were human, fallible and fundamentally imperfect. This notwithstanding, they had one thing in common with the superheroes of the small screen – they were ready to sacrifice their own comfort and reputations in order to bring justice to their victims and the victims' relatives.

Chapter 2

*"Life is the art of being well **deceived**; and in order that the **deception** may succeed it must be habitual and uninterrupted."* – William Hazlitt

Three days had passed since the brutal murder of the Japanese student Castor. (The victim had an Americanized name, while his twin brother was known as Pollux. From now on, those will be their official names.)

In the meantime, no new evidence had emerged or new determining facts come to light. Everything seemed stagnant, irresponsive and leading to nowhere.

Ken Fresco assembled his team for a strategy session. It was urgent to revive the investigation by injecting some energy and enthusiasm into his men.

He presented a brief summary of their findings indicating viable directions for their future work.

There was a possible suspect, Pollux, but not enough evidence to treat him as such. They were in possession of the murder weapon and the discovered motive appeared plausible enough. However, the alibi, even if contradicted by an eyewitness, seemed so solid it could demolish any adverse evidence and withstand any prosecutorial storm.

In this quasi-perfect picture, a grey-area background required immediate attention. That strange symbol on the wall resembling an X needed a scientific description and a possible source of origin.

Was it manmade or just the unintended result of blood splattering?

Was it related to some underground organization or international criminal group?

Did it have any correspondent symbol among the many Japanese characters?

The blood relation of the twins presented a seemingly disconcerting puzzle as well. In fact, they were completely ethnically dissimilar. Only a paternity test could dispel any doubt on the subject.

Finally, was the middle-aged couple who made the alibi almost impregnable in any way connected with the student?

At the end of his presentation, Ken requested some input from the members of his team. During the heated exchange that ensued, an ill-disguised tension between Mary Rosenthal and Charlie Wilson could not be overlooked.

Charlie accused Mary of being partial to Pollux. He described her as emotionally attached to him. That was obviously clouding her professional judgment and jeopardizing the case. Mary did not hesitate to defend herself by portraying Charlie as jealous and resentful. In fact, she had constantly refused his not-so-veiled sexual advances and was tired of putting up with his male aggressiveness.

Finally, the tension, sexual in nature, was in the open. Now the imperfect team was starting to show its raw humanity and its true colors.

Not that before nobody had noticed anything, only it was regarded as a private matter, without consequences within the professional sphere. However, after those public accusations that was no longer the case.

Nobody of sound mind would dare to dismiss it as inconsequential, much less Ken, so uneasy with office dramas, personality clashes and go-getting careerisms.

The chief detective publicly formulated a stern warning against Charlie to stay away from Mary and to invest his exuberant energies in something more constructive, like salvaging his second marriage, after having sunk the first one.

As tangible punishment and to remove any possible temptation he would never partner with any female in the foreseeable future. At the present time, to facilitate the return to the path of righteousness he should be relegated to office work for six months. On top of that, an internal affair panel would evaluate his performance with appropriate recommendations.

It was obvious Charlie would not get a commendation for Detective of the Year anytime soon, nor for Husband of the Year.

On the other hand, Mary received her admonition too. Any kind of sexual harassment had to be reported at once. Her conduct should be professional at all times with no attachments or favoritisms of any sort.

Openness and forthrightness should be a basic trademark in her dealings with superiors.

After this public rebuke that left everybody on edge, Ken adjourned the meeting believing order and trust had been restored and smooth sailing lay ahead.

He could not have imagined how wrong he was.

The news of Castor Ishida's murder hit the Land of the Rising Sun hard. All of a sudden, the nation was totally gripped by an insatiable curiosity. Everybody, from street people to politicians, from common folk to professionals, was taken in by that unbelievable story on foreign soil.

The victim was the son of a prominent industrialist family that commanded respect and admiration at home and abroad.

Who could possibly have dared to provoke and antagonize that distinguished dynasty in such a senseless way?

Castor's mother, heiress to a huge economic empire, did not waste any time or money sending a private investigator, by the name of Jinpachi Nemoto, and a lawyer, Taisuke Fujii, both bilingual, to America. Besides assisting their counterparts in Pittsburgh, they would carry out research at their own discretion and in complete secrecy, sending daily reports of their findings to the distrustful family.

The visual and written media did not spare any effort or financial resources either. An army of reporters, writers and correspondents landed in the "Steel City," exhausting all possible accommodation in town.

Every restaurant, café, or meeting place swarmed with people in black suits. They were armed with cameras and microphones, repeating with politeness and annoying persistence, "Please, please."

The Pittsburghers had never seen such a bizarre spectacle in their quiet city. After learning the powerful connections of the unknown student, they could make some sense out of it.

The police too, clueless up to that point, appeared restless and unsettled. The small internal problems subsided and Ken Fresco and his team had to refocus.

Being under the foreign press' microscope was not the most conducive atmosphere. The murder of a foreign student was no longer a local affair. It possessed incredible ramifications, reaching the State Department and affecting the good relations between two economic superpowers.

Strings were pulled subtly from both sides and a considerable amount of money flowed from one pocket to another.

The first person feeling the pressure was obviously Ken Fresco, whose superiors demanded a speedy and impeccable resolution to the case. His only fear was that the notoriety of the case would bring in the FBI. It was already bothersome and annoying to deal with two meddling Japanese experts. However, it would be much more aggravating and disturbing to share authority with a federal investigator.

Ken's initial confidence and determination in solving the case quickly and with diligence went out of the window.

The media coverage, so persistent and pervasive, had to be kept on a leash, imposing a total blackout on the dissemination of any findings or rampant speculations. Easier said than done.

Would the local detectives abide by the stringent rules imposed by their boss? Or would somebody, at the glitter of money, cave in, selling sensitive information?

Besides the personal reputation of every member of the team, something more important was at stake. The whole nation was being scrutinized and its detective skills and methods put to the test.

Would they withstand the inevitable attacks and criticism pouring down from the foreign press, so emotionally invested and so difficult to please?

The race was on and the outcome unforeseeable. Too many variables surrounded that cause célèbre and what would happen next was anybody's guess.

Ken Fresco, on tenterhooks for the unpredictability of the situation, had a long, circumspect talk with the newcomers, the private detective and the lawyer, establishing the ground rules.

Jinpachi and Taisuke, who preferred to be called Jin and Tai, during Ken's long conversation, maintained poker faces, at times even condescending.

The American did not want to read too much into that perceived unfriendly posture. He knew he was facing a different culture and could easily get carried away by cool, reserved body language.

He also had been informed that Jin and Tai had a separate encounter with their client over a lavish Japanese dinner, where sushi and sake had been served in abundance.

Jin and Tai were two worlds apart, for the social status of their family and for their upbringing. Tai belonged to a Tokyo dynasty, with numerous lawyers, politicians and diplomats among its ranks, while Jin derived his roots from rice-farming peasants. With views culturally and ideologically irreconcilable and with contradictory manners, they had to accomplish the same mission. They had to provide their distinguished client with the best investigation and a superior defense. Anything below that standard would be unacceptable.

Tai was well mannered, sophisticated and possessed a sharp mind, while Jin appeared sloppy, a simpleton and with scarce intellectual resources.

Nothing could describe them better than a court TV drama with Perry Mason and Colombo working side by side.

Regrettably, this was not a beautifully pre-packed make-believe drama of the small screen. It was a real life-and-death situation, where the future of a young man, the offspring of a prominent family, hung in the balance.

Jin and Tai, however different, even contrasting, in their styles and methods, had their work cut out for them.

Both had long private conversations with their client. The version presented by Pollux contained stark differences with the police reconstruction. Obviously, they had great faith in their young lad, despite the powerful motive and the murder weapon. The whole matter, besides being out of character and culturally improbable, had all the signs of being a Machiavellian setup, a criminal trap, purposely set to ensnare the naïve foreigner.

The investigation should pursue different avenues, exploring, for instance, the sign on the wall and unearthing possible underground organizations among students and outside the academic world, within organized crime.

When Ken met with Jin, something unexpected happened. Ken listened, with a sympathetic ear, to every single word pronounced by Jin and agreed wholeheartedly with his point of view. However, he had in mind a different set of priorities.

In the spirit of collaboration and avoiding any confrontational posturing, so common in those circumstances, Ken tried to incorporate his Japanese counterpart, assigning him a very specific task.

That move, underhand to all appearances, could produce beneficial results for all parties involved.

Jin's task was delicate but essential in solving the ethnic puzzle, which so bothered the American detective. His mission was to return to Japan with a DNA sample of the twins and compare it with a DNA sample of the parents. If any discrepancy should arise, Jin had to dig into the marriage history and possible extramarital affairs.

Being a prominent family, the utmost discretion and delicacy was necessary. Could that man, a little sloppy, rusty on the outside, and acting in a rough and awkward way, accomplish the miracle?

Was Ken Fresco sending a bull into a china shop? That seemed like a real gamble and optimism in a positive result a luxury.

For Tai, the lawyer, there were no special requests, just friendly handshakes and polite smiles. But the well-mannered, high-profile attorney wasted no time. With punctilious accuracy and surgical precision, he started evaluating every shred of evidence given by the police and his client, weighing up the pros and cons.

Under the acumen of his bright intellect, words and events acquired unsuspected dimensions and showed unbelievable connections. The jurisprudence expert, like a scientist with an atomic force microscope, imaged, measured and manipulated to his advantage every move, shade and projection of that highly disturbing murder, bringing out from the crime scene and its protagonists, real or imaginary, a symphony of possibilities, which would please the most discriminating criminalist's ear.

Tai, more conscientious than a brain surgeon, worked tirelessly, burning the candle at both ends.

Somebody else was also working her way through the huge amount of information, but with a different purpose and intensity.

A young reporter from *The Pittsburgh Gazette*, by the name of Lilly Porter, was faced with fierce Japanese competition. To be first in reporting something new was all that mattered in that kind of business. Regrettably, whether it was accurate or not did not amount to much.

Her youth and looks worked like a charm with Charlie Wilson, recently demoted to a desk clerk. He had easy access to any police information and was extremely vulnerable to her feminine allure.

Lilly, who had inside knowledge of the man through her friend Susan, had him under her thumb with a skirt and a smile.

It was a sad spectacle to see the scorned detective fall blindly for a peppy, vivacious reporter, ready to betray the most sacred thing in his life – his marriage – and dance, like a subjugated bull, to her tune.

An invitation to dinner was a standard practice for the venal police officer. Obviously, that was Lilly's coveted plan. With a good meal and an extra glass of wine, Charlie would sing like a canary and the sneaky reporter would obtain the latest scoop.

Pollux, virtually under house arrest, on his counsel's advice suspended all academic activities. His dream of becoming a researcher in molecular and pharmacological biology remained a pure abstract entity in the realm of possibilities.

His heart's desire of working with his twin brother was tragically cut short by a cruel destiny. It lay at his feet like a broken piece of fine porcelain. He felt completely impotent to put it back together.

Confusion, desperation and hopelessness were mild words to describe his inner feelings.

Without Tai's legal assistance and warm support, the poor lad could have easily broken down under the pressure of public opinion and the rough handling from law enforcement.

Those were trying times for the student who had seen nothing but comfort, love and understanding during his entire life. Nobody and nothing had ever prepared him for such an unpleasant predicament.

If he had a choice, he would have returned precipitously and without a second thought to his beloved homeland, putting an end to that misery.

Mary Rosenthal, the only one with a human face, after Ken's criticism became cold and distant. The legal battle had not even begun, and an adversarial psychological barrier was already in place.

The passing of the days was remarkably slow and Pollux's gloom deepened, sinking him into a state of depression and despondency.

His brother's corpse was kept at the city morgue, depriving him of grieving properly at his tomb. Everything seemed to be conspiring against him. An unbreakable chain of adversities was forming around his neck, leaving no room from any daring escape.

The investigation was dragging its feet. After a week of conjectures, new theories and suppositions, our sleuths did not stumble on any new forensic evidence, nor could they detect any promising clue.

All appeared stuck in time like the morning of the crime. The results of the expert on blood splatters, examining the X-looking symbol on the wall, came back inconclusive. More likely than not the sign was handmade, but it could also have been sheer chance.

With this ambiguous and double-edged pronouncement, there was no room for celebration.

This information, albeit inconsequential, was intended exclusively for the investigators. However, the press got hold of it, and in an exclusive article *The Pittsburgh Gazette* disclosed details only an insider could have known.

As soon as the paper reached the police station, an enraged Ken went on a rampage of recriminations and threats. Whoever leaked that particular piece of information would pay dearly. He was dead set on uncovering the mole and flushing him out of the force.

In his professional opinion, some insubordination, some sexual advances and even a serious mistake could be condoned. However, fragrant breaches of secrecy or deceitful snitch activities were inexcusable and unpardonable. It would destroy the morale of the team and send the wrong message to aspiring moles for hire.

It would not take long to unmask the responsible party. Then the punishment would be swift and exemplary.

The most expeditious method of dealing with the situation was to establish some connection. Charlie had been seen hobnobbing with the young reporter Lilly Porter.

In view of that, Ken entrusted Mary Rosenthal with the secret mission of tailing the flaky Charlie in his rendezvous with her friend Lilly from *The Pittsburgh Gazette*.

Mary did not have any trouble at all with her undercover assignment, for the simple reason that her friend Lilly disclosed the source of her information, without even being solicited.

Nobody was taken by surprise when the chief detective announced in a public meeting the name of the mole. Despite his public denials, Charlie was sent packing in disgrace.

However, removing the bad apple did not purify the contaminated basket. Charlie's legacy, in fact, would float around for quite a long time, like a black cloud of poisonous gases.

He had left in everybody's mouth a real bad taste of what a detective, who had sworn to uphold the law, shouldn't be.

He was a remarkable manipulator, a born deceiver, a male chauvinist pig, and a racist redneck.

An example comes to mind that seems to epitomize his fundamentally twisted nature.

One day, back in his rookie years, when he formed part of a canine unit, something scary yet hilarious at the same time happened, according to his partner. While patrolling a commercial street in Pittsburgh, Charlie spotted a black teenager stealing from a concession stand. Immediately he unleashed his dog on the unfortunate adolescent.

The well-trained canine reached his target in the blink of an eye. Grabbing with its powerful teeth the left ankle of its victim, and uttering a dreadful howl, the animal threatened to dismember him.

The poor terrified lad screamed at the detective, begging him to call off his dog. Unmoved, the officer kept his composure and staring at him in a contemptuous manner said, "Do not worry. My dog is allergic to black meat." The remark, heard by several bystanders, provoked hysterical laughter, diffusing the tension and leaving his companion speechless and dismayed.

That was the racist Charlie Wilson at his best. As a manipulator and born deceiver, he was the reincarnation of several historical figures – Don Giovanni, Casanova, Charles Manson and the Boston Strangler – all packed into one body. It is impossible to describe his amorous adventures, his masochistic sexual deviations and his extended repertoire of entrapments.

After his departure, would the team regain confidence, reestablish itself and take control of that runaway investigation? Only time would tell.

The reenergized team of detectives worked sedulously, interviewing everyone directly or indirectly involved with Castor's murder.

Among the persons of interest, Susan Bajouke stood out. She was the victim's girlfriend and the alleged cause of the rift between the twins.

Mary Rosenthal conducted an extensive interview with the girl. It was a rainy day in Pittsburgh and Susan, circumstances notwithstanding, appeared radiant, ready to smile to the media and clear up her role in that sordid affair. Her gothic look, accentuated by heavy, dark makeup, black leather attire, unusual piercings and loose hair, gave an overall impression of a person with a definitive lifestyle.

The detective made an effort not to be put off by her bizarre appearance and keep an open mind. She tried to appear normal and genuinely interested in the girl's personal life, quizzing her about her family, studies, hobbies and friends.

Nothing remarkable stood out in those areas. Her family was not rich. At school, she was getting passing grades. Her hobbies and friends had an unambiguous right wing leaning.

However, the unimpressive normalcy ended there. As soon as Mary started closing in on Susan's love life, some disturbing peculiarities began to show up. The gothic girl was more attracted by money than by looks. Not a long time back, she had broken up with her Caucasian boyfriend, choosing instead Castor. The white boy was not solvent in the economic department, while the Japanese student belonged to a rich industrialist family.

On top of that, the new unlikely couple seemed to complement each other. Reserved, withdrawn and painfully introverted, Castor was a perfect match for the blonde, extroverted, easygoing Susan. He found in her what he was missing in his own personality. He felt as if he had been extracted from his natural shell and propelled into a new world of opportunities and surprises.

Susan saw in Castor the ideal companion, whereby her dominatrix instincts would exercise their baleful influence, and her insatiable appetite for money would be abundantly satisfied.

According to street gossip, the Japanese family had more material riches than time to spend it. Castor's attraction for that unusual specimen of female was sincere and genuine. The same cannot be said for Susan's attraction. This was a weird oddity, sustained only by convenience and blind self-interest.

The more the interviewer quizzed the girl, the clearer the picture became. It was a one-sided relationship, lacking intellectual and emotional involvement. Susan's previous boyfriend, Rudy Streaker, was a skinhead, strongly motivated by a racist ideology and politically violent, while the new flame, so to speak, was a shy lad, undefined and easily led by any ideological current.

Even to an inexperienced detective, Susan's choice would present all the characteristics of an unexplainable irrationality. Nobody of sound mind goes overnight from a Nazi type to a spineless jellyfish.

If she did not have a hand in Castor's brutal murder, how can anybody exclude her ex-boyfriend? A rejected man, full of hatred and bad tempered, would seem an ideal suspect. Certainly, he had a motive. Did he also have opportunities?

When Mary Rosenthal reported back to her boss, one thing became clear. A second suspect was in the picture. There was no time to waste. Rudy, a notorious troublemaker and bully, was immediately notified to appear at the police station for questioning.

Ken Fresco conducted the interrogation personally. He was eager to put the squeeze on the racist boy. Using all the shock tactics at his disposal, Ken encountered a solid wall. Rudy's alibi for the time of the murder stood seemingly impregnable.

Eyewitnesses, mainly friends, swore he was in a motel with a prostitute until six in the morning. In no way could he have perpetrated the horrendous crime. The manager of the establishment was ready to swear to it on the Bible.

Regrettably, nobody seemed to know the woman's name, preventing the police from verifying the validity of that alibi. Would this be the Achilles' heel of Rudy's excuse?

The cut-and-dried case envisioned by Ken Fresco and his team at the very beginning was starting to unravel under their eyes, showing unsuspected ramifications and previously neglected possibilities.

Chapter 3

"*Oh what a tangled web we weave, when first we practice to* **deceive**." – Sir Walter Scott

In the spirit of an unprecedented collaboration, Jinpachi Nemoto flew back to Japan with a simple mission – to solve the mystery of the Ishida twins. Their physical appearance was in fact anything but similar. No brothers on the planet could have looked so different, let alone twins. Their dissimilarity, one Asian, the other Caucasian, could have puzzled many in the past. However, at present it ceased to be a curiosity, becoming a serious problem in need of an immediate solution.

Under any circumstances, the goal had all the characteristics of an extraordinary simplicity. A DNA test on the parents and their embattled siblings would solve the mystery.

The Japanese detective, lacking in social skills but endowed with a sharp intuition and fine understanding of human behavior, had a long talk separately with Kimiko, the mother, and Hiro, the father.

Having been hired by the family and paid handsomely, anybody would have expected the best of cooperation by both parents. If they had been straightforward and forthcoming, no test would have been necessary.

To Jin's chagrin, that was not the case. After the usual exchange of condolences on the detective's part and politeness on the parents' side, some reticence seemed to emerge on the twins' paternity. Kimiko gave the clear impression of hiding a dark secret, while Hiro showed some confusion and embarrassment on the subject.

Putting undue pressure on the parents would have been neither diplomatic nor conducive. Jin was left with only one choice, the test. With extreme caution, alien to his nature, he collected samples from the mother and father. In conjunction with the brothers' samples, he sent them to the lab.

While waiting for the results, the sagacious sleuth had informal talks with relatives and friends. His suspicions of some dark family mystery appeared justified by some random comment on the physical appearance of the twins. This was frequently pointed out, but never satisfactorily explained.

The powerful family did not have to give explanations to anybody, much less give credit to the many rumors circulating. Unless somebody could prove the contrary, Kimiko was above suspicion and unworthy of nasty rumors.

Shielded by money and might, heiress to an immense fortune, she could look into the future without fear. Secrecy, silence and a supercilious attitude, typical byproducts of an innate deception, reigned supreme in the Ishida family. The honor and prestige of their dynasty was of paramount importance and should be preserved with any means at their disposal.

Kimiko's father, who adored his daughter and treasured his grandchildren, in the presence of that tragedy ran for cover and tried to cut his losses. In absolute secrecy, he summoned Jin, the detective who was on his payroll. He made him swear absolute discretion on whatever result the DNA test would produce. Moreover, he should keep under wraps any unfavorable findings arising from his investigation.

Non-compliance with those rules would result in an abrupt termination of his assignment. Jin was quite aware of the perils of dealing with the powers that be and knew any misstep would cause a catastrophe. Fairly new in that high-profile job, he was still finding his way. Besides, Japanese society has its unspoken code of conduct, which should be abided by, no matter what.

Since the very beginning, he never thought of his appointment as a walk in the park, but he never imagined either that it would be an obstacle course. That case could make or break him as the shrewdest investigator in the whole nation.

He assured Kimiko no breach of confidentiality would ever occur under his watch and any information obtained would be kept privileged. This way, Jin tried to obtain her complete trust, while at the same time tearing down an imperceptible wall of secrecy and reticence she unconsciously erected in self-defense.

The young, still charming mother appeared consumed by fear and destroyed by intense pain. The happy days of her adventurous youth had long gone. What was left, parental responsibilities, family honor and prestige to uphold, were falling like autumn leaves, leaving behind naked branches and empty spaces. None of those values could be considered an easy burden for her fragile constitution.

However, that was not all. A terrible secret, kept intact and hidden for years, was eating away her peace of mind. As a stolid woman, she would not mind this persistent torture of her conscience. Putting up a marvelous front of resignation was her sacred duty, from which she would never shy away.

In spite of Jin's assurances of confidentiality, she would reveal voluntarily to no one the natural freakishness of her twins' ethnic dissimilarity. In all probability, she was not even able to explain to herself that oddity, although she had some inkling of its origin.

All was so obscure and incomprehensible, so shrouded in mystery and nebulousness, that her being was shaken to the core by the very thought of it. Her passions and desires had crossed all natural boundaries, penetrating the forbidden zone of the capricious, illicit and sacrilegious. In return, nature outdid itself, producing a hybrid, previously only envisaged by mythology.

Was she a monster, a freak of nature, a repugnant human being, or a simple variation in the tapestry of infinite possibilities of the always-evolving universe?

Kimiko, whose beauty and irresistible attractiveness had superseded any legendary and ancient standard, found herself trapped by her cultural ties and at the same time alienated and allured into a modern world, where permissiveness and unrestricted freedom reigned supreme.

Tossed like a twig by the blind, contrasting forces of nature and society, she could find an anchor of salvation only in the strict rules of conduct of her ancestors. Nothing was more stifling than that, yet similarly, nothing was more protective than that.

It was a mixed bag of curses and blessings, a heavy armor, which protected the body but restricted its movements.

Kimiko, so far, had successfully defied nature, society and family. However, her beloved son's premature death had turned the clock back, and a new risky, underhand game was about to start. Who would play the winning card – the gawky, graceless detective or the intriguing lotus flower emerging from a turbulent pond?

Jin came to a sudden realization of the high stakes involved in his mission. He could be dismissed as fast as he got the job. In the blink of an eye, he could plummet from the pinnacle of his career to the depths of misery and anonymity.

Kimiko too could have lost her respectability, her fame and good name in attempting an impossible balancing act between burying a troublesome past or letting it emerge from the rubble, between sheer deception and murdered reality, between what it is and what it should be. The line between licit and illicit, acceptable and unacceptable had never been so blurry and undistinguishable.

No ancient traditions, no religious dictates, no moral imperatives could guide her through that inextricable maze of blind impulses, gut feelings and feminine emotions. It was a crossroad with no indication and multiple choices.

Kimiko remembered a scary episode of her early childhood when she strayed far from her mom while collecting flowers in the woods. The path had suddenly disappeared and numerous trees and bushes obstructed her view. Unable to find her way back she erupted in a cry of anguish and despair, convinced of being lost forever. Fortunately, her terror ended when her mother, attracted by the baby's piercing screams, came to her rescue.

Now, after so many years, her internal screaming was as loud as ever, but at this juncture there was no Mom ready to save her. She was all alone, unable to decipher her destiny.

In her subdued but determined fashion, she would face the wrath of God and the scorn of man, like a noble Japanese samurai, ready to end his existence with a ritual suicide or *seppuku*.

Her secret was sacred and she would guard it with her life. Not even her son's death, no matter how painful and devastating, would break her determination to go to her grave with it.

She would arrange her daily routine as if nothing had happened, keeping her solemn composure. A dark storm was brewing – her friends' and relatives' gossip and the whole atmosphere around her like the four horsemen of the Apocalypse, forerunners of conquest, war, famine and death.

Who could have survived the impending devastation, looming large on the horizon? One son dead, the other facing fratricide charges, family and acquaintances stonewalling any effort at rapprochement, made her stoic and impenetrable.

Her husband, partially cognizant of the family's terrible secret, made every effort to save her sanity and mental balance, showering on her precious gifts of affection and devotion.

His unfaltering support was admirable and like balsam in an open wound. Ultimately, Kimiko was the only one responsible for that disheartening predicament, and she would remain virtually alone in the battle for survival. Always in nature, birth and death are solitary events. As such, one has to face them solo, unaccompanied and unsheltered.

Days of intense pain and numbness preceded the arrival of the DNA tests. Finally, the results were delivered signed and sealed to the detective. As an act of supreme courtesy, he arranged a meeting with his client and only in her presence would he open the envelope.

Sitting in the living room, with the walls as silent witnesses, Jin looked at Kimiko, like a son ready to address his mother with reverence and admiration. She stared blankly at the paper in front of her. She knew in her heart that her secret was about to be violated, that her world would be turned upside down and inside out. If that was her destiny, there was no way of stopping it. No money or power in the world would be able to change the natural course of events. Without whispering a syllable, and with her eyes on that yellowish envelope, she observed Jin tearing it open. He politely handed the contents to her.

Motionless, like a statue of alabaster, she sighed deeply. After an interminable pause, she returned the paper to Jin, and with a gentle, imploring voice, she asked him to read and explain it to her.

The detective, touched by her gesture of confidence, laid his eyes on those results with extreme curiosity and trepidation. Not believing what was written, he went back and forth in his reading several times.

Finally, with a look of total disbelief on his face, he opened his mouth. As if deciphering an ancient cryptic oracle, he said, "With an accuracy of 99.9% the tests reveal that you are the biological mother of the twins. Your husband, Hiro Kimura, however, is not the biological father of Castor or Pollux."

This revelation, albeit shocking, did not seem to affect the oriental woman in the least. Apparently, she was already aware of that reality. However, what came next hit a sensitive nerve, throwing her into mental disarray.

The detective concluded his reading with this revolutionary and seemingly incomprehensible sentence.

"With an accuracy of 99.9% Castor and Pollux have a different biological father."

Kimiko appeared genuinely shocked.

How could it be humanly possible for twins to have a different biological father? Isn't that a flagrant contradiction? How could science explain that freakish product of nature?

Jin, the shrewd detective that could find an explanation for almost anything, this time was at a loss for words.

Addressing his client with humility and humanity, he said, "Honestly, I don't know what to say. What might seem an oddity for a traditional way of thinking might not be impossible after all. Perhaps you are the only one holding the key to this mystery. I encourage you to examine the events of that extraordinary conception and retrieve the source of that duality."

He bade farewell to Kimiko, after assuring her of his complete discretion. Obviously, he needed some time to reflect on those results, and make some sense of them, if possible.

Jin's brain and imagination went into overdrive. Not only was he picturing the existence of two men, with legitimate claims to a biological paternity, but he was also imagining the infinite possibilities of strained relations and awkward probabilities, in case the two men had some knowledge of the existence of their sons.

Where were they? Did they vanish into thin air after consummating the act, unwilling to assume their responsibilities?

Alternatively, God forbid, had Kimiko been a victim of group rape, and therefore totally devastated by indescribable pain and unutterable shame?

In all likelihood, her impenetrable silence and saturnine muteness harbored a terrible secret that could have destroyed the reputation of her family. In such a case, who would dare to blame her for being hermetic and tight lipped?

One way or the other, the detective had to get to the bottom of that conundrum. That was his mission. That was what he was being paid for. To renounce the truth was not an option. The harder his job, the shinier could be his reputation as a shrewd and sagacious investigator.

With an unassuming, almost naïve, disposition he would attempt to gain Kimiko's heart and make her give away some insignificant clues, which ultimately could lead to the very entrance of the dreadful mystery.

For her part, the grieving mother was fighting the battle of her life. Caught between a rock and a hard place, she did not know where to turn. On one hand, she was determined to keep intact the reputation and honor of her family. On the other, she was dying to know the reason for her son's senseless murder.

However, in this existential dilemma there was an enormous question mark. Was her son's death in any way related to his conception? If the answer was negative, why reveal to the world what was hidden in her heart?

To add more perplexity to the situation, she wasn't totally sure of what happened that blistering night of yesteryear. She remembered exactly, detail after detail, what she did, but she ignored the consequences of her burning desire.

Something more troubling was on Jin's radar. Why did Kimiko name her twins Castor and Pollux? Was she infatuated with Greek mythology and in love with Leda, the legendary heroine, wife of Tyndareus, and mother of Castor and Pollux?

Was she fully aware that the twins Dioscouri had different fathers? Castor was Tyndareus' child and mortal, while Pollux was the son of Zeus and by divine nature immortal.

Was it pure coincidence that her firstborn Geminis were named after those mythological figures, whose origin from a dual paternal sperm constitutes an unsolvable mystery and a total wonder in nature?

On the other hand, did she have an inkling that the fruit of her womb defied all conceptual laws, breaking natural barriers and originating new wonders?

What was the frail Japanese beauty hiding in her heart? She did not look or act like any ordinary mortal because the DNA test revealed a blunt abnormality, a riddle that would leave any expert in shock and awe.

Maybe Jinpachi Nemoto, in his unorthodox ways of conducting investigations used to break conventional methods and approaches, could have a crack at it.

Certainly, this case constituted a real challenge for him. He welcomed it and embraced it with the fervor of an "Illuminati."

He would tackle it not head-on like a ram, but circumventing obstacles like a wily old fox. His apparent clumsiness and awkwardness were a real plus in his business. Like an apprentice magician, failing to produce a rabbit from a hat or a dove from a sleeve and provoking unintended laughs for the failure, he would twist the final outcome in his favor, melting the icy psychological barriers away and creating ideal circumstances for his client to open up, and reveal her darkest secrets.

Relying on his customary philosophical slow approach, he let a few days pass, giving Kimiko ample time to recompose herself.

In the meantime, he mentally played out a strategic plan that would keep the Pittsburgh detective hopeful in some meaningful results and the grieving mother yearning for solutions.

To transmit the DNA results to his colleagues in America could seriously jeopardize the secrecy he had solemnly promised his client. Evidently, he could not trust the Pittsburgh team, given the previous experience of a venal detective ready to sell information to an attractive female.

Close collaboration was his aim, but within an intelligent and cautious framework.

If his strategy with Ken Fresco and his men was to buy time, with Kimiko he tried to play around her family feelings and sincere devotion to her friends and acquaintances.

In a cozy, intimate tea ceremony, where a few members of the powerful family were present, initially the conversation was steered toward the traditional topics of types of tea, calligraphy, kimonos, flower arranging, ceramics and incense. Soon after, the traditions of the past became the focal point. To better illustrate the subject, some albums with black-and-white pictures were brought in.

Instantly, Jin saw his window of opportunity to pry discreetly into Kimiko's youth. Perhaps, in that vast array of people and places frozen in time, some indicative clue could emerge, leading the cunning detective in the right direction.

Kimiko possessed an entire album dedicated to her trips abroad. At that time, she was still single. Between a sigh of nostalgia and a phew of jubilation, a spontaneous comment came out of her mouth. "Those were happy days!"

Jin combed through those pictures with a subtle, disguised interest. Did they hold the key to the puzzle he was attempting to solve?

In the very last section, dedicated to Italy, several photographs portrayed a joyful Kimiko standing between two young men, one Asian, the other Caucasian. Now Jin remembered seeing a similar framed picture on display on the living room mantelpiece.

Struck by a lightning bolt, the detective pointed his index finger at the picture and asked Kimiko, "Who are those two handsome gentlemen?"

A veil of mist seemed to cover the brightness of Kimiko's eyes, plunging her into darkness. After a long pause, she murmured, "Those were two very dear friends of my youthful past. Their memory is still vivid in my heart." By saying this, a hint of embarrassment seemed depicted on her delicate face. Did she involuntarily give away a painful secret?

Jin knew immediately he had discovered a pot of gold and the possible origin of the family mystery. He was determined to pursue that clue, no matter the consequences. Would that lead him to the ends of the earth? So be it.

He breathed deeply before speaking again. Uncertain whether that was the right moment to pursue such a delicate matter, he tried his hardest to conceal his understandable curiosity. With an unnatural tone of voice, that could be detected miles away, he adventured the decisive question.

"Do you still remember their names?"

"How could I ever forget them?" was the immediate answer. For an instant, Kimiko seemed to relive the indescribable joys of her love life's golden era that no one could ever bring back. After that, in fact, an autumn of lukewarm affection had stiffened up her sweet heart, still yearning for intimacy. National and family traditions had harnessed her unbridled passion, while compromises had tied her down to a respectable position as a wife and mother.

If her soul could have channeled the overflowing amount of sentiments and converted them into words, no poem could have been good enough to convey them. Jin might not have detected the volcanic movement inside that fragile human being, but he was certainly aware of having hit a delicate button.

Kimiko paused for a few moments, savoring the memory to the fullest. The chalice of the past still contained the sweetness of the rarest alpine flower, inebriating her with its potent aroma.

Finally stepping back from that oasis of remembrances and reinserting herself in the aridity of the present, she revealed the identity of her friends. "Their names are Peter Egger and Takeo Shirieda."

The initial fire in her eyes dimmed considerably and a languid look took its place. The magic moment with all its emotional charge had vanished forever, leaving a handful of discolored pictures and an empty fist of memories.

"I met them several times in Torino, Italy, while they were studying theology in a Pontifical Institute. After a few brief encounters, our communications mysteriously ended. I never heard of them since."

The detective had sufficient information to launch a formal investigation. He thanked Kimiko profusely for her hospitality and mainly for her rare moment of candor.

Taking leave from her, he said with a smile, "I shall keep in touch. Do not worry." She bowed ceremoniously. He did the same and departed from her with no regret.

He had accomplished his mission without incident and without raising too many suspicions.

The elements in his possession contained a generality that he could not pinpoint with accuracy. What was a Pontifical Institute for Theology? It was certainly connected with religion and more precisely with the Catholic religion, Italy being the place and pontifical the qualification of the institute.

The subsequent question was more intriguing. Were the students seminarians preparing for the priesthood, or simple laymen interested in theology? If they aspired to be Catholic priests, did it not seem quite odd to have them fraternize with an oriental female, so dissimilar in costumes and beliefs?

What was the real connection between these two contrasting worlds? Was it platonic or carnal, intellectual or sexual, business or pleasure?

The mystery was thickening and the probabilities scary. Jin was hypothetically entering a universe unknown, where strict prohibitions, blatant transgressions, high moral standards, degrading mortal sins, purification and degradation, Good and Evil went hand in hand.

He could never imagine the road ahead, full of disappointments, surprises and even miscalculations. That experience would certainly forever mark his career as a detective and change his outlook on many world realities.

Before leaving for Europe, the continent he always dreamt of visiting, he had ample time to brood over strange amorous liaisons, blind passions and murderous betrayals, medieval style. Castles and nights, witches and goblets, kings and popes suddenly populated his mind, tossing him into a surreal atmosphere.

Not happy with the products of his vivid imagination, he acquired some European literature apt to enlighten him over the background of his investigation.

On the eve of his departure, Jin arranged a brief encounter with Kimiko, clarifying the scope of his trip and asking her politely whether she had anything to reveal about her two friends that could facilitate his research.

A mute attitude was the answer, accompanied by a slight gesture of dejection. Was the detective prying into her personal life, violating her privacy and feeding his morbid curiosity? Was it indispensable to pursue that line of questioning?

Sensing an underlying hostility, not conducive to a relaxed rapport with the client, the detective apologized in an oriental manner. He bid farewell to Kimiko, promising strict confidentiality on every finding. Moreover, he assured her he would keep her abreast of every single development in his investigation.

It was pouring with rain on that farewell visit. Was it any indication of the stormy relations ahead or just an unrelated atmospheric phenomenon?

He felt somehow disappointed, not with the weather conditions but with the strong resistance from his client. Would he face a similar wall of mutism on the Old Continent, where traditions and religious superstitions were as vigorous as in his homeland?

Who were those two smiling students with their arms around Kimiko's neck, as if holding a pricey conquest? One pertained to the Aryan family while the other belonged to the Asian race. Did they share a common bond of friendship or were they entangled in an explosive love triangle, whose forbidden fruit had a mythical name?

Finding the men and getting their DNA would solve the intricate puzzle. However, would what looked relatively simple turn out complicated and troublesome?

As always, there were more questions than answer to Jin's uncontrollable inquisitive frenzy. Ranting and raving like a madman did not help. All that had to stop if he wanted to restore some sanity in his life.

Back home, wet and uncomfortable, he grabbed a bottle of sake and pouring a generous shot of that liquor, he sipped it with gusto and vengeance. While time slipped away, he kept pouring and sipping, until his mental clarity disappeared, and a warm fogginess clouded his awareness, wrapping him in a comfortable dream of endless possibilities.

The following morning, the embattled detective woke up with a monstrous hangover. His head hurt and his body was unwilling to perform the most basic movements.

The booking of his trip to Torino, Italy, had to be postponed until his physical condition was back to normal. In the afternoon, he made a couple of phone calls, one to a local travel agency and the other to Ken Fresco in Pittsburgh.

There is nothing like a sober good night's sleep. Jin had wasted twenty-four hours, but he had recovered his sanity and equilibrium. With an unusual celerity, he was once again on top of his game.

Finalizing the last details and taking some precautions, he left for the airport, carrying a mid-sized suitcase and a thick wallet.

Unlike on his flight to America, this time he experienced some strange feelings of venturing into the unknown. Maybe the language barrier had something to do with that uncomfortable state of affairs, maybe his diminished enthusiasm for the mission, or maybe the possibility of dealing with men of the cloth threw him off completely. Whatever the reason, Jin would not bet a dime on the success of his European trip.

Would he ever come back to his beloved country unscathed and in one piece, or for some freak accident or hidden vendetta would he pay the ultimate price, like the protagonist of his investigation?

What kind of forces were at work in that mysterious murder – blind forces of nature, invisible forces of some supernatural entity, or just an eternal destiny embedded in the chromosomes of the Ishida family?

Even the modern tools of communication, with their lightning speed, would not be able to protect him against mythical perils and unleashed monsters from the underworld.

Assuming a fatalistic attitude and a stoic outlook, congenital to his Shintoistic philosophy, Jin momentarily overpowered his fears. Still a sea of turbulence and intranquillity agitated his horizon, announcing rough sailing ahead.

While he attempted to recompose his disturbed mind and uneasy heart, and in between short spells of sunshine and sudden downpours, the taxi he was traveling in landed him, with Swiss watch precision, at Narita Airport.

The embarking procedures, so cumbersome for the many restrictions imposed on passengers, were unusually smooth and expeditious.

The anxious detective had no time at his disposal, not even for a quick prayer of propitiation to the divinities of his ancestors, because the airport loudspeakers were announcing his flight. A jumbo jet, belonging to a Japanese airline, was ready for boarding.

Finally and with no regret, Jinpachi Nemoto was off to Italy. As the plane took off, from his seat he waved nostalgically to his homeland. Would he ever be back, or was this his final farewell?

His destiny was sealed and nobody knew the outcome of that risky adventure.

Chapter 4

"*The true hypocrite is the one who ceases to perceive his* **deception**, *the one who lies with sincerity.*" – André Gide

Back in Pittsburgh, the investigation had stalled once again, for lack of significant discoveries and tangible progress. The reenergized team, made whole after the amputation of the cancerous mole Charlie Wilson, had fallen into a routine mode, losing purpose and enthusiasm.

The complete absence of new findings, of possible clues and potential eyewitnesses was devastating for the detectives' morale.

The helping hand so eagerly awaited from Japan never materialized. Everything seemed to conspire against the speedy resolution of the case.

Ken Fresco, with the intent of salvaging the sinking ship of his investigation, temporarily switched the attention from the murder to the victim.

Castor's corpse had been examined thoroughly by the forensic pathologist and meticulously preserved in the local morgue. There was no need, neither scientific nor tactical, to keep it there indefinitely.

The time had come to ship it back to his family in Japan, for a proper burial. That was extremely hard for Pollux, whose physical proximity to his twin brother was a source of comfort. On the other hand, it was an overdue gesture for the family, still bleeding emotionally for the criminal act, and unfairly hit by the void of a grieving ceremony, where the mortal remains were present.

At the Ishida family's expense, Castor's body was flown back to his homeland. Only the brother was present for the last farewell, accompanied by his lawyer and Detective Mary Rosenthal.

When the plane disappeared into the sky with the corpse, Pollux dried some silent tears from his face. Sadly, he went back to his apartment, halved by destiny and numbed by pain. He would never understand the meaning of that senseless tragedy, because, maybe, there was no meaning at all.

Life, usually so simple and transparent like a clear water stream, can become inexplicably twisted and entangled, so much so that any attempt at explanation ends up in sterile platitudes and commonplaces.

Pollux did not possess any philosophy of life or for that matter of death. Instead, he was possessed by a potent desire to live, and a compulsive zeal to fight against all forces of the underworld.

While his brother was laid to rest in an intense religious ceremony at home, he, in a foreign land, felt a piercing sadness, an unquenchable longing and an unrequited love. He could not explain that mixed bag of feelings, as he could not abolish the immense distance that separated him from his family.

He wanted to be present at that family gathering. He wished to experience the subliminal connection with his ancestors and pour his heart out to them. His brother was already in their company. In all probability, he was playing the role of ambassador, conveying the obscure layers of his soul never revealed to anybody.

Even absent and far away in time and space, he was present through his brother, fully participating in that ritual banquet, in that communion of spirits and bodies. He could smell the ceremonial incense, hear the rhythmic and repetitive invocations, and exchange sighs and laments.

Their mother, who conceived them in an unforgivable Bacchanalia of sex and liquor, and gave them birth under the pretense of a respectable marriage, was the central point of that somber gathering. Everybody had their eyes on her, observing her every expression and move.

She had irreparably lost what she desperately wanted and treasured most in this world. Maybe her obstinate passion had stolen something that did not belong to her. Finally, the immortal gods, so jealous of their prerogatives, had taken back the abusive property, reestablishing a lost equilibrium and restoring justice.

Kimiko, overwhelmed by guilt and subdued by fear, could not shed a tear. She looked at her son, lying motionless in that coffin, an ethereal serenity on his face. She could not avoid the thought of a terrible punishment inflicted by enraged divinities. Any prayer coming from her lips, any invocation from her heart probably would go unheard.

More tragically, what she smelled was not the incense coming from the sticks, what she heard were not pious supplications from the mourners, and what she saw was not Castor's pale face.

Her lively imagination, in a miraculous transfer, had transposed the present with the past, the muzzled suffering with the unbridled passion, the pervasive incense with the fumes of potent potables, the lamentations with immoderate laughter. In that whirlwind saraband of odors and rumors, the distinct acridness of sex and the joyful moans of copulation stood out.

Did her mind go insane, rebelling to a cruel destiny? Was Kimiko unconsciously erasing the painful present and reliving in that somber moment the beginning of a mysterious journey, known to her alone? At that moment, she looked more like a wild lover than a grieving mother. Had all the passions, energies and wild impetus of yesteryear come back, or was it just a pile of embers still glimmering under the ashes of time?

In that rare occurrence, it was impossible to discern the world of feelings from the world of facts. Against all the laws of nature, the real appeared evanescent, and the unreal, lively and vibrant.

The fantasized place, so vivid and compelling, was a distant land, where tragic stories of love had been immortalized by poems, and young lovers had met their cruel destinies.

While in that bizarre, dreamlike state of a seeress, a relative whispered something in her ear. Pollux was calling from America. Coming out of her induced trance, she sighed deeply. After all, part of her romance was still alive. Her story had not ended yet.

She grabbed the phone and with unusual sweetness uttered the words, "Mushi, mushi." Her son came through immediately and asked affectionately, "Okasan, how are you?"

"I am fine," she answered, "and I love you."

"I love you too, okasan. Do not worry. When I come back, I will take care of you. My brother is alive in me and I will live for you. You are my strength."

As soon as Kimiko heard those tender words, she broke into tears, unable to refrain from showing her emotions. A long pause ensued. Finally, she recovered her serenity. With all the dignity she could muster, she thanked her son, telling him she missed him terribly.

After that, her heart still pounding in her chest, she hung up the phone and returned among the mourners.

During the funeral procession, the extended family was silent and reserved. In the cemetery, there were a few more prayers and a few more tears. Castor was solemnly entombed beside his grandparents, and Kimiko, as a last gesture of affection, laid a beautiful wreath of white chrysanthemums at his mausoleum.

The viciously slain student rested in a peaceful setting, far away from the clamoring and wrangling of detectives, lawyers and judges. The world had stopped for him, while for the survivors the battle raged on.

Pollux, who had never been physically separated from his twin, was in the middle of it, fighting for his life, and for the honor of his family. Without being officially indicted, he was going through the sheer hell of uncertainty.

His lawyer tried to explain the American justice system to him, and the police procedures in similar cases. It could take months, even years, to collect evidence and file charges.

In his case, as in many others, all the findings pointed at him as the only suspect. Unfortunately, there were no leads for other possible suspects. If somebody else had committed the crime, he had done a superb job in framing Pollux. He had masterfully covered his tracks, killing one twin, and ruining the other for life by stacking up the evidence against him.

Only a professional killer, with a very sick mind, could have arranged such an elaborate tapestry of deception and deceit. Pollux's alibi was the only thing that kept him from landing immediately in a court of law and ultimately in jail. The eyewitness couple never faltered in their testimony. Their story was linear and believable. The description of how Pollux was dressed that fatal morning, and the unusual hooting of an owl, added a touch of irrefutable truth.

For this reason, Detective Ken Fresco and his team were dragging their feet, unable to reach any positive conclusion. Obviously, that was not the first case with similar characteristics, but it was the first affecting a foreign national from a powerful family.

The lawyer from Japan, Taisuke Fujii, made the best out of a bad situation. He reassured Pollux the American detectives were up against a brick wall and any law enforcement agent in the world would be in serious difficulties if he or she decided to ask for an indictment.

Pollux felt comforted on one hand, but on the other found himself plunged into an eternal limbo of legal wrangling between the District Attorney's Office and the police department.

Even the cruelest, most sadistic person could not have devised such excruciating torture. No money, fame and power in the world could have freed the poor Japanese student from the asphyxiating tentacles of a judicial system believed perfect and almost infallible.

The creeping deception of many human moral convictions goes unnoticed daily, sowing distress in many noble souls. Daily people stick to longstanding convictions, and sacrifice their lives, coming up at the end empty-handed and brokenhearted or cynical and defeatist.

Consequently, there is a necessity for a constant critical analysis of traditions and convictions, religions and cultures, legal systems and operational procedures. The perfect, the absolute, the sacred, the immutable, does not exist among mortals, and it will never exist despite humankind's desperate yearning for it.

Our protagonist, submerged under an avalanche of contrasting beliefs and judicial tenets, was incapable of processing his personal reality in the crucible of a critical mentality, reinventing himself at every twist and turn of vicissitudes and events.

To step out of that obscure tunnel and look dispassionately at his situation would have been a miracle. No wonder, for lack of vision and good judgment people fall constantly into fictitious traps, remaining permanent ideological prisoners.

However, to circumvent this depressing reality come the multifarious tentacles of deception. Under cover of fisicious and fallacious justifications, they attribute meaning, sense and purpose to what is totally irrational and inexplicable.

All the history of humanity should be rewritten as if God, supernatural forces, justice, fairness and many other big abstractions did not exist. The author says this not because he does not believe in them, quite the contrary; but because those awesome realities, wrongly manipulated by humans intent on preserving their privileged status and selfish ways, instead of offering the right interpretational key, generate spurious substitutes and poisonous ideological assertions.

But enough of these impromptu thoughts, ideological by nature and subscribing to the theory of moral relativity. It is time to return to the story.

Pollux, still considered a person of interest in the murder of his twin brother, Castor, was on edge and in considerable emotional pain. The investigation had lost its steam, going nowhere. The Pittsburgh team, initially so motivated and reenergized, for lack of tangible progress, had reached rock bottom. The District Attorney's Office, so eager to show the world its efficiency, had toned down its political rhetoric, and assumed a dormant attitude.

In opposition to all this acquiescence, the external pressure, non-existent at the beginning, started mounting with vigor and determination. First, the Japanese consulate, later the State Department, initiated their offensive, demanding a quick resolution to that embarrassing homicide. For them it was not primarily a question of justice, but a serious issue of credibility and saving face, at home and abroad.

The Ishida family made their powerful economic influence weigh on the decisions at every level. Money talks louder than words and threats.

While the machinery of justice, well oiled by secret funds, began moving again, rhythmically and speedily, something unexpected happened.

Susan Bajouke, Castor's greedy, demanding girlfriend, was found murdered with her tongue cut off. Was this second crime related to the first, or just an unfortunate coincidence? Was the perpetrator, whoever he was, trying to confuse the primary investigation and throw the detectives off the right path?

Was Susan an inconvenient witness or just an unintended target of the rampant criminality in the city? The timing was certainly disturbing.

The way Susan had been murdered did not bear any resemblance to her boyfriend's execution. The perpetrator had strangled her to death with his bare hands, while Castor had been clubbed to death with a baseball bat.

In Castor's case, there was no doubt the intention was to erase the ethnicity of the student, by disfiguring his face, while in his girlfriend's murder it seemed apparent the criminal intended to take exemplary revenge by cutting off his victim's tongue, silencing her permanently.

Did the different methods suggest two murderers, or was it just an ingenious device to confuse law enforcement?

This was exactly what the Fresco team tried to determine right from the outset of the investigation. The elements at their disposal would suggest a connection between the two crimes. Consequently, they would proceed on such an assumption.

The marks left on Susan's neck indicated a muscular man with a powerful grip. Any fiber, hair or bodily fluids left on the crime scene would take the investigators back to the origin.

Susan's body and the surroundings, where her corpse was discovered, underwent a prolonged and thorough examination. Ken Fresco personally combed the area for any possible clues. After exhaustive research, a few fiber fragments were found. However, the most exciting discovery was under the victim's fingernails. Probably in the struggle for her life, she scratched the assailant. Ken Fresco found tiny particles of skin, some stains of blood and miniscule pieces of hair. Whatever he dreamt of for the successful resolution of a case was right there, under his own eyes, ready to reveal to the world the name of the perpetrator.

The primary suspect in this crime had been Rudy Streaker all along. Susan's former boyfriend, violent, bad tempered and with a criminal record, had plenty of motives, and opportunities. With those findings, it would be extremely easy to trace back the DNA. A positive match with Rudy would leave no doubt.

However, when something appears too simple, it never turns out that way. Unfortunately, this case was a confirmation of that rule. Rudy's DNA was absent from those fragments. Fresco's initial optimism and jubilation were premature. The plot was thickening and the solution was far from being quick and simple.

Once again, there was a corpse and an abundance of evidence, but no clear suspect. Rudy, the hirsute neo-Nazi, poster child for trouble and insubordination, seemed to have a good alibi. A couple of his friends were willing to vouch for him. According to these eyewitnesses, at the time of the murder Rudy was in a nightclub playing poker and fooling around with strippers.

Facing an imminent fiasco, Detective Fresco pounded his fists on the table and cursed everything under the sun. It was frustrating to watch such a turn of events and it was irritating in the extreme to feel powerless.

What happened to the beautiful theory that the murder scene had a story to tell? It was true Susan had trodden on many people's toes, and therefore many could be suspects. Nevertheless, a very serious motive would have driven somebody to perpetrate such a heinous crime. Only one person was known to have a powerful reason to kill Susan, and that was the infamous Streaker.

Despite all the evidence, in Fresco's book Rudy was still a suspect, perhaps the only suspect.

It was up to him to prove with facts that his theory was a valid one. Would he be able to meet the many challenges ahead, and pull a rabbit out of the hat?

The slaughter of a young woman, so soon after the Japanese national, became highly explosive for the media. A brutal frenzy of speculations, accusations and derisive comments on the police's handling of the case exploded in the local papers. A public opinion tsunami was sweeping away the good work so far carried out by the detectives.

Fresco was honestly appalled by the insensibility and viciousness of the public opinion trumpeted so blaringly loud by the media. Against all odds, he was determined to stick to his guns. Nothing and nobody would force him to change direction or methods. With the determination of a wild animal hunted down by predators, he would fight tooth and nail to solve the case and gain respectability. It was a question of survival.

Rudy Streaker, an unsavory character well known by the public at large, was his main suspect and would be treated as such.

Obtaining the necessary search warrants, and planting secret devices on his premises, he put a tail on Rudy and some of his friends. He was almost certain the constant surveillance would come up sooner than later with some startling revelation. A slip of the tongue, a wrong move, an act of sheer bravado would land the untouchable punk in the police snare.

Patience and perseverance, in conjunction with subtle shrewdness, would work like a charm.

Sooner than expected, a secret conversation in Rudy's bedroom gave him away shamelessly. While drinking and fornicating with his latest conquest, he started boosting his ego for the clean job he did in disposing of the overbearing Susan.

His ruthless henchman, by the name of Stavros Kalidopulous, had executed his orders to the letter. Since Stavros never had any run-in with the law, his DNA and fingerprints were absent from the National Database. Nobody would ever suspect his involvement in that crime. The logical conclusion was that Rudy was home free. Or so he thought.

He had grossly underestimated the detective's determination to catch the culprit and put an end to the mounting pressure.

Nobody could imagine his astonishment the day the police came for him and his partner. To his dismay and everybody's amazement, the police arrested him. Among the bombastic orders of the agents in uniform and the flashlights of the unscrupulous media, they handcuffed him and took him to police headquarters.

All had been staged down to the last detail and executed with precision. After reading him his Miranda rights, Ken Fresco took the man into custody in the company of his pal Stavros. With one shot, the police had caught the two birds of prey. Their heyday was over and everybody in town breathed a sigh of relief.

The rapid resolution of Susan's murder did not open the door to a resolution in Castor's case. On the contrary, it produced an increased grey area due to the disappearance of a fundamental witness, so close to the victim and so involved with Rudy.

Ken Fresco and his team were painfully aware of this predicament. Any reminder would have been an added insult to the existing injuries.

While the press had softened its criticism, the powers that be escalated their pressure to the point of becoming brazen and impudent.

For the veteran Fresco that was certainly the most disturbing aspect of his job, to have some zealot superiors breathing down his neck during the most crucial period of the investigation. As badly as he wanted to control the press, he wished he could muzzle the public authorities the same way. Unfortunately, he was powerless in both cases.

If he wanted to succeed, he had to work around them, paying lip service on the outside while on the inside ignoring them. That was obviously a dangerous strategy. Any indiscretion, in fact, could have provoked his immediate demotion.

To leave the force in disgrace was not his ultimate goal. He was eager to retire after the crowning achievement of solving Castor's murder. Only then would he rest satisfied. Anything short of that would have been a resounding defeat.

Chapter 5

*"Truth lives in the midst of **deception**."* – Friedrich von Schiller

Jinpachi Nemoto had left Japan, his beloved country, with a small suitcase, and a big duffel bag of ambitions and illusions.

However, cautious as he was and keeping his feet on the ground, he did not want to feed his curious imagination with extemporaneous and delirious assumptions and conjectures.

The circumstances, albeit adverse, would dictate the proper course of action. He would not be influenced by a spurious personal agenda, or by presuppositions or fantasies of any kind.

The facts and only the facts would guide him through the meanders of reality. Optimistic but not super-confident, he looked forward to the inception of his mission.

The flight, although long and tiring, did not present any particular challenge for Jin. Except for a few interruptions, he slept soundly all the way to Rome. When the arrival in the Eternal City was announced over the intercom, the private detective found himself rested and restored. With a joyous smile, he greeted the ancient monuments and their garrulous dwellers, unaware of the awesome weight of their glorious past.

Jin was totally captivated by the relaxed demeanor of the Romans and their fruition of the present. Their motto seemed to be "Enjoy the present because the future is uncertain" or expressed in their classical manner, "Carpe diem!"

Reminiscing on the old aphorism, "Cum Romae sis, Romano vivito more" ("When in Rome, do as the Romans do"), the oriental visitor made a supreme effort to assume a "not a worry in the world" attitude.

That approach came in very handy when he tried to book a flight to Torino. The pilots of the major carriers were on strike. Unable to continue his journey to the northern city, capital of Piedmont, he had to spend the night in a Roman hotel, hoping that the following day the union dispute would be resolved.

Obviously, he was not the only one stranded. It happened that a reporter from *La Stampa* took notice of his predicament and invited him to spend the night at his hotel. In a taxi, they reached their destination. In broken English, the Italian tried to explain some basic Italian customs to the Japanese.

At the same time, he wanted to know the purpose of his visit to Italy and Torino in particular. The shrewd detective, smiling politely, said, "Strictly pleasure. I needed a vacation with good food and beautiful views. And here I am."

The reporter did not inquire any further and gave the Japanese a few tips where to dine and what to visit in his endearing northern city, strategically located at the foot of the Alps.

Jin did not have to work hard in assuming a tourist mentality and showing a relaxed attitude. The unfortunate inconvenience of the air strike did not irritate our man. Deep down his philosophical nature was full of resources. He could face a mountain of difficulties without getting deterred or discouraged. Certainly, he possessed the right stuff to navigate the rough Italian waters unscathed. Any irritation would compromise his mission and ultimately his career. A skillful pilot, he would steer his ship unharmed between Scylla and Charybdis and safely reach the desired port.

In the morning, a subtle smile of fruition was painted across his face. A double shot of espresso added the vital energy that would propel him into an overdrive mood.

A few phone calls resolved the sticky situation of the impasse, revealing the resumption of the flights, and bringing back a more cheery mood among the stranded travelers.

Around mid-day, the plane took off from Rome and ninety minutes later landed in Torino. Everything went smoothly. Indescribable was Jin's joy in setting foot for the first time in that noble city, so rich in history, culture and tradition. The day was splendid, without smog and with crisp air. People felt good to be alive.

He booked a room at the Golden Palace (Via dell'Arcivescovado, 18). The location was ideal for his investigation. Not far from the Archbishop's residence, it would provide Jin with his first and most important source of information.

The Curia would certainly know the exact address of the Pontifical Institute, where Kimiko's two friends received their theological formation.

The hotel accommodation was fantastic, and it did not take very long for our tourist-detective to settle down and feel at ease.

A shower and an excellent meal contributed to a rosy outlook and great expectations. "La Vecchia Signora" ("Old Lady"), as Torino was nicknamed, was there to be discovered and enjoyed.

There were still a few hours before sunset, so why not call a cab and take a leisurely tour around the city? On his way, he could drop by the Archbishop's residence and make an appointment for the following day.

While awaiting his ride, he received a phone call from Kimiko, asking about his trip and his location. She sounded anxious, almost scared. Jin assured her everything was fine and that he was breathing Piedmontese air. She immediately realized he was already in Torino. The reminiscence of that name sent shivers down her spine and an inner excitement shook her fragile body.

All was coming back to her in an emotional flash of memories. Powerful sentiments mixed with romantic longings agitated her heart. Visibly moved and incapable of controlling that avalanche of emotions, she wanted to ask more questions, but was only able to utter a few disconnected words that did not make much sense. Polite in the extreme, and fearful of any indiscretion, she abruptly terminated the conversation by wishing him a pleasant stay and a fruitful investigation.

She certainly wanted to know much more but her strong feelings were giving her away. Under no circumstances would Kimiko allow that to happen.

Jin could sense the anxiety coming from the other end of that strange communication, but he was unable to quantify or qualify it.

A dark past seemed to dangle over that place and the key to that mystery lay in the lives of those two students. It was imperative to find their whereabouts and their unlikely relationship with a Japanese heiress.

Notified by the concierge that his taxi had arrived, he walked speedily through the impressive entrance and exited to the street. With his oriental ceremonial manners, he greeted the cab driver and showed him on a hotel letterhead the address of the ecclesiastical Curia.

Extremely courteous but reserved the man drove toward the destination. The traffic was not bad and the congestion quite manageable. It took only a matter of minutes to get to the Curia. He asked the driver to wait for him. He rang the bell and a middle-aged woman opened the door. He asked to see the Archbishop's secretary. After a telegraphic phone call, she told him to follow her.

At the end of a dimly lit corridor, on the right-hand side was the secretary's office. Introduced by the housekeeper, Jin explained the purpose of his visit and asked for a formal appointment. Mons. Franco, the secretary, appeared surprised by the visitor and curious at the same time. In elementary English, the clergy explained there was no need to come back. Jin could present his request right there and he would do his best to satisfy it.

Happy with that turn of events, the undercover detective dismissed the cab driver and initiated his conversation with the secretary. This was a man of few words but of great determination and clarity.

Jin, quite aware of the delicate subject he was dealing with, tried to concoct a palatable story, in order to get the information he needed.

He started his narration by saying, "A Japanese woman, from a rich and powerful family, many years back was befriended by two students of theology. At that time, they were studying at a Pontifical Institute in the city. Unfortunately, with the passing of time, she lost track of them. Still very interested in their career and because of her charitable sentiments, she was very eager to locate them and find out whether they were in need of anything."

The Monsignor listened attentively to every word pronounced by that mysterious man. Finally he said, "If my memory serves me correctly, the only institution that comes close to what you mentioned is the former Pontificio Ateneo S. (Via Caboto, 27), which is no longer in existence. It was a temporary residence for students from all over the world seeking a Master's degree in theology. In 1965, it was moved from here to Rome (Piazza dell'Ateneo S., 1), where a magnificent building had been built. A year later, it was inaugurated by Paul VI and in 1973 it was elevated to the rank of Pontifical University (Pontificia Università S.), conferring degrees in several ecclesiastical disciplines. The old records from the faculty were transferred to the new entity."

When the secretary read that information from a webpage, Jin didn't even blink. Blown away by the reading, he remained immobile in his chair, adding a touch of drama to his proverbial oriental impassiveness.

Everything seemed so unreal, so unpredictable, and so capricious that the talkative detective was at a loss for words. He smiled at the clergy and thanked him sincerely. Mons. Franco printed the information out on a sheet of paper and handed it to him.

Jin bowed respectfully and took leave of his helpful host. Back at the hotel, he breathed deeply. Italy was for him the land of surprises. Curiously enough, instead of cursing his bad luck, he felt the urge to visit the old building on Via Caboto, 27.

Stepping out of the cab, he took a long look at the grey brick building. It bore a striking resemblance to a correctional facility. For an instant, he thought how many dreams of young lives with passionate hearts had been housed and sheltered inside those walls. Oh, if those cold bricks could talk! Probably they would be able to narrate infinite struggles and sublime sacrifices. Probably, they would re-echo with multiple aspirations of their dwellers that at one time or another had burned their candle at both ends there.

Jin would later learn that burning the midnight oil was a common occurrence in those days. The motto of those indefatigable students was "Pane, Lavoro e Paradiso," ("Bread, Work and Paradise"), reminiscent of their founder's program.

In that garden of noble ideals, unimaginable pursuits and hard work, was a disruptive romantic liaison with a fragile, vulnerable Japanese girl possible? Was it even conceivable, or just the outlandish, bizarre fantasy of a sick mind?

Given any resemblance of verisimilitude, what a fascinating story it would have been for the media!

Refusing to let his imagination go down that slippery road, Jin looked around anxiously, almost awaiting some ghost from the past to show up and reassure him. A few more seconds of that palpitant expectation and the down-to-earth detective was on his way back to the hotel.

Sometimes places have the power to transport people into another dimension and make them feel strange sensations. That former Pontifical Institute was no exception, not even for a man immune to easy suggestions.

The mixture of sex and religion, the clash of cultures and the powerful thrust of instincts and nature never ceases to amaze and intrigue humankind.

In his hotel room, while packing, Jin felt a surge of contrasting emotions. Was this investigation beyond his expertise and capabilities? Was he transgressing the boundaries of decency and desecrating holy things?

Would he be able to stop in time? Conversely, would people and circumstances toss him around in a whirlwind of life's vicissitudes?

The Japanese detective had never before faced radical dilemmas or frightening choices. Probably, during this adventure, unlike any other in the past, he would test his stamina and determination and reveal new facets of his personality.

Armed with patience and protected by a funny smile on his face, he would go to the ends of the earth, with no regrets. It was a kamikaze mission with only two outcomes, total suicide or complete success.

Highly motivated by his sense of duty, Jinpachi flew back from the "Old Lady" to the "Eternal City." Before visiting the S. Pontifical University (Quartiere Nuovo Salario), the inquisitive detective wanted to know some basic beliefs about the religious congregation that ran that center of superior studies.

He booked a room at Milani Hotel, in the proximities of Stazione Termini and very close to Sacro Cuore, the famous basilica founded by St. John Bosco and run by the members of the same congregation, in charge of the university in question.

The intent was clear. Jin wanted to become acquainted with that powerful religious society, with a noticeable presence all over the world, to which Kimiko's friends belonged.

Bred and fed by that organization, they were supposed to possess all the main characteristics of the founder and be a standard-bearer of his ideals.

On his visit to the basilica, he approached a seminarian from Australia, doing a kind of internship, in that sanctuary, during his summer vacation. It was very coincidental that the young Aussie was majoring in pedagogy (the theory or principles of education) at the S. Pontifical University.

The long conversation was a real revelation for the foreign private investigator. He learnt that the basic mission of the congregation was the education of youth. Don Bosco, the founder, had placed extreme emphasis on purity and chastity, without which, in his conviction, it was not feasible to become his follower and carry out an educational mission. He used to quote the following phrase from the Book of Wisdom (7, 11): "Venerunt autem mihi omnia bona pariter cum illa" ("Now all good things came to me together with her.")

While in the Bible "illa" ("her") refers to wisdom, Don Bosco interpreted it as "purity" and "chastity" making them the cornerstone of his educational system, and the most important prerequisite for any of his followers. Without purity and chastity, nobody should dare to join his religious order and become an educator. The opposite would be the mockery of all mockeries.

The young student from "down under" explained to his listener the main tenets of Don Bosco's pedagogical system. But Jin, from the Land of the Rising Sun, was frozen by the Biblical quote and could not swim his way out from an ocean of perplexity.

His malicious supposition of a love affair between Kimiko and the two students, in light of this doctrinal revelation, was unbelievable. How could it have even been thinkable that two students, members of such a religious congregation with so high a moral standard, could have entertained an illicit liaison with a female, during the most sensitive and spiritually intensive period of their priestly formation?

All the odds were heavily against similar conjecture. In a state of mental shock, the oriental detective shook off from his mind that persistent and impertinent presupposition, focusing instead on the points his improvised guide was trying to elucidate. Obviously, it was hard to do, but it was necessary for appearance's sake.

Following that formal meeting and in a more familiar setting, Jin talked about his intention to visit the S. Pontifical University. Very pleased, the Australian student offered to accompany him personally to his alma mater on his day off. Such a kind offer pleased the detective enormously. Suddenly he found himself in a favorable position. The records of those students were pivotal to a successful resolution of his investigation.

No sooner was the student free from his duties than he showed up at the Milani Hotel. Jin was ready and waiting for him. The weather was splendid and a great desire to live permeated the atmosphere. Everything was conducive and inviting. Not a cloud in the sky would suggest an ominous outcome to that search and retrieve mission.

During the trip, the conversational Aussie kept his host entertained and relaxed. Through his sagacious words, a new world of values and visions was opening up to Jin. He never thought, not even remotely, of real parallel ideological universes, where people live and breathe, operate and conduct their business, inspired and motivated by principles so alien to his own way of thinking. If their daily necessities were the same, their motivations and inspirations were disparate.

At the root of their vocation was not a generic veneer of philanthropism that could easily crack under pressure, but a sincere surrender to a mission of dedication and love on behalf of underprivileged youth, with nothing to lose and everything to gain.

He admired the zeal and fervor of that rare human breed, so genuine and uncommon at the same time. In his experience, he had only one point of reference, his kamikaze compatriots – ready to die for their country and their emperor, for the salvation of souls. Different missions, same commitment.

Penetrating the psyche and demeanor of that enthusiastic Aussie, it was amazing to capture how real and true was his altruistic spirit. It was not a sticky pietistic posture, but a sincere, humble projection, a live and dynamic human project, capable of miracles.

The more he came to admire this laudable model, the more reluctant he was to dig into the past of two of his confreres.

Their names were sculpted in his mind with indelible characters. Kimiko's sweet voice caressed them like a gentle breeze. The weeds of time hadn't outgrown them. Could he discover their origins, their astonishing development and their magical impact on a fragile yet determined young oriental woman?

Jin was about to find out. The taxi in which he traveled with his guide had reached the entrance of a magnificent new building. He paid the driver and ventured into the bowels of that impressive giant.

The lack of mundane noise was overwhelming, despite the numerous people crisscrossing corridors, riding elevators, entering, and exiting offices.

Maintaining a religious composure, they neared an office with a simple name on the door: Rev. Michele Frattini, Administrator. The man was very amiable. However, under his gentle demeanor and unassuming attitude there was an iron-like determination and a bloodhound nose.

Rev. Michele received them courteously and followed every single word the pseudo representative of an unknown benefactress uttered.

The story, so cleverly manufactured by that strange man, had a hollow ring to it. How could a real benefactor stay in hiding for more than twenty years, without the intended beneficiaries ever mentioning him or her, and without ever appearing in the official list of benefactors?

The administrator smelled mischievous treachery. Nevertheless, with the most convincing smile on his face and the most reassuring tone of voice, he said, "Before releasing any information on two members of my order, I would like to contact this admirable Japanese woman and verify in person that she is what you say she is."

Jin, not prepared for such an answer, remained speechless. Recovering quickly from that unexpected punch in the stomach, he replied, "I will do my best to put you in touch with my client, but first I need to confer with her. Thank you for your help and I will see you soon."

Jin's strategy had been a complete failure. Rarely in his career had he suffered such a resounding defeat. He was learning that religious people were not so gullible after all.

It was time to regroup and with the help of his resourceful Aussie find a new way to reach his goal. An excellent starting point would be to retrieve the present domicile of Kimiko's friends. That strategy turned out to be a very simple and effective one.

At the beginning of each year, all Catholic religious orders issue a yearbook containing the name, address and occupation of every single member.

How silly of them not to have thought of that in the first place!

The student had a copy of the yearbook in the library of his residence. The only thing left was to consult it. Jin did not have to invent any fancy story in order to access it, nor beg anybody, or use sneaky subterfuges. Everything was plain and simple. To release such information did not imply any impropriety or illegality.

Jin breathed a sigh of relief and thanked his guide. Finally, he could lay his hands on that precious information and start his investigation in earnest.

To his amazement, those two names were written with bold characters. Takeo Shirieda and Peter Egger not only possessed a prestigious address but also held a preeminent position within the order.

The carefree students of yesteryear, with great looks and superior intelligence, had reached the pinnacle of authority in their region. Both were provincials, Peter in Austria and Takeo in Japan. Moreover, according to curialist indiscretions, Takeo Shirieda would soon be nominated as a member of the pontifical congregation Propaganda Fide, and Peter Egger Bishop of Salzburg.

From mere high-ranking officials of a religious congregation, they would soon be part of the powerful Catholic hierarchy.

Still, according to well-founded rumors, a pontifical commission was investigating their past, leaving no stone unturned. Any tiny shred of impropriety, any youthful indiscretion, would have immediately frozen their ascent to the prospected position.

Jin came to the painful realization that he was treading on a minefield and discretion was of the utmost importance. Any misplaced word on his part, any unwarranted inference, any slip of the tongue at all, could have ruined those two rising stars. The ecclesiastical firmament, so bright and enticing, does not admit black holes or falling stars among its ranks, nor out-of-orbit asteroids compromising its heavenly harmony.

All had to fit properly in its place and all had to work in perfect synchronicity. The Vatican diplomacy and its commissions were the supreme watchdogs. They had to ensure even the slightest appearance of impropriety or irregularity was banned from their universe.

To get in touch with these future high-ranking officials he had to forgo the planned game of cat and mouse, waiting for the propitious time. A face-to-face interview was completely out of the question. Moreover, any mention of an old friendship with a Japanese woman or any acknowledgment from her of their affection could have been catastrophic.

It was imperative to alter the course of the investigation by working in absolute secrecy. At this point in time, the only thing that really mattered was to anonymously obtain some DNA samples from both clergies and discover whether any biological connection existed between them and the twins Castor and Pollux.

The first half of the new mission took Jin to the beautiful city of Salzburg, Austria. By train, he reached that jewel of alpine beauty and world-famous baroque architecture, birthplace of Mozart. On his arrival, his first impression was of sheer amazement and fascination. Enchanted, dreamlike scenery appeared to his astonished eyes, making him forget the purpose of his trip.

He had a reservation for the Crowne Plaza Salzburg Hotel, ideally located next to the magnificent Mirabell Gardens and opposite the Congress Center in the very heart of Salzburg.

After settling down in his tastefully decorated room, he walked to the nearest café for a cup of coffee and a generous portion of apple strudel. The locals were friendly but reserved. Talking casually to a waitress, by the name of Brigitta, he received some valuable information. The following day, Sunday, the Rev. Peter Egger, rumored bishop *in pectore* of Salzburg, would celebrate the eleven o'clock Mass in the Cathedral. They were expecting a high attendance with a consequent rise in business. Eatery establishments had hired extra staff for the occasion. Excitement was in the air. Everybody was dying to see and hear the future shepherd of the Catholic Church.

What a magnificent opportunity for the undercover detective! With impeccable accuracy, he could obtain the exact schedule of the future bishop, the places he would visit, and among them the convent where he would stop for lunch.

Wasting no time, Jin, through a friend Brigitta had, contacted a dishwasher that for many years had worked in the convent where the visiting ecclesiastical dignitary would stop for a frugal meal. With precise instructions, the simple woman received a substantial sum of money. If everything went according to plan, the reward would be doubled.

The task was extremely easy and perfectly harmless. She would keep separate, in a safe place, a glass or cup used by the reverend and an unknown collaborator would collect a DNA sample. Unnoticed, the simple woman, who firmly believed in admiration and religiosity, performed the maneuver without a hitch.

For the DNA exam, the detective used a famous lab in town and to avoid any tampering, the sample had a fictitious name.

By any standard, the operation appeared flawless in its execution. No wonder Jin was ready to wrap up his stay. However, all hell broke loose when the results came back. More accurately, there were no results, because there was no DNA on the glass. Nobody would ever know what happened.

The Japanese detective went in a matter of seconds from a euphoric mood to a deep depression. Was he fighting against an invisible enemy, smarter and shrewder than he was? An ecclesiastical conspiracy would be improbable but not impossible.

At the risk of making things worse, Jin poured out his troubles to Brigitta over a cup of coffee. She in turn confided the failed secret operation to an old nun, who had been her catechism teacher. There is nothing out of reach for women who put their mind to it. Their mysterious ways can find a path in the most impenetrable jungle, or on the faceless horizon of a burning desert. In the face of adversity, their courage and inventiveness are admirable.

That frail, humble servant of God looked into the eyes of her former pupil and her face irradiated with a sparkle of inner joy.

"Not to worry, my child," she said with a benevolent smile. "I have the perfect solution for your problem. During the Mass, the Reverend wiped some sweat from his face using a monogrammed handkerchief I provided. I kept it as a relic. You can borrow it and return it as soon as possible."

The young waitress hugged the sister with the affection of a daughter. With the precious memento in her purse she ran joyously to the detective, who was becoming increasingly despondent.

However, Brigitta, before leaving the nunnery, received a valuable lesson from her former teacher. The nun, as she had done in the past, did not pass up such a marvelous occasion without handing down a pebble of her wisdom.

Staring into the distance and holding Brigitta's right hand, she started lecturing her pupil by quoting in Latin from Matthew's Gospel (6, 24) a saying so dear to her heart.

"Sufficit diei malitia sua," which literally translated means, "Sufficient for the day is the evil thereof." Expanding on that obscure concept, open to several interpretations, the old teacher proposed her own personal interpretation, matured during many years of sweat and toil, of hardships and suffering.

"Dear Brigitta, every day has its trouble. It is unavoidable. We must face it and believe it is proportionate to our capabilities. Without magnifying it with our worries or belittling it with our simplistic ideologies, we must take care of it. There is always a solution, which is not permanent or good for every occasion.

The mistake of our society is to believe that with a law, a disposition, we can prevent future occurrences of failures, disasters and criminal acts. That might be partially true, but it will never hold in a universal sense. Moreover, this can create a false sense of security, which in turn strengthens a spurious optimism of a better future. Unfortunately, the truth is that no man can have total control of what surrounds him. Blind forces of nature, human's free will, and even personal instincts, more often than not are beyond our personal control.

If so many fundamental variables are outside reason and law, how can anybody expect a harmonious society, a peaceful future and a worry-free life? Every day has its own troubles, every day will always have its own problems, there will never exist a "happily ever after" situation. By rejecting this Pollyannaish vision, and accepting the "readiness to fight every day the good fight," inherent to our human nature, we can survive. The painful disappointments, frustrations and depressions will not overwhelm our natural instinct of survival. The successes, joys and euphoric exultations will never blind or obscure our troubled realities, always lying in wait for a new challenge, a new obstacle.

The preachers of an insured life, free from economic or psychological pressures, of a never-ending stability and happiness, of an esoteric moral righteousness or of an exclusive path to salvation are false prophets. They might be politicians, religious people, academics, businesspeople or simple, common charlatans; they still are and remain false prophets.

Their secret weapon is deception. Consciously or not, they sell illusions and false hope. Under the cover of noble ideals, they seek their own advantage, their own interest. Power and prestige, fortune and enjoyment are their drugs of choice.

Inebriated by such poisonous motivators, they lead the masses, even whole nations, astray. It is time to regain our personal independence and build our own vision of life. Let us get rid of our idols with feet of clay, of our specious ideals and values, of all the counterfeit merchandise accumulated by centuries of indoctrination and let us breathe anew an air of renovation, of sincerity and authenticity.

My dear Brigitta, we must wake up from our illusions and dreams and look at our always-changing reality, filled with difficulties and vicissitudes, successes and misfortunes, joys and sufferings. Nobody will fight for us the good fight, and nobody can make us immune from our share of troubles."

The venerable nun stopped uttering sounds. Her facial expression and demeanor was that of a post-trance experience. On the threshold of her life, had she briefly crossed over to the other side and looking back discovered the pathetic fallacies of this world?

It is hard to imagine a religious woman with a long life experience painting such a grim view of our society and culture. Not even a prophet of the Old Testament would go as far as proclaiming our reality a cruel deception, smoke and mirrors and a total lie.

A woman who had dedicated her entire existence to serving God in humankind, was she qualified for such judgments and pronouncements?

Maybe, just because of her lack of studies she could better tune in to nature. Maybe, divested of ideologies and superstructures she could better feel the true pulse of reality.

Regardless of her qualifications or sensitivities, she was not alone in that kind of queerish thinking. From Plato to Calderón de la Barca and beyond numerous people have conceived our reality as a shadow, a dream, something inconsistent and deceiving.

Our reality is unreal, our perception fogged and distorted, our convictions misleading.

The frail nun, gasping for breath, looked benevolently into Brigitta's eyes, as if she wanted to ask forgiveness for her extemporaneous outburst of pernicious concepts. She concluded her unintended conceptual rebuke by repeating twice the initial quote, "Sufficit diei malitia sua."

Whether that was a statement of intent, an involuntary justification of her behavior, or a motherly admonition to her listener, nobody would ever know. She had spoken her mind. She had poured her heart out and she felt better.

Finally telling the truth was a great weight off her shoulders. She felt her time on this earth was up. One step away from the grave, she breathed an incredible sense of tranquility, peacefulness and heedlessness, unthinkable in the heyday of her youth. With a serene smile on her face, she told Brigitta, "This is my testament to you. Treasure it and share it. Your Japanese friend might understand it, or he might not. Whatever the case may be, it will give him a broader perspective and a wiser approach to his daily pursuit of clues and explanations. Go, and give him the special handkerchief."

Brigitta, still stunned and bewildered by what she had heard, ran off with the precious object. Jin had been waiting impatiently for quite a while. When he saw her, an intense anxiety overtook him. However, all changed in an instant when the young woman produced the surprising personal effect.

The detective remained ecstatic, with an incredulous look. He could not believe his eyes and his good fortune. Brigitta had obtained what his careful planning could not. Needless to say, his sense of gratitude toward his improvised assistant was indescribable. As a gesture of sheer joy, he forgot to bow to her; instead, he hugged and kissed her with all the effusion of his heart.

That was a remarkable attitude in a traditional oriental man, always attentive to traditions and etiquette. Brigitta was surprised too and contrasting emotions encircled her small world, tossing her on a capricious whirlwind of wild speculations.

With that incredible show of raw feelings and emotions one departed from the other, leaving a strange taste of something unresolved. That spontaneous kiss had created a new parallel universe, where the impossible assumed the appearance of the possible. Not only had Brigitta forgotten to convey the prophetic nun's message to Jin, she also found herself lost in a quagmire of sentiments that tore her soul apart. All had been so sudden, so unexpected and captivating that she did not have time to separate the wheat from the chaff.

Did Brigitta, in a fit of irrationality, want more of that sweet honey? Did Jin imply anything else in his gesture besides a genuine outburst of gratitude?

For the young woman the atmosphere remained charged with powerful currents, while for the seasoned detective a great sense of accomplishment filled his spirit. The same act had given origin to contrasting interpretations.

Neither was totally wrong or totally right. Each read the same reality according to his or her personal resonance.

In possession of that special trophy, Jin told Brigitta to hurry to the lab for the examination. This time he was really anxious to know the results. Would frustration set in once more, or would resounding success crown all that hard work?

He did not have to wait long for the final report. When Brigitta got the results, she made several copies for her personal use. After that, she returned and handed the envelope to the tense detective. To nobody's surprise, the handkerchief contained the Rev. Peter Egger's DNA. However, the detective was completely taken aback when he read the conclusions. The comparison between Pollux's DNA and Peter's DNA revealed, without a shadow of doubt, a biological connection. It was evident Peter Egger was Pollux's real father.

Did Peter know of this paternity? Did he at least have some suspicions of having fathered a child in his tormentous youth? Undoubtedly, Kimiko wasn't in the dark. She had a lot of explaining to do. Her mysterious behavior, her induced reticence, her clever façade, her alleged platonic friendship with the young seminarian, masked a monstrous secret, a painful, yet cherished past.

The admired religious man, who came from an order that held purity and chastity as the only essential thing for pastoral success and survival, and who was about to become Bishop of Salzburg, was equally concealing a passionate event that if known could easily destroy his brilliant career.

From the revelation of those DNA conclusions, nobody would gain anything. Probably the most affected would be Pollux. He had been lied to and cheated by his own mother. His family, so traditional and exemplary, would collapse like a house of cards. An alienated mother, a putative father, a dead brother and an unknown father would constitute his new grim reality.

In an instant, all would be swept away by a violent hurricane, leaving behind debris of insanity and a swamp of treachery. All too often, the truth is more destructive than a lie. Continuous deception would appear as the only salvation table.

Jin had a lot of thinking to do before any sudden rush to reveal the stark truth. Still in a state of deep shock, he could not halt his unbridled imagination.

He started comparing father and son's physical characteristics. Peter Egger was incredibly handsome. A powerful allure, in fact, emanated from his person. His blue eyes and blond hair enhanced his magnetism. Pollux, on the other hand, possessed two big round eyes, whose color was quite difficult to typify, a mixture of hazelnut and greenish with no well-defined boundaries. The hair too escaped any traditional classification, being of smooth texture and light chestnut brown color. Pollux was definitely more Eurasian than Asian. However, one single feature, the nose, gave him away and made him unmistakably Peter's son of Aryan descent.

In the light of such evidence, why did nobody ever suspect Pollux's spurious origin? Was there a conspiracy of silence, a mysterious pact, a superimposed coercion?

The wealthy and powerful have always possessed means and ways of imposing their vision of reality. In this particular case, the mystification of Pollux's conception had been deliberate and masterfully planned. The family's honor and integrity had to be upheld for all eternity. Pollux was the legal heir to the Ishida's vast fortune and as such had to present immaculate birth credentials.

Jinpachi Nemoto's investigation was unearthing inconvenient and disturbing facts that threatened to jeopardize the stability and continuity of a famous dynasty.

However, that was only half the truth. The other half, belonging to Castor's origin, probably could be found in a prominent Japanese clergy, ready to become a member of a Vatican congregation, Propaganda Fide. The detective could not erase the reappearance in his mind of a famous picture, enshrined in Kimiko's living room, where she appeared surrounded by two smiling seminarians, Peter Egger and Takeo Shirieda. Was Takeo the father of the deceased twin, Castor? How could that be even imaginable? Twins with a different biological father? Only Greek mythology could offer a similar abstruse fabrication.

The probability of that myth being scientifically true was one in a trillion, which in practical terms meant zero.

Mythology and probabilities apart, the simplest way of verifying the bizarre supposition was to obtain Shirieda's DNA and check the hospital records where the twins were delivered.

The baffled detective had to proceed with extreme caution and have a sincere talk with Kimiko.

He put a stop to his delirious raving. In a hurry and without a second thought he booked his flight back to Tokyo.

The enchanted hills of Austria, the lovely Brigitta, and the prominent clergy Egger, with his scandalous story, were soon forgotten. The second part of his mission was in a familiar territory, where the shrewd sleuth could maneuver at his pleasure.

Chapter 6

"*The only thing infinite is our capacity for self-deception.*"

It was a typical fall day in Kyoto. The sky was overcast, the temperature mild and Jinpachi's expectations extraordinary.

Upon his return from Austria, the Ishida family greeted him with sympathy and curiosity. No sign or indication of something abnormal transpired from his usual ceremonial demeanor.

He was in no particular rush to reveal the findings of his investigation to the interested party. There were two fundamental reasons for that decision. Firstly, Lady Kimiko Ishida was experiencing a frightening spell of depression that kept her reclusive and incommunicado. Secondly, he wanted to check the hospital where the twins' records were kept and obtain the DNA of the prominent clergy Takeo Shirieda.

Having friends in high places and knowing people with the right connections was Jin's sure ticket to a successful mission. However, what seems easy on paper oftentimes turns out to be, if not disastrous, surely treacherous and perfidious.

While strategizing in the quest for the hospital records, he received a letter from a European organization, whose name was absolute hogwash. In-depth research came up with no clue. The "Organization for the Defense of Clergies" was a no show, probably just a fictitious tool of intimidation by some deranged fanatics.

In that letter, addressed personally to Jinpachi Nemoto, a serious threat on his life was made in the event he should reveal the results of Peter Egger's DNA test. The shadowy organization was adamant in its request. Any disclosure would be met with the loss of a limb or his life itself.

The style and content of the letter bore a striking resemblance to the mafia's unscrupulous and bloody methods.

No religious organization would operate along those criminal parameters, let alone a Catholic association, or would it?

Deeply disturbed and profoundly shaken, the seasoned detective felt like a rookie in the first days of his career.

Had he touched a sensitive nerve of the Catholic hierarchy, or just infringed on a delicate personal area, forbidden to outsiders?

Was that letter a believable threat or just a desperate attempt to scare and gag the private investigator? Most importantly, who was the source of the leak? Only two persons knew of the DNA test on Peter Egger, Brigitta and the old nun, and only one had cogent reasons for betraying the Japanese.

There was no need for great intuition or special powers of deduction to reach the obvious conclusion. Brigitta was the informer.

Jin's abrupt departure from Salzburg, without even saying goodbye, left the charming café waitress in a complete emotional shambles. She felt used and abused, like a piece of clothing or a kitchen tool, ready to be disposed of as soon as it no longer serves a purpose.

Obviously, she felt entitled to sweet revenge. Without wasting any time, she wrote a letter to the Rev. Peter Egger, detailing the steps taken by Jinpachi Nemoto with the precise intent of obtaining his DNA. For obvious reasons she omitted the nun's and her collaboration in that evil plan and her resentment for the treatment received.

The Reverend did not need to be a genius to connect the dots and discover the real intentions of his enemies. By uncovering the prevarication of his ebullient youth, they intended to discredit him and forever close the door to his imminent ascent to the Salzburg Episcopal office. Bewilderment and panic followed among his close friends, as soon as the influential clergy revealed the content of the letter. They had to mount a prompt, effective defense, which resulted in the threatening letter, the authors of which nobody would ever know.

The polite, always ceremonious investigator had not only underestimated the Austrian woman, he had forgotten a basic tenet of a private eye. Any collaborator must be bound by the same vow of secrecy as the private investigator. On top of that and out of deference and gratitude, he should have kept cordial relations.

That implausible slip in his professional etiquette was costing him a serious headache that would not go away with a simple pill.

In both quarters, Salzburg and Kyoto, fear and panic were rampant. Rev. Peter Egger saw the apogee of his career darkened by an ominous cloud. The days of his triumph, supposed to burst with joy and merriment, were instead dripping with tears.

On the other continent, Detective Nemoto had dreamt of comfortable days in his homeland with a very successful conclusion of his investigation; instead, like a hunted animal, he avoided daylight, public places and interaction with people.

A simple disclosure by an unknown waitress had changed the rules of the game forever. The world they knew and were used to no longer existed. A disgruntled woman, innocuous to all appearances, had subverted their universe, sowing confusion and disarray.

On top of that Jinpachi had another potentially explosive front to deal with – the Ishida family, and more specifically the beautiful but disturbed Kimiko.

As had happened often in the past, she was experiencing a severe bout of depression that rendered her almost unmanageable. Instead of seeking professional help, she was auto-diagnosing her condition as a transitory mood swing and self-medicating with a healthy dose of seclusion and mutism.

When she was young, her parents did not attach much importance to her moody behavior, believing time and age would modify that abnormality. Her father, in particular, to alleviate her depression, bought her things and took her with on his frequent trips abroad.

Unfortunately, with the passing of time her condition worsened considerably. Parental guidance and friendly advice were insufficient to produce a tangible change. In her glorious moments of euphoria and elation, she was charming, seductive and irresistible. During the long spells of depression, she would become irrational, despondent, destructive and extremely irritable.

Even a profane eye, not clinically trained, could have detected a serious chemical imbalance, a very abnormal mental condition.

In short, Kimiko showed all the symptoms of a disease called bipolar disorder. The way she dealt with it had been wrong all along, as had her father's cures been erroneous and misguided.

Now, despite her family's understanding and sympathy, she was languishing in a frightful isolationism, ready to explode in extreme acts of self-mutilation or suicide.

Jinpachi followed those aberrant manifestations closely. Grasping the severity of Kimiko's condition, he was impotent in his desire to help her. Like a bystander, he looked on at the inevitable demise of a beautiful human being. He dreaded the moment in which he would have to reveal the results of his investigation. Would that be the final straw? Obviously, he did not intend to be instrumental in breaking that noble soul.

While waiting and hoping for a miracle, the private investigator obtained, through an Ishida family member, a copy of the twins' birth certificate from the hospital where they were born.

According to the document, they had come into this world the same day, a few minutes apart. The mother's name was Kimiko Ishida and the father's name Hiro Kimura.

Jinpachi knew the father's name on the document did not square away at least with one of the twin's biological father. The family was covering up some dark secret, the eventual disclosure of which would cause serious damage.

Kimiko's delicate mental condition and the family's threatened image did not deter the intrepid detective from pursuing the last part of his mission – discovering Castor's biological father.

The solution to that puzzle had always been in that famous picture, where two smiling seminarians had their arms around Kimiko's waist.

The second prominent clergy, on the greatest upswing of his career, soon to be nominated member of a Vatican congregation called Propaganda Fide was Rev. Takeo Shirieda. Respected and admired, he lived a frugal life, far away from the spotlight and totally dedicated to his pastoral mission.

Nobody could ever fathom the devastating consequences if the news of fathering a child turned out to be true. An obscure and painful incident during his formative years could bring him down and bury him under a pile of mud.

Knowing perfectly well the catastrophic consequences of his investigation, Jinpachi pushed forward with an unprecedented determination, unaware that devious, sly figures were following him, observing his every move. Against all odds, he wanted to get to the bottom of a confusing reality.

In the parish church where Rev. Takeo lived as resident pastor and provincial of his order, an important annual celebration was coming up. He would preside over a solemn Mass and after that a splendid banquet. The highest local authorities would be present, along with other dignitaries and celebrities.

Through the services of a very close friend, it would not be difficult for the detective to obtain a glass with the Reverend's DNA.

The operation, mounted without any showy or eye-catching apparatus, proved to be simple and effective. The results of the lab analysis, although not completely unexpected, were startling.

Rev. Takeo Shirieda was indeed Castor's biological father. If science was adamant in proclaiming a double biological paternity in the same set of twins, the same accurate science did not have an answer on how that could be possible or even thinkable.

The private investigator had never before had such a mysterious and burning reality on his hands. Only Kimiko held the key to that puzzle. Only Kimiko knew the sequence of events that led to such an outcome. Only Kimiko could shed some light on the improbable double paternity of her twins.

Confronted with a reality she never wanted revealed, would she finally come forward with the truth? Alternatively, would she crash under the monstrous deception and innumerable lies woven by her family over so many years?

Given her psychological condition, any prediction was a total tossup. Contrary to her family's fears, Kimiko emerged quicker than expected from her depression. She showed a luminous face, an expansive mood, and a great desire to engage people and circumstances.

Jin saw a marvelous window of opportunity and arranged for a meeting at the end of the week.

Unfortunately if, on one side, the sky seemed to open up and present a chance of a lifetime, on the other side, dark clouds covered the horizon and rumbling thunder deafened his ears.

No sooner had he wrapped up his investigation and obtained the results than another letter reached his address. This time there was no threatening content, but a sure promise of a swift revenge. He had blithely disregarded the first warning and the punishment was upon him.

Confronted with a faceless enemy, the detective became timorous, feeling, for the first time in his career, unprotected and at the mercy of the unknown. If his life was at risk, he had to cover all the bases and run immediately for cover.

With no time to waste, he made a copy of all the lab results. By certified mail, he sent them to Ken Fresco, the chief detective in Pittsburgh.

The two prominent clergies, Peter Egger and Takeo Shirieda, would also receive a copy of their paternity test. If they never knew or had doubts about having produced an offspring, now they would know for sure. Their uncertainties would be laid to rest.

That secret incriminating document would not only put a damper on the most significant day of their careers, but also might forever ruin their lives as men of the cloth.

Forced by adverse circumstances, Jin was precipitating events that should have unfolded slowly and painlessly. At this point, a deadly machine was moving, and nobody had the power to stop it.

Would it sow death and destruction, purification and regeneration, or both?

When human free will is involved anything is possible, and no prediction is ever accurate.

If he had received the old nun's message that everything is lies and deception, would he have acted differently? Would he have conducted himself with more caution? Had the religious woman foreseen something frightening in Jin's immediate future? Was he dealing in a thoughtless way with an explosive reality, ready to blow up in his face?

While those explosive documents flew to their intended destinations, something terrifying and appalling happened.

There was no doubt a mysterious organization, author of a second threatening letter, meant business. The day before his meeting with Kimiko, the fearless private detective Jinpachi Nemoto was found dead on the driveway below his apartment.

In a pool of blood, with a fractured skull and a smashed body lay Jinpachi, lifeless, eyes open, almost begging for mercy. To all external appearances it looked like suicide. In his seventh floor apartment there was neither sign of forced entry, nor any indication the motive was a robbery or some vengeful act. Everything was in order. There were no visible signs of a struggle. The only indicative thing was the open window, which did not lead anywhere for the lack of fingerprints.

If it was not suicide, the job had been carried out with surgical precision and immaculate professionalism. At first, nobody knew the sensitive documents were missing, among them the two paternity tests and the two threatening letters. Only when the Pittsburgh detective, Ken Fresco, notified the Kyoto police he had recently received the DNA test results from Jinpachi did they realize the inconsistency of a suicide hypothesis and the probable cause of that sudden death.

Despite that communication shedding some light on the matter, the Kyoto police had a hell of a case on their hands that could take months, even years, to reach a satisfactory solution, because they were in the dark, as was everyone else, concerning the letters and the specifics of Nemoto's investigation.

That horrible death filled everyone with dismay, fear and suspicion, starting with the Ishida family. Needless to say the main protagonists, Peter Egger and Takeo Shirieda, already in possession of their paternity tests, were also extremely shaky and fearful.

They were faced with an unprecedented choice, to reveal their secret paternity to their superiors and consequently incur severe punishment, or to keep lying to God, to themselves, and to the Church and suffer the constant torment of their consciences.

Another tactical choice was available, if the two ecclesiastics were concerned about a likely disclosure and divulgation of their ignominious secret – early retirement. Fading into anonymity with no fanfare or publicity would leave intact their scandalous conduct and resolve the problem, sparing the Church from humiliation and ridicule.

To voluntarily give up power is never a viable option for a man in a position of authority. For Peter Egger and Takeo Shirieda it was even more difficult. They had coated that intoxicating pill with religious justifications. God had called them to shepherd his flock. Nobody on earth had the right to terminate that divine mission. Since its origin was from God, only He could put an end to it.

Blinded by a similar pseudo-theology, so widespread among religious people, a voluntary withdrawal from public office – much less a public confession of their shameful past – was unthinkable.

The matter was becoming unmanageable and out of control. It was clear the police would interrogate the clergies and possibly indict them for their connection to the two murders. The proverbial Church silence regarding its subjects and its traditional praxis of sweeping their misdeeds under the carpet would further complicate their investigation.

At the end of the day, nobody would come out as a winner. The police would look like intruders and violators of the Church immunity, and the Church like a protector and refuge for criminals.

Would the two authorities give up some of their prerogatives and reach a workable compromise? Alternatively, would they prefer a frontal collision in order to uphold their positions and save face?

Jinpachi's assassins, whose aim was to suppress any possible connection between the two eminent clergies and Kimiko's sons, obtained the opposite effect. Contrary to their abominable plan, they let the cat out of the bag. Everybody knew now the Ishida family possessed a shameful secret and that two renowned members of the Catholic Church had been involved in an immoral, sinful affair.

The Pittsburgh police had another lead to follow, a possible international crime organization – so far never taken into consideration – going under the name of the "Organization for the Defense of Clergies."

Was it directly or indirectly affiliated with the Church, or a private criminal enterprise composed of a handful of zealots? Was there any record of this underground movement, or was it just a fancy front to mislead law enforcement?

Whatever the case, it was worth looking into it through Interpol.

The Kyoto Police, already in touch with their Pittsburgh counterpart, would notify the Salzburg detectives and coordinate the efforts spanning three continents.

This unprecedented effort rattled the Ishida family, whose foundation seemed to shake badly under the undue burden. Money, prestige and connections were not enough to arrest the monstrous machinery. The efforts of many years of hard work and skillful planning would vanish like a chimera. A youthful indiscretion would bring down a powerful dynasty. Nothing but misery and disgrace would accompany Kimiko until the end of her days.

As soon as the papers in Kyoto started unveiling some unbelievable details of the paternity tests, intense curiosity and unending gossip began mushrooming not only all over the city, but also all over the country. The initial small snowball was becoming an overpowering avalanche, burying people and things in its wake, leaving a trail of indescribable destruction.

The first victim was obviously Kimiko, followed by Peter Egger and Takeo Shirieda. The picture of yesteryear showing three smiling faces all of a sudden became a mug shot kept in police records.

It is not easy to narrate their ordeal, their sufferings and their outcome.

Before assisting their precipitous demise, a look at their past will put things into perspective, toning down harsh judgments and ruthless critics.

Chapter 7

*"We are never **deceived**; we **deceive** ourselves."* –
Goethe

In an enchanting village, called Mondsee in Austria, there
was happiness and celebration in the air. Frau Theresa
had given birth to a healthy, seven-pound baby. She was
the mayor's wife and after a prolonged labor, she could
finally hold her firstborn in her arms.

Fighting back the tears, she could not remove
her eyes from that little bundle of joy. As a woman, she
felt fulfilled and as a wife proud of giving her husband an
heir.

For the whole Egger family that was the day that
the Lord had made. It was a time for jubilation and
merriment. The entire community joined in with
manifestations of joy.

The baptism ceremony in the historical cathedral
saw the majority of the population gathered around the
baptismal font. The ritual possessed the mystery of a
time when the sacred was revered and feared.

The celebrant, an old priest with a husky voice,
called the newborn Peter, a name chosen unanimously by
the family.

During the rite, something very unusual and
foreboding happened. The minister was pronouncing
those threatening words, "Exorcizo te, immunde spiritus,
in nomine Patris et Filii et Spiritus Sancti, ut exeas, et
recedas ab hoc famulo Dei...: ipse enim tibi imperat,
maledicte damnate... Ergo, maledicte diabole, recognosce
sententiam tuam... et recede ab hoc famulo..." ("I
exorcise thee, unclean spirit, in the name of the Father
and of the Son, and of the Holy Spirit, that thou goest
out and depart from this servant of God...: for He
commands Thee, accursed one... Therefore, accursed
devil, acknowledge thy sentence... and depart from this
servant...") when an altar boy inadvertently knocked over
a flickering candle.

A few among the participants raised their
eyebrows in amazement. However, panic replaced

surprise as soon as a sacred linen caught fire. Flames and smoke engulfed the altar and tabernacle. Only the prompt action of a handful of courageous, faithful congregants averted a sure disaster.

In ancient times, people were very superstitious and attached special significance to any out-of-the-ordinary phenomenon. Still in those days, some individuals, known as the voice of tradition and interpreters of the future, would dare to venture some dire predictions.

How could anybody of sound mind look at that cherubic face, and predict evil deeds and fiery destruction? Ominous presages, gossip and rumors do not die easily in traditional villages. However, the occasion was too festive to hang on to scary thoughts and negativities.

The day was gorgeous, the atmosphere relaxed and the expectations very high. The villagers quickly forgot the mishap inside the cathedral and threw themselves body and soul into the lavish festivities. A band played traditional songs in the main square, while numerous folks danced to their tunes. All seemed spontaneous and sincere and the whole world seemed to dance with the small Austrian village.

The celebrations dragged on until midnight and the following day, Sunday, everybody's favorite conversation was the christening of the mayor's son.

No one would probably ever forget that joyful event. The Egger family, in fact, was not only influential but had been well respected and a focal point for generations.

The infant Peter could not have hoped for a better or more loving family. Mother, father, grandparents and other relatives poured on the new member all the affection they could muster. He was destined to carry on the family name and uphold the village's noble traditions.

Certainly, a heavy burden was laid on those fragile shoulders. Would the newborn prove himself worthy of all the attention and hopes bestowed on him?

According to his secretary, Peter did not have many memories of his childhood. However, a few stood out, like a milestone on the Appian Way.

He remembered with fondness his deceased grandmother taking him to church every Sunday. She would dress him up with the best clothes he possessed in his small closet, walk him to the imposing cathedral, put his fingertips in the holy water, kept in a font near the entrance, make the sign of the cross and kneel down on an oak pew. Those were little steps that would lead him psychologically only in one direction.

The ceremonial Mass was interminable for the small child, but a great peace and reverential awe would fill his heart, molding his soul. Like other children, he would not fuss, talk or cause a disturbance, but he would stare at the altar and follow every movement of the celebrant. Grandma was so proud of him and he loved her in return with an endearing simplicity.

Regrettably, she passed away before he could manifest his desire to become a priest. Then she would have beamed with joy and satisfaction.

Another moment that stuck permanently in his mind was the first day of school. Instead of being a traumatic day, as it usually turns out to be for many children, for Peter it was a glorious day. The reason was very simple. The first grade teacher was one of his aunts, and three of his female cousins were his schoolmates. On top of that, he felt important and grown up, wearing a school uniform and carrying books and pencils.

As soon as he stepped into the classroom, accompanied by his mother, he felt at home. His aunt greeted him with a big smile and assigned him a seat near her desk.

Did his physical location, next to the teacher, invest him with a special responsibility of supervision? As a born leader, he felt that way, even if in reality his aunt did not attach any special meaning.

His leadership role came to prominence during fifth grade when his schoolmates elected him class president. His duties were spelled out in a long list of tasks that can be easily summarized in one basic mission

– to keep order and discipline. At his tender age, he took seriously his assignment to the great satisfaction of the teacher and students. In fact, he was able to command the respect of his class and obtain incredible results. With the authority came the perks. Pupils looked at him with admiration and in particular a girl, named Susannah, seemed to have a terrible crush on him.

Her behavior, with the peculiar characteristics of puppy love, caused great confusion in Peter. Much to his embarrassment, he realized he too had feelings for her. She appeared to him like a little princess in the flesh. Every one of her movements, words or gestures were extremely cute and lovely.

Her hair, her eyes, her lips possessed the hidden fire of a thousand volcanoes, her melodious voice the enchantment and spell of countless sirens and her gaze a piercing arrow penetrating deep into his heart.

During the night, she would appear in his dreams and during the day, she would not miss an occasion to approach him with some nice gesture or comment.

Authority and physical attraction can be a deadly combination. Could Peter walk the walk and show good judgment and impartiality?

He was still a boy when his desire to become a priest materialized. In view of this, those feelings were becoming a menacing obstacle. In the small world of his comprehension, he saw clearly the incompatibility between God and Susannah, his vocation and that fatal attraction. Heaven and hell had never come so close and disputed the supremacy of his heart.

The dilemma was radical, abnegation and renunciation, or surrender and enjoyment; celibacy or marriage; Church or woman.

Despite his tender age, Peter grasped this dichotomy with meridian clarity. Would he be able to walk away from his mundane tendencies and cut himself off from all human desire? Would that cut be radical and permanent or just superficial and temporary?

The last two months of fifth grade were rocky and turbulent, to say the least. Not without difficulty, he asserted his leadership role, putting to rest idle gossip and mean remarks.

He bravely distanced himself from the tempting apple. Nevertheless, some sentimental attachment lingered on, leaving an emotional scar on his psyche.

In this childhood drama, it is worth noting that Peter was not the instigator of the fire of passion. He was clearly a victim of circumstances. However, contrary to all human predictions, he was first to cut that strangling cord, setting himself free and flying to better pastures.

A young priest, belonging to a religious congregation unknown in those regions, came to Mondsee.

Invited by the local pastor, he gave some impassioned talks to a group of elementary school children, in preparation for the Holy Week. However, he had a hidden agenda – to recruit possible candidates for the priesthood and his order.

The topic of his fervent, fiery sermons was the cleansing of the soul from any impurity and sin, and God's call to a higher mission.

In order to be able to listen to God's voice, man needed to be spotless inside. There was no better or nobler profession in life than to dedicate one's existence to the Almighty, sacrificing everything from material possession to the legitimate desire to form a family. No sacrifice would ever be huge enough, considering the reward of an eternal life in heaven.

Among those young listeners was Peter Egger, who had already decided in his heart to follow the priestly vocation. Those inflamed words strengthened his determination, setting his heart on fire. He could barely wait to tell the visiting priest and his parents about his decision.

The preacher was elated by that revelation, but not so Peter's father, who saw his dreams vanishing in a puff of smoke. No words of discouragement, no enticing promises, no fatherly effort were able to reverse Peter's decision. His mind was firmly set on the priesthood, becoming blind and deaf to any other call, no matter how reasonable and thoughtful it was.

In his tender age, he seemed to follow an inescapable logic. God, the Supreme Being and the Ineffable Good, He constitutes the highest priority. Consequently, his call supersedes everything else, supplanting any other pretense and making null and void any human claim or right.

With this ironclad argument, Peter felt invincible. Any other reason, whether logical or sentimental, would be dismissed *a priori*.

Similar rational mentality in embryo, so pervasive in religious people, will develop, with ecclesiastical education and theological instruction, into a full-blown blinding dogmatism.

The enticement of the flesh, embodied by the charming Susannah, not only paled into insignificance when compared with God, but also became a devil's ally to be avoided at any costs. His eternal salvation was at risk, together with his priestly vocation.

His perspective on human relations had changed considerably, inverting priorities and leaving his previous world upside down. Family ties and any type of emotional attachment had to be subordinated to God's demands.

Jesus had been uncompromising on this particular issue: "Another of his disciples said to him, 'Lord let me go first and bury my father.' But Jesus answered him, 'Follow me and let the dead bury their dead.'" (Mt 8, 21-22).

Jesus' call overrides even a filial obligation of the highest importance, considered sacred in the Jewish and Hellenistic worlds.

Imbued with this teaching, Peter would dismiss any consideration or appeal coming from mundane sources, whether family, friends or simply people interested in his welfare.

The young preacher, with his impassioned sermons, had left a lasting impression on Peter, molding his soul and spirit irreversibly.

At the end of that historic summer, the Egger firstborn left his native land with its placid lake, and like a devoted little soldier marched into the seminary. He was ready to undertake the most grueling training of any human profession.

Bravely and without a tear in his eyes, he said goodbye to his parents, relatives and friends. Susannah was not included in the emotional farewell. Purposely avoided, she would however remain, for years to come, a calculated risk, an impending danger, a tormenting allure.

The crescent moon shaped like the serene lake, the gentle slopes of the hills surrounding the valley, the woods and the orchards beautifying that surreal landscape were observed mutely by the departing son.

No singing birds, no mourning bells, and no rumbling thunders marked the sad event. Just an overextended silence seemed to overtake, for a short while, the usual joyful life of the villagers.

Peter Egger, from the window train, saw his native land disappear in the distance, while in front of him a new landscape opened up like a book full of magnificent pictures. Was that a beautiful dream, a journey of a lifetime, or the biggest illusion of his childhood?

He was accompanied by a handful of schoolmates, all eager to consecrate their lives to the mysterious God of the young priest that had captivated their imaginations.

As soon as they were exposed to the building, called a seminary, which was going to house them, their hearts sank. Unadorned and austere in its structure, it gave the impression of a reformatory.

The comparison was not far from reality. Like troubled youth are reformed in those facilities, the same way the seminarians are restructured and reshaped to fit Christ's image. They must divest themselves from the old sinful habits and embrace the way of the cross, which inevitably will lead them to the supreme sacrifice on behalf of their brethren.

Were Peter Egger and his schoolmates up to this enormous task, and did they have the right stuff to engage in such a superhuman adventure?

Peter had his mind and heart set on the priesthood. Nobody and nothing would ever deter him from reaching his final destination.

The seminary, like any other boarding school, had its advantages and inevitable drawbacks. Educational theories rarely stressed the latter, always painting a rosy picture of those establishments.

Eager to please and succeed and due to inexperience, Peter embraced without reservation the totality of the system, overlooking the serious flaws that plagued it.

Any uncomfortable feeling, any out-of-the-ordinary tendency, in his perception was a byproduct of his weakness and not a direct result of the system. Peter was convinced, like any other around him, of the absolute perfection of the institution.

Later on in life, looking back at that supposedly idyllic stage of his formation, he would discover the inherent deficiencies of seminarian life. However, it would be too late for any remedy. The damage had been done and there was no possibility of turning back.

Meanwhile these first crucial years left an indelible mark on Peter's psyche, converting him into a convinced crusader and an inflexible doctrinarian. The Church was above human frailties, saintly and infallible, and he, as its elite member, participated fully in those prerogatives.

If at times he could not live up to that high standard, he would instinctively cover his wrongdoings with deceptive ingenuity and misleading justifications, always presenting a perfect façade and an immaculate standing.

Unconsciously and over time, deception became an integral part of his personality. In the name of God and the Church, he had to cover stains and filth, which was required by his vocation.

The easygoing boy, with leadership qualities and invaluable resources, would slowly undergo a radical transformation.

Cooped up in an unnatural, unauthentic environment, he experienced a deviation in his sexual tendencies, and a need for spurious sentimental attachments. A continuous struggle followed him day after day, hour after hour. He was happy to constantly renounce his sentimental needs. He was glad to stack up sacrifices and mortify his natural necessities, because only in that way would he resemble Jesus, the supreme model.

Not everybody in the seminary had Peter's determination and courage. Only a few months had passed and around the feast of the Immaculate Conception (December 8) of the Virgin Mary, according to the official explanation, a handful of unworthy and unclean subjects were swept away.

They had been discovered engaging in filthy actions, contrary to the purity and sanctity required in a seminarian. Peter would never know which type of impurities they had involved themselves with and how they became to be known. It was apparent an underground network of spying was at work and nothing against the rules and regulations would ever go unpunished.

The moment that intimidatory system with its disreputable tactics came into the seminarians' radar, a sudden panic surfaced among the students, spreading like wildfire.

No one felt secure or immune from intimidation and retaliation. Anyone could be the next victim. If the fear of God was not enough, the system had provided them with the next best thing, the fear of man, more precise and effective.

Peter was utterly intimidated by that shocking reality. However, having nothing to fear, he overcame his hesitations and uncertainties, embracing the concept.

One day the director of the seminary called him into his office with a surprising offer. He invited him to become a member of the secret society of the so-called Untouchables, in charge of monitoring any suspicious activity or dubious conversations.

On one hand, Peter felt privileged, but on the other, he was frightful of the consequences. The time had come to choose sides – either be an integral part of the system, or be exposed to its devastating attacks. The election was not easy for his honest, transparent conscience. However, after weighing all the pros and cons, a sense of practicality prevailed. It was preferable to work within the system than to fight it as an outsider.

In an exclusive ceremony, Peter was anointed as a member of that elite team, whose existence was never officially acknowledged and whose activities were always denied as bogus.

The system had absorbed and integrated him in a way he never thought possible. He would become a convinced underground activist with enormous potential.

Endowed by nature with a keen sense of sleuthing, the new inductee wasted no time in becoming operational. If any minute was precious, any small finding could be vital to the good name and survival of the establishment.

Not only were students under scrutiny by this invisible but all-pervasive vigilante squad, but also staff members were closely scrutinized. No one was above suspicion, and anyone was fair game.

More than a year had passed without any spectacular public lynching, when Peter came up with a formidable lead. A staff member, with the basic duty of assisting the students, showed signs of a predilection for a seminarian with a delicate physical constitution, but who was particularly good-looking and thirsty for affection.

At first, nothing appeared out of the ordinary. That delicate creature, in fact, attracted everybody's attention. No one was immune from dispensing him with special favors.

However, on closer scrutiny, Peter discovered some well-disguised sensuality under apparent forms of accepted behavior. The preferential treatment on full display in every occasion, the closing of an eye and sometimes of two on clear faults and transgressions were nothing compared to the numerous private meetings behind closed doors. Everybody murmured and gossiped about the two lovebirds but nobody dared to do anything to stop that scandalous behavior.

Peter, accompanied by another member of the moral militia, planned to burst in on one of those meetings and unveil any alleged turpitude.

In the dormitory where the assistant carried out his supervisory duties, he had his bed, nightstand and dresser. For privacy's sake, four white curtains, similar to a hospital bed's enclosure, protected him from indiscreet eyes. Unwisely enough, he used that hideaway for his suspicious rendezvous with the youngster.

It was easy for Peter and his vice squad member to storm in and surprise the two transgressors. The daring plan was implemented with the righteous determination of an inquisitor. As soon as they stepped inside the enclosure, they could not believe what their eyes were seeing. The two suspects were engaging in clear immoral behavior, touching and caressing each other inappropriately.

The intruders, shaken to the core, immediately smelled a miasma of sexual decay and, horrified, started screaming incomprehensible words and ran away. Innocent bystanders, attracted by the noise, confirmed their suspects.

Meanwhile the two public sinners, caught in *flagrante delicto*, remained frozen, as if a divine punishment had paralyzed them instantly. Ashamed and speechless, they pulled back the curtains, and remained in silence for an undetermined lapse of time.

No length of time, no attenuating circumstances could ever repair the immense damage provoked by that impudent act. The gossip and rumors were no longer gossip and rumors; they were gospel truths.

What happened next is extremely painful to narrate. The student was expelled on the spot, and the assistant was found dead a few hours later, due to a massive overdose. His still-warm body lay lifeless on the same bed he used to satisfy his needs. From his open eyes transpired a sense of doom and total desperation. A promising life, full of energy and ideals, had been wasted on the altar of lust and irrepressible passion.

No public funeral with wreaths, no private Mass with eulogies, not even a secular farewell, was ever held for the public sinner, the pedophile, the damned soul. He was a cancerous disease that only the fire of hell could have kept from spreading.

Such a terrible ending overshadowed the unmentionable action and its devastating effects, spreading the fear of God and the reprisal of man.

Peter had scored valuable points by adding to his résumé a brilliant operation. In recognition of his merits, he was elected master of the secret organization, a position he would hold until the end of his high school years.

Nothing of all this spilled over the four walls of the seminary, and nothing ever reached his family's ears. It was his life, his secret.

Every summer, Peter returned to his village to spend a one-month vacation with his relatives. His participation in local life was kept to a minimum, while the religious activities were the center of his attention. He was a model seminarian, helping his pastor in everything pertaining to liturgical ceremonies and youth activities.

He maintained a safe distance from Susannah, the seductive girl, who, in the past, had captured his imagination and imprisoned his heart. Nevertheless, he had to confess to himself that the attraction, instead of decreasing, was gathering strength with the passing of time.

Unfamiliar with the laws of human nature, whereby self-denial and abstinence increase the appetite, he was not afraid to engage in mortal combat against the pleasures of the flesh. That was his fight that only God and he would witness during the long spells of insomnia at night, and the interminable hours of inactivity during the day.

Susannah, on the other hand, bound by no religious restrictions or mental convictions, did not miss an occasion to chase after him. His soft, well-mannered rejections did not deter her; instead they gave her wings.

The only effective maneuver Peter knew was a simple one, suggested by the founder of his order. Don Bosco had said clearly, "Do not face this enemy and do not engage him in any type of dilatory tactics, retrieve instead swiftly and disappear."

The only way to salvation was to escape. This method of fighting the temptations of the flesh might seem cowardly and laughable, but it is perfectly in line with an old popular saying – "Out of sight, out of mind."

However, as pointed out above, the daily experience would suggest the opposite. The more one starves himself, by constantly denying his sexual tendencies, the more needy and aggressive he becomes, creating a volcano of passions, ready to unleash its destructive power at any time.

One of the reasons is that the enemy is inside oneself, and nobody on earth can escape from himself. The so-called enemy, which in reality is a powerful primeval instinct, is an essential part of man's physical and emotional makeup. No one can totally suppress it without defacing his human nature, creating a rare monster in the process.

All sexual deviations, from the most bizarre to the most pitiful, are the result of some mishandling of this irrepressible thrust, which cannot be ignored or underestimated.

Peter had embraced his founder's doctrine, becoming a fugitive from sex. He would bravely stick to it until an unforeseen event would earthquake his magnificent scaffolding, bringing down his theory and praxis.

There is no need to anticipate the future by putting the cart before the horse. During this basic formation period, Peter seemed to have found a rare equilibrium in his world of feelings, tendencies and spirituality.

School year after school year, summer vacation after summer vacation, and Christmas after Christmas the promising seminarian was growing in stature. His leadership qualities, his commanding personality and his expanding knowledge attracted everybody's attention.

His superiors beamed with satisfaction and pride, his parents too, even if with some mixture of reservation, incomprehension and doubt.

A maternal uncle by the name of Luther was the most outspoken critic of Peter's religious choice. He could not conceive of the idea of a young boy, so talented and good looking, embracing a career where money and sex were totally marginalized.

Luther's concept of the Church and its ministers not only amounted to very little, even worse, it was nurtured in scorn and deep hatred. Whether that was a product of a life experience, an anticlerical atmosphere in his workplace, or some other imponderable factors, nobody would ever know.

What everybody knew was that his family was very religious and that he had been brought up with the fear of God and respect for his representatives on earth. On the other hand, what appeared certain is that his job, in the construction business, had converted him into the black sheep of the family, although respected and even admired for the huge amount of money he had accumulated in a few short years.

Every time he had a chance, he would not hesitate to warn his nephew against the Church, using any argument to discourage him from following his vocation. As expected, every single word fell on deaf ears. Peter was convinced of the sacredness and legitimacy of his position, while regarding his poor uncle as a mundane subject intent only on making money and satisfying his base instincts.

Definitely, Luther was no role model for young people, but he was certainly a persistent, annoying voice in Peter's conscience. Since he was neither a saint, nor insensitive to the call of the unclean spirit, he would have to fight constantly against the weakness of the flesh and the magnetic allure of the world, like Jesus did when tempted by the Devil.

The only comparison that could make perfect justice to the magnitude of this fight would be that of David and Goliath. The all-powerful, invincible giant would succumb to the ingenuity and resourcefulness of a young lad, whose trust was in God and not in man. In the same way, Peter would overcome the enormous obstacles thrown in his path by family, friends and his own flesh.

Like a well-trained soldier, he would march proudly, holding his head high. Two strange occurrences might typify the monstrous struggle that went on for years without visible clashes or clattering swords.

Peter loved to spend time reading or meditating in his favorite childhood hideaway. It was a secluded spot in the woods of an overlooking hill. All was quiet and serene in that place. The only signs of life were the chirping of the birds, the rustling of the leaves and the buzzing of insects.

While there, Peter never failed to sense the omnipresence of God and his benevolent hand protecting him from invisible falls and spiritual dangers.

One day, during the last summer vacation before entering the novitiate, while in a pensive mood and absorbed in a challenging reflection, something extraordinary happened. Regrettably, that was not a manifestation of God's presence, quite the contrary.

All of a sudden, an unusual noise startled him, interrupting his concentration. He lifted his eyes and a real apparition had invaded his space – a smiling Susannah stood in front of him in a provocative pose. Without uttering a sound, she lifted her skirt well above the knees enticing him with the most provocative and explosive part of her body.

In that crucial moment, Peter, totally lost and with his heart ripped apart by a violent tornado of conflicting emotions, wanted to say something, but no words emerged from his mouth.

Finally, the temptress Susannah broke the deadly silence and said in a softly mellifluous voice, "If you desire me, you can have me. You will be my first."

She waited for an answer, which was never formulated in words. Instead, she saw the object of her love jumping up like a wounded animal. He staggered momentarily, but recovered immediately, running away as fast as a cheetah. It is impossible to describe the anxiety, confusion and fright inside that perturbed soul.

However, in that unlikely commotion, one thing was clear, Peter stuck to his founder's directives. Escape is the only way to salvation.

That crucial moment of Susannah standing in front of him with such an instigating and incendiary attitude would remain indelibly stamped in his memory and soul.

No other memory would ever overshadow this one, except the one that caused his downfall years later. Although this second one would remain memorable for different reasons.

A second episode, of quite a different nature, would challenge his determination to become a priest. This time it was his uncle Luther putting him to the test.

Together with Peter's parents and other relatives, the anticlerical uncle invited him to a sumptuous dinner, where he put on display the wealth and opulence he had achieved through his profession. The purpose was clear: to entice his religiously fanatic nephew to turn back on his obstinate decision and retrace his steps toward a more sensible and profitable way of life.

To that end, he proposed a toast with an appealing offer. "To my sagacious nephew and his new future in my construction company, as my right arm and factotum."

In spite of the looseness of the moment, due to the abundant beer ingested by the guests, everybody was taken aback by the impudent proposal, a sense of disorientation and confusion showing on their faces.

Obviously, the most shaken among them was Peter Egger, on the threshold of entering the novitiate and consecrating his entire life to the service of God and the salvation of souls. Astounded as he was, he did not lose his composure.

After regaining full control of the situation, he looked around that selected gathering. In particular, he directed his gaze at his uncle in a mixture of amazement and complacency, like somebody about to accept the Trojan gift.

With an indescribable finesse, far superior to his age and mundane experience, he formulated his original toast. "To my shrewd uncle, successful in business and in love with admiration and deference. If, in the future, misfortune and failure are to befall him, he will always find a position as sacristan in my church."

Roars of laughter saluted the inventive and imaginative response. The uncle gracefully accepted defeat. He dismounted his high horse and never again tried to outsmart or sneakily ambush his nephew.

Peter had overcome two of the biggest obstacles that threaten a priest's life, money and sex. He had not even been anointed as a priest yet, nor had he pronounced his religious vows as a member of an order, but he was surely ready for both. Theoretically, poverty, chastity and obedience should not constitute a grave challenge for the young clerical recruit in the near future.

However, the clear intellectual knowledge of something does not mean a peaceful possession of it. Real life is always unpredictable and subject to change, whether one likes it or not.

What seems facile and easily attainable at one stage in life can become difficult or even impossible at another. People change, and reality and all that goes with it change. Everybody's mental attitude should be to expect the unexpected and be ready for anything destiny throws at him or her.

With these obvious, self-explanatory remarks, the time has come to narrate the childhood vicissitudes of Takeo Shirieda, who mysteriously fathered Castor, according to the DNA test.

Chapter 8

"If it weren't for our illusions we'd be free from **deceptions***."*

It was a cold, foggy morning in November. The piercing cry of a newborn baby disturbed the peace and quiet of a family in Otsu, a city near Kyoto in Japan.

The young woman, in her first birthing experience, did not scream or shout even once. Not a slight complaint ever came from her dry mouth. Obediently, she followed the midwife's instructions clenching her teeth and swallowing her pride.

At the sight of her baby, her face irradiated a rare luminosity. None of the people assisting the event had seen anything even remotely similar. All the circumstances surrounding that joyful moment possessed a magical aura.

Indeed, in spite of appearances, there was something magical and spellbinding about that place and those ordinary folks.

The house, more like a small fortress than an ordinary dwelling, was perched precariously on a steep hillside overlooking Lake Biwa. The building seemed to have been designed to blend in with the surroundings. Hard to reach and with a spectacular view of the city and the lake below, it had certainly once been the target of armed raiders and soldiers of fortune. If those solid walls could talk, how many happy stories and tragic events they would reveal! How many intrepid men and fascinating women had woven their way through life creating legends and sheer magic there!

Among the many historical inaccuracies and legendary feats, one thing was certain, the existence of a sixteenth century samurai, by the name of Thaddeus Shirieda. He was one of the newborn's ancestors, who more than any other would condition his future.

That ancestor, whose life was shrouded in mystery, and whose first name bears no resemblance to any Japanese name, one day had a striking encounter with a famous *gaijin* (foreigner), a Jesuit missionary, who had come from Europe with the clear intent of introducing Christianity in that mysterious land.

The fierce samurai was captivated by not only the original ideas and values of the new religion, but mainly by the imposing authority of Jesus. That meek man, who had shed his blood on a cross for every human, instantly became a powerful magnet for the young Shirieda. Without abandoning his bellicose profession, he embraced the new religion with passion and conviction.

In a moving ceremony he received the Christian baptism and with it a new name. From that moment on, his profession would receive a new direction. He would fight for the weak and defend the rights of the oppressed. Christian charity, not pagan pride and vengeance, would be his motto.

In the last two decades of the sixteenth century, Japan saw a remarkable growth of the new religion introduced by St. Francis Xavier. After his death in 1552, the number of Christians had grown to more than 200,000. Among the converts, there were several influential political leaders, nobles, samurais and merchants.

While the Jesuit mission prospered and Christian communities were multiplying, a sudden panic spread among the ruling classes. Buddhists feared the rapid spread of Christianity was a clear sign of a hidden political agenda. The Spanish Empire was trying, under the cover of religion, to swallow their country.

In 1587, an edict was issued, ordering all the missionaries out of Japan. A few Jesuits obeyed the order and left the country. The majority, however, remained and went undercover to continue their mission.

The untapped human riches of the Japanese population impressed the European missionaries. Loyalty, word of honor, a strong sense of duty and even the sacrifice of life on behalf of family and country were a superb foundation for the new religion. The better the human qualities, the more grounded would be the Christian values. In other words, Japanese soil was the most fertile for the new religious seed.

Proof of this was the numerous indigenous vocations to the priesthood. Among them, one shined through like a bright star. It was the son of a well-to-do military chief. His name was Paul Miki and he lived near Kyoto. Converted by St. Francis Xavier, he expressed his desire to become a priest. Noble and bright, while in training his impassioned sermons helped to convert many people. Thaddeus Shirieda was one of his first conquests. Both samurais, they felt a great affinity for one another.

In 1597, Miki, a few months shy of his priestly ordination, witnessed something very tragic. The authorities, made suspicious by his fiery preaching, could no longer allow the devastating effects of his religious propaganda. The renegade samurai had too many followers. He had to be stopped immediately.

The police arrested him, along with two other Jesuit companions. He was crucified in Nagasaki, along with 25 other Christians, Thaddeus Shirieda among them. Bystanders described Miki's remarkable composure during the cruel crucifixion. Dressed in his Jesuit cassock, although he had the right to dress as a samurai, he delivered one last moving sermon from the cross.

Both Miki and Thaddeus in their dying breath pronounced Jesus' last words, "Father, forgive them, they know not what they do," (Luke 23, 34).

They were beatified on September 14, 1627 by Urban VIII and canonized on June 8, 1862 by Pius IX.

Like Tertullian had said in the second century, "The blood of martyrs is the seed of new Christians," the conversions did not cease with the persecution. On the contrary and against all odds, a thriving underground community kept its traditions and preserved its precious faith.

The Shirieda family, following the example of their co-religionaries, became crypto-Christian, practicing in secret their religion and hiding any external sign of Christianity. Even their noble and ancient lineage became a mystery, buried under the appearance of commoners.

Centuries later, when the fear of persecution had vanished, the Shirieda family, like many others, kept their true identity under wraps, practicing discreetly and far from the eyes of strangers.

Only the nearest and dearest relatives knew their past and shared in their religious beliefs. When the time came to baptize the newborn, both parents wanted to call him Thaddeus, after his famous ancestor. However, still afraid of public opinion and possible discrimination they chose the name Takeo, the closest homophone to the Christian name.

If the very welcome offspring was spared an embarrassing name, he was certainly not kept in the dark about the family's past. Everyone in the family made sure he had a clear knowledge of their religious tradition.

When he was small and thirsty for magic tales and fantastic stories, Mom and Dad fed him abundantly with amusing events of their rich history. He loved those moments of family intimacy and grew up with a great admiration and respect for his ancestors.

Unlike many of his predecessors and living relatives, he did not show a vibrant personality, a strong character and a fearless attitude. On the contrary, the older he got, the more apparent became his shyness, pusillanimity and faintheartedness.

Bashful and introverted, he was considered a pushover. To his parents' dismay, he was a frequent object of ridicule and bullying in the school playground. For this reason, he avoided the company of or association with others like the devil avoids holy water.

His heart, however, was in the right place. Attentive and considerate, punctual and meticulous he was a model student. With a sharp mind and a delicate sensibility, he made great strides in school, martial arts and sport. He preferred reading, composition and meditation to the last two activities. Nevertheless, his parents insisted on those physical activities, because they wanted him to build a strong character and physical stamina.

The religion of his ancestors, practiced in the utmost secrecy, was of great comfort to his soul. Moreover, the martyrdom of Thaddeus Shirieda, crucified on a cross like Jesus, was a constant inspiration for Takeo, who longed to follow his example.

In his eyes, nothing was nobler and higher than that. He wanted to fulfill his deepest aspirations by assuming suffering and humiliation like a precious gift.

One day, during a school break, two students got into a heated argument over a pretty girl. In no time at all, the verbal skirmish degenerated into a violent fistfight. Takeo, the sworn enemy of any violence physical or otherwise, intervened on the spot. Putting to good use his martial arts, he broke up the fight. What was most astonishing to students and teachers observing that unusual scene was the shy Takeo convincing the two combatants to apologize and reconcile.

The curious spectators broke into rapturous applause, saluting the newfound humble hero. That valiant action gained him respect and admiration but did not propel him into a leadership role.

Takeo, faithful to his nature and inclinations, kept his distance from crowds and easy popularity, mindful of his role models, Jesus and Thaddeus.

His family was proud of him, and was not surprised when he disclosed his desire to become a priest.

A local priest, who through the years had catered to their spiritual needs, rejoiced in Takeo's decision and took upon himself the duties of private tutor, teaching him Latin and Religion.

At the end of his high school years, the young Shirieda was ready to enter the novitiate of a relatively unknown order. That was not his first choice; it was the only choice. In fact, he would have preferred the Jesuit Order. Unfortunately, there were no Jesuit formation houses in his area, preempting his wish and dashing his hopes.

However, his unwavering faith made him discover the invisible hand of the providence in that turn of events. God was guiding him firmly, despite his mundane desires and tendencies.

According to his tutor, he had to be on the alert because his spirit was ready but his flesh was weak. This simple lesson, of distrusting his own feelings, stuck with him as long as he lived, even if in some crucial moments he totally disregarded it.

He would regret such a careless attitude and in due time would shed bitter tears of remorse.

The departure from his native land, so serene yet surreal at the same time, assumed neither the characteristics of a traumatic event, nor the aspects of a painful estrangement; on the contrary, it encapsulated the cozy feelings of a harvest time, when the farmers pluck the ripe fruit from the trees and take it to its rightful destination.

Takeo was mature for his mysterious journey into a world whose existence was almost totally unknown. Neighbors and acquaintances thought of a special technical school where students, through an apprenticeship, learnt a trade.

It was certainly a rigorous apprenticeship, but not for an ordinary type of profession. From now on, his specific business was to save his soul and that of his fellow human beings.

On the pews of the novitiate, he would learn adoration of the Blessed Sacrament and meditation of the *last truths* or *novissimi*: death, judgment, hell and paradise.

Takeo felt extremely comfortable in this spiritual environment. It suited his nature and his deepest aspirations perfectly.

Later on in life, he would remember fondly those sweet days of innocence and union with God. No mundane worries, no material temptations, no power struggles for advancement, just prayer and dialogue with the Almighty.

Like a docile child, he accepted the spiritual guidance of his Master of Novices, whom he admired and respected. The Master in turn nurtured a sincere appreciation for that promising youngster, who had all the signs of a future pillar of his congregation.

Takeo passed the weekly and monthly tests, whether written or practical, simple or complicated, with flying colors. Only one time he encountered an insurmountable obstacle, which put his complete spiritual scaffolding in serious jeopardy.

A young novice, with angelic looks and a delicate physical constitution, fell gravely ill. Fainting, loss of balance and strong migraines were the most visible symptoms of his illness.

The house physician, from the old school of medicine, diagnosed the patient a little hastily. As a possible cause, he indicated the rigorous religious training, the poor diet and the insatiable appetite of the novice for physical mortification, depriving himself of essential nourishment and rest.

During that nebulous period of uncertainty and misdiagnosis, while the poor novice was suffering the torments of hell, Takeo became his bedside assistant as per instructions of the Master.

Attentive and solicitous, he spared no means or sacrifices to alleviate the patient's suffering. In the process, his emotional attachment grew slowly but strongly, to the point of forgetting his basic duties and general responsibilities. He was like a brother to him. He was convinced he needed his constant, undivided care.

After a battery of tests, among them an MRI of his brain, in a specialized hospital the unfortunate novice was diagnosed with an incurable brain tumor. Takeo's reaction was one of bafflement, shock and desperation.

Faced with the most painful experience in life – death – not only did he lose confidence in human nature, but his strong faith in God and religion seemed to vanish in a mist of doubts and general distrust.

A fierce battle erupted in the dark meanders of his soul. His serene posture and positive attitude gave way to an anxious, anguished demeanor. A somber mood marked his days and actions.

The Master of Novices, always on the lookout for any unusual behavior amongst his pupils, could not fail to notice such a change. In their monthly colloquy, Takeo opened up without any reservation to his spiritual guide.

It was clear to the introspective Master the poor novice had reached a critical stage in his purification journey, called by experts the "night of the senses."

In the history of Christianity, all the great mystics have undergone that terrifying experience, where God and men seem to have abandoned the tormented soul in the hands of its worst enemy, the Great Tempter himself, the devil.

It was up to Takeo to extricate himself from the tangled, collapsed building of his previous existence and inaugurate a new form of living, not restrained by human attachments, sentimental feelings and prefabricated religious tenets. Was he able to live up to such an expectation and step into the unknown? Blind faith, total abandonment and supreme sacrifice were the requirements for the new soldier.

The trying test, so arduous and toilsome, became even more grueling and punishing when the news of his co-novice's death reached him. The last days of the dying patient had been ones of excruciating suffering, mitigated only by powerful painkillers.

"Why is that innocent youngster going through such a hell of miseries?" was the spontaneous question in Takeo's mind. No explanation – rational, religious or otherwise – appeared satisfactory. The discriminatory existence of cruel pain and undeserved punishment, which had afflicted humankind over the centuries, remained a mystery.

Takeo, with his visceral world in turmoil and rebellion, his heart in total disarray and his mind in a terrible morass, did not know whom to turn to.

Was there any Good Samaritan ready to extend his arm and rescue him from the edge of the abyss? Trembling and confused he approached his Master of Novices. There was no need for him to utter a word of lament or shed a tear of confusion. His spiritual guide, just by looking at his facial expression, captured that moment of desperation.

He grabbed a large crucifix lying on his desk and with a silent gesture showed it to him. He did not possess any explanation for the human suffering, just a symbol, an example, Jesus dying on the cross. He was the supreme model to whom everybody had to conform if he wanted to become his disciple.

Either you embrace that model, or you renounce being a Christian. It was as simple as that. A great leap of faith was necessary in order to avoid the precipice. That was the only anchor of salvation at Takeo's disposal.

The Master smiled fatherly at his novice, patting him consolingly on the shoulders. He was sure his subject understood the message.

After a moving ceremony in the novitiate chapel, the funeral procession and burial for the departed companion took place. The immediate family of the deceased was devastated, along with other relatives and acquaintances.

It took time for the sad reality to sink in. Regardless of the Master's reassurances and the numerous pious explanations, Takeo never wholeheartedly accepted the death of his friend, and never made peace with that inexplicable reality. He kept paying lip service to the beliefs of his religion, but inside he was restless and rebellious.

Would time eventually heal those wounds or would the days ahead rub salt into them, making them bleed profusely?

Takeo was a resilient and resourceful boy. He put up a valiant front and pretended to sail full steam ahead. Unconsciously, a subtle veil of deception blanketed his ordinary existence, like snow on a winter's day. All the ugly things that soiled the terrain of his life disappeared instantly, giving the impression of a picture-perfect landscape.

Family members and religious superiors were taken aback by that stolid attitude. The only one not impressed or convinced was Takeo himself. Prayers, meditation, physical mortifications and excessive abnegations did not restore serenity or peace of mind; on the contrary, they exacerbated the volatility of his spiritual equilibrium, bringing moments of exuberance and tragic instances of depression.

In his inner sanctum, Takeo was a changed man. He was no longer the role model envisioned by his Master, but a slender twig at the mercy of oceanic waves, slammed back and forth, with no direction and no finality.

However, outwardly he was always on his best behavior, not showing any of his tumultuous inward movements.

His spiritual weather forecast was always sunny on the surface and tempestuous deep down.

The training days of his novitiate came to an end. Some time before the solemn ceremony of the vows, where each novice would solemnly promise to be chaste, poor and obedient for life, Takeo had his final conversation with his Master.

It was more than customary; it was a requirement *sine qua non* for the novice to reveal, in a confession fashion, with all the implications involved, all his sins past and present, all his shortcomings be they spiritual, psychological or physical, all his doubts, hesitations, fears and the like. The Master would have an unprecedented and final picture of his subject, on which he would deliver the ultimate judgment. Only two outcomes were possible – acceptation or rejection.

That was certainly an awesome responsibility for the superior and an extremely difficult duty for the subject.

Takeo, in an unprecedented manner, opened up his troubled soul to his Master without any reservation. He laid on the table the full map of his tormented journey, honestly expressing his inadequacy, at that moment in time, to take the sacred vows. Not only was he afraid of breaking his sacred promises in the future, but of betraying his vocation, becoming a public scandal.

In conscience, he did not have the courage or strength to assume the grave responsibilities of the religious profession. He was clearly in favor of an honest retrieval instead of a certain betrayal.

The Master, who secretly favored the candidate, regarding him as the best and brightest hope of the new generation, looked intensively at Takeo, scrutinizing his troubled heart. Instantly he sensed the power of the Eternal Enemy at work and the sincerity and ingenuity of that noble soul.

Any true, sincere human would have felt inadequate for the job, regardless of his confused situation or the taxing obligation implied in the profession.

Contrary to Takeo's fears of being discarded as damaged merchandise, the Master regarded his doubts and insecurities as the best foundation for his future life.

No one with that honest disposition would ever dare to deceive himself or the order. He conformed perfectly to Jesus' first beatitude, "Blessed are the poor in spirit, for theirs is the kingdom of heaven" (Matthew 5, 3). Takeo felt so spiritually poor and humanly destitute that he was unworthy of entering God's Sanctuary. What better psychological disposition than that? Jesus, during his earthly life, always regarded the humble in spirit as the only ones worthy of entering his Kingdom.

Would it be any different for one of his representatives on earth? Would he dare to go against the Supreme Master's teachings?

The Master of Novices, after listening attentively to Takeo's unabridged confession, so full of negativities, uncertainties and indignities, held the shaky novice's hands in his, as a sign of complete trust and confidence. As Jesus did with his disciples, the Master told Takeo, "Come, and follow me!"

The deeply troubled novice could not believe his ears. He had received the green light to enter the order despite his chaotic situation.

He did not jump for joy, he did not thank his spiritual guide, he did not shout in jubilation. He left the confession room, which he expected to be his place of liberation, and wandered aimlessly for a long time through the beautiful garden. He felt chained for life to a secular tree that gave him strength but restricted his movements and freedom.

Security, stability and final salvation were the positive aspects, while the negative spelled out constraint, limitation and possible eternal damnation. Certainly the last one was not a consoling thought. Similar terrifying prospects would have deterred anybody from rebelling or jumping the fence.

On balance, Takeo decided it was wiser to enter the order by taking the vows than to face a world full of dangers and temptations.

Therefore, the model novice, whose future appeared more than promising and glorious, approached the great day of the profession in an apprehensive mood.

It was a hot summer's day that August 15, the Feast of the Assumption of the Blessed Virgin Mary. The small group of novices, whose religious training during those twelve months had been arduous and rigorous, were more than eager to become members of a fairly unknown Catholic order.

Their parents and relatives, gathered in the chapel, were anxious to see the culmination of their sons' dreams.

The Mass started with the singing of a solemn *Te Deum*, the official thanksgiving hymn of the Church. The sermon, inspiring and uplifting, followed the reading of the Gospel.

After that came the long-awaited ceremony of the individual emission of the three sacred vows. One after another, the novices came forward, kneeled in front of their provincial superior, and with trembling voices promised solemnly to be poor, chaste and obedient to God and their superiors until death.

After that, there was no turning back. Even if the emission of the vows was temporary for three years, the intention was to be forever, according to the spirit of the order's rules.

Exhilaration and intoxicating euphoria was in everybody's face, except for Takeo. The novices seemed to have touched heaven with their fingers, except for Takeo. The superiors were ecstatic in the presence of that modern miracle, except for the Master. The parents' jubilation was indescribable, except for Takeo's mother. Along with the Master of Novices, she did not notice in her son's eyes the sparkle he exhibited on previous occasions.

When he entered the novitiate and previously when he revealed his desire to become a priest, his completely joyful universe was on display in his demeanor and in his look. In those great moments, he appeared to jump out of his skin, ready to conquer the world. Now, instead, he gave the impression of somebody reluctant to come out of his shell and show his true sentiments.

The mother, observant as she was, understood immediately that something serious had happened to her son. He was a changed man, but not for the better. Unfortunately, she could not pinpoint with accuracy the determining factor of such a mutation.

When the solemn Mass was over, the celebration continued with a sumptuous banquet. All the participants experienced a surreal atmosphere of celestial proportions. For a few fleeting moments happiness was real, even for Takeo and his family. There were no menacing clouds on the horizon, no fears in their hearts and no creeping up deception in their minds.

As was customary, the new members of the order were assigned to a formation house for their junior college. A decisive chapter ended in Takeo's life and with it a testing ground for his vocation.

Chapter 9

"*Life is the art of being well **deceived**.*" – Goethe

The charming, attractive, and seemingly innocent café waitress by the name of Brigitta, described in Chapter 5, was not simply a casual or extraneous player. Her full name was Susannah Brigitta Müller.

Years back, when she left her picturesque village of Mondsee in search of a job, she landed in the historic city of Salzburg with a new identity. Using her middle name, Brigitta, she hid a failed marriage, a son born out of wedlock, and numerous tumultuous liaisons.

Still young and good looking, she was more than eager to start a new chapter in her life. The enchanting city and waiting tables at a famous café offered her many opportunities to meet interesting people and interact with a great variety of customers.

Years before leaving her village, she suffered a crushing heartbreak by a presumptuous youngster, who in the name of God had looked down contemptuously on her, rejecting her desire to surrender completely.

Susannah never overcame that humiliating rejection. A mental inadequacy overtook her personality and an inferiority complex marked all her future attempts to find love.

An untapped rage was ready to explode in self-destructive gestures and insane acts of revenge. She would probably never act upon those deep-seated feelings of retaliation and reprisal, unless something unexpected and miraculous happened.

But what was the chance of that? To any impartial observer, none. She had already resigned herself to her miserable fate of an inconspicuous existence deprived of glorious feats, of some retributive justice and a deserved appeasement of her soul.

In her poor, frail estimation destiny had been very unfair to her. Would it ever redirect itself, righting the wrong and reasserting some degree of fairness on her tormented, little planet?

Occasion after occasion passed her by, like the hundreds of casual customers bagged snuggly into their worries, unable to capture their neighbor's secret needs.

One day, similar to thousands before that, all changed under the magic spell of a goofy foreigner from Japan. The last thing she expected to hear from him was the name of Peter Egger.

At that sound, even if slightly adulterated by an unmistakable oriental accent, an avalanche of emotions and memories overwhelmed the Austrian beauty and an old wound started bleeding again.

She could not connect her first true love to a Japanese tourist, much less understand his interest in collecting a DNA sample from him.

Was destiny knocking at her door? Was fate presenting her on a silver platter a chance of a lifetime for an overdue retribution? Was that a blessing in disguise, so many times implored and never obtained?

With simulated interest, and concealing her past connection to Peter Egger, she played along with the detective's scheme.

Brigitta was dying to find out more about the undercover operation that seemed to fulfill her repressed aspirations.

When the first attempt to obtain the DNA of the prominent cleric failed, Jin sat down with the lovely waitress and went into detail about his secret operation. The possibility of Peter fathering a child with an influential Japanese woman shocked Susannah Brigitta Müller. The revelation that the Reverend had possibly been involved in a sordid affair was earth-quaking.

If the test results confirmed the damaging suspicions, Susannah would have a very explosive tool on her hands, one that could potentially destroy all Peter's ambitions and his existence as a man of the cloth.

She promised Jinpachi Nemoto her full cooperation, assuring him absolute secrecy. The detective, in the dark about her tumultuous past, admired Brigitta's initial commitment. Her subsequent zeal in pursuing the objective stunned him. Was he just lucky or the victim of a feminine trap? His experience in that kind of business made him always distrustful of easy gains.

However, he put aside his common sense and gut feelings in the presence of a valuable ally. Susannah was witnessing a complete reversal of fortune, from underdog to master, victim to executioner, impotent to omnipotent.

Entranced by that awesome power and inebriated by the simple smell of success, she could not sleep at night and barely functioned during the day. Like a zombie, injected by a powerful sedative, she was pursuing on automatic pilot an elusive dream that had failed to materialize during her entire productive life.

Now she had regained complete control and nobody on earth would ever deter her from her path of sweet revenge and destruction.

She could not imagine, not even in a million years, her former handsome Adonis, so puritan and with high morals, being the victim of an amorous entanglement, resulting in him fathering a child.

How could it have happened and how did he keep it a secret for so long? The whole yarn was unbelievable and beyond reason, defying all the laws of human nature.

Susannah, as she had solemnly promised the mysterious detective from the Land of the Rising Sun, made sure everything worked without a hitch.

In fact, with the collaboration of an old nun, her former teacher, everything proceeded smoothly. The venerable sister had dedicated her life to eradicating the bad weeds and corruption from the Church. At her age, one step away from the tomb, she was extremely happy to give her last contribution to the purification of her beloved Church and avoid the tremendous scandal of a corrupt and unworthy cleric.

The two women, so opposite in their moral standing – one a prude and humble, the other wicked and unprincipled – had the same purpose and the same enthusiasm. Their reasons, however, differed like night and day – revenge on one side, the good name of the Church on the other.

Peter Egger, at the apogee of his career, was clueless about the secret operation mounted by two seemingly innocuous females.

He was breathing deeply the inebriating air of success, so far removed from common mortals and so appealing even to religious people.

He was looking forward, with great anticipation, to the day of his consecration as Bishop and to the solemn ceremony of installation as Archbishop of Salzburg.

Finally, his dream was within reach. All his supporters and friends were jubilant. No doubt, he was the best and brightest candidate for the office.

The festive atmosphere surrounded by frantic preparations for the big event all of a sudden came to a screeching halt. Somber faces and nervous attitudes supplanted the jovial smiles and friendly handshakes.

What had happened? An anonymous letter had reached Peter Egger's address. If the content was true, he was in for a tremendous shock. The moment he finished reading it, he collapsed into his chair.

Shaking like a leaf, he felt his harmonious universe crashing down in front of his very eyes. Evidently, the rabid writer not only knew what he was writing about, but he had proof. For some unknown reason he or she was determined to destroy the cleric's career and his very respectability.

Obviously, the anonymous writer was Susannah Brigitta Müller, who had an old score to settle with the prominent clergyman. Scorned and rejected once, she was more than eager to turn the tables on the presumptuous Peter.

Instructed by the detective Jinpachi, she went to the lab to collect the results of the DNA test. It was there she secretly made several copies for her personal use. Jinpachi never suspected the attractive café waitress had a hidden agenda.

The Japanese detective, as mentioned previously, was so impressed Brigitta had obtained Peter's DNA sample that he forgot the most elementary etiquette. He embraced and kissed her in such an effusive way that she was completely taken in by his charm and love.

More demonstrations of affection befell Brigitta even after delivering the results. It was like a tender scene of a mature man courting a damsel head over heels in love. Acts and perceptions have different meanings for different people.

Jin's embraces and kisses are a typical case in point. For him, his emotional exuberance did not entail any sentimental attachment; they were merely a spontaneous manifestation for the operation's success. For Brigitta, it went beyond the moment, establishing an unintended love connection.

The gullible waitress' deceptive interpretation became painfully clear when Jinpachi, after concluding his mission, left Salzburg without even saying goodbye.

Deceived once more in her life, she turned cold-bloodedly thirsty for revenge. She had suffered so much and waited so long it was time to take decisive action.

With the calculated precision of a brain surgeon, she sat down and wrote three letters. The first was addressed to her old enemy, Peter Egger, the second to the retiring Archbishop of Salzburg, and the third to the papal nuncio in Vienna. The three letters were anonymous, and all contained a copy of Peter's DNA results and a copy of Pollux's DNA, showing without a shadow of a doubt their blood relation. The letters manifested a deep concern for the future of the Church in the event Peter Egger was consecrated Bishop and promoted to Archbishop.

Despite the anonymity and the lack of diplomatic phraseology, those inflaming documents ignited a devastating fire.

As mention, Peter, after reading it, collapsed into his chair. The retiring Archbishop was appalled to see in his successor a corrupt, unworthy clergy and swore to God to do everything in his power to prevent that nomination. For his part, the nuncio forwarded the explosive documentation to the Vatican Secretary of State with a stern warning. Too many sexual scandals had plagued the Church lately. A special commission should investigate every single candidate nominated for office within the ecclesiastical hierarchy.

Brigitta, unaware of the effects of her underhand actions, not only buried Peter's religious aspirations, but also jeopardized Jinpachi's life. It was a classic case of killing two birds with one stone.

Here are the details of the vigorous action mounted by the three abovementioned personages.

Peter's secretary found him lying on his chair, almost lifeless. The unprecedented blackout had paralyzed all his senses, converting him into the living dead. Still holding the letter in his hands, he stared aimlessly into space while an imperceptible breathing emanated from his nostrils.

How long he stayed in that unconscious state, nobody would ever know. Maybe the noise of the secretary, or some other somatic factor, brought him back to consciousness. Ashamed of being found in that deplorable condition, he told his worried secretary not to get alarmed, but to read the letter that had caused him to faint.

The secretary's facial expression turned from curiosity to shock and dismay. He immediately realized the gravity of the situation and the full potential for impending doom.

The first things to do were run for cover and stop any possible leak. Examining the document containing the lab results, two things appeared indisputable – the name of the lab that performed the DNA test, and the man who ordered it.

Through the first, the secretary obtained the address of the second. Both received a stern warning with dire consequences.

Unfortunately, it was too late, because the cat was already out of the bag. In fact, the retiring Archbishop and Rome had already received the infamous documents.

Peter Egger and his friends, despite the corrosive panic infecting their psyche, enjoyed a few days of calm. It was an ominous calm before the breaking of a violent storm. The elderly Archbishop sent a special pleading to the papal nuncio, who forwarded it to the Secretary of State.

Rome, overwhelmed by the documentation, abandoned its proverbial lentitude, suspended any nomination's proceedings and sent a commission to investigate the case.

When the bumptious clergy heard the emissaries from Rome knocking at his door, he experienced the last judgment's pangs.

Completely unaware of the secret war waged against him, he unconsciously perceived imminent danger. Apparently, the fight he and his staff had put up to suppress any possible leak did not work, and the time to be accountable had come.

One of the two investigators, tall and not deprived of certain nobility in his manners, skipping any preamble, addressed Peter.

"The Secretary of State, having received damaging information about your past, sent us to verify the accuracy of the facts. Have no illusion, one way or another we are going to get to the bottom of this. It is better for you to be completely forthcoming with us and tell us the whole truth. Only sincerity and honesty will be rewarded, while deception and lies will be severely punished."

The previously snobbish clergy found himself forced into a corner with no room for maneuvering. All of a sudden he saw himself fallen from grace and at the mercy of two bureaucrats, whose only interest was not his psychological well-being, his peace of mind or his future, but their ability to conduct a thorny investigation and succeed. According to their mentality, nothing succeeds like success and nothing is more pleasant than the smell of success.

Out of his comfort zone and in very unfamiliar territory, Peter's palms were sweating and shame and confusion filled his heart.

It was such a surreal mix of raw emotions and dreamlike fantasy to go back more than twenty years and recount, for the very first time, the most dramatic moment of his existence.

Year after year, he had tried to bury himself in the illusion that nothing ungodly and despicable had ever happened. Now he was forced to unearth the putrid remains of a skeleton covered by a mask of clever deception and a pack of lies.

In a penitent posture, like a medieval flagellant, Peter, between sighs of grief and death rattles, initiated a succinct, sanitized account of a party at a luxurious mansion in Turin during his theological formation.

At the end of his public confession, he appeared exhausted. The hidden demon had been exposed and the monstrosity of the past unveiled. Finally telling the truth had removed a great weight off his shoulders. Peter was the perfect image of a broken man, with a free spirit. Liberated from the ballast of an embarrassing past he could soar above the mundane worries and show his true self. The crazy run for power and prestige had left his troubled soul, and a more serene aspect seemed to exude from his persona. He had lost his cloak of untouchability and an extreme vulnerability became his daily suit.

Human perception and external reality do not always coincide. However, this time perception and reality formed a symbiotic relationship full of gloom and doom. There was no future of prestige and glory for Peter, just lonely days of shame and punishment ahead.

The two Vatican commissioners had listened attentively to the skimpy narration of Peter's lurid sexual entanglement with a young Japanese woman. No sign of disgust or disapproval transpired from their facial expressions.

At the end, the one in charge sealed the encounter with these words. "From this moment on, while waiting for His Holiness's final decision, you will refrain from any public statement or appearance. You will remain incommunicado and sequestered in your own home. The Church will do the impossible to protect your privacy, but more than that its own reputation. Before leaving Salzburg, we will issue a statement to the media, announcing your non-acceptance of the impending nomination, and your early retirement. Nothing from your past should be leaked to the press and public. We bid you farewell."

No handshakes or special greetings marked that departure, so cold and business-like. They had done their job and obtained the truth without much intimidation or scary tactics. Figuratively speaking, not a drop of blood was shed, even if a prelate *in pectore* had been left behind, bleeding to death.

Thousands of miles away from Salzburg, in the mysterious land of samurais, a dirty war was raging against Jinpachi Nemoto, the easygoing detective, and Takeo Shirieda, the somber and introverted clergyman, rumored to be a sure candidate for the Vatican Congregation called Propaganda Fide.

Unconsciously, Nemoto had opened hostilities against the most revered clergyman in Kyoto.

The private detective, in fact, was dead set on discovering the biological father of the slain twin Castor, as he had with Pollux. The innocuous but highly probable clue he was following were the two smiley faces in Kimiko's picture, so proudly displayed in her living room. The heiress possessed innumerous photos of her much-traveled past, but the one she treasured most was the one portraying her with the young theology students, Peter Egger and Takeo Shirieda.

Every time she looked at those two handsome men, her heart skipped a beat and her mind wandered back to her youth with intensely romantic longings. That had been her paradise lost, her best of times, and her secure refuge during her frequent spells of depression.

For Jinpachi the same picture represented something completely different, an unmistakable footprint of Kimiko's tumultuous past, where passion, femininity and maternity found their common thread.

Chasing that suggestive lead, the detective had already solved half the puzzle. If this first result had earned him a threatening letter by an obscure group called "Organization for the Defense of Clergies," which in reality was Peter Egger's inner circle, the attempts at solving the second half not only earned him a second warning, but ultimately a premature cruel death for his persistence in tracking down Castor's biological father.

A different group, self-proclaimed "Samurais for Honor and Honesty" was the sender of the second letter. Jinpachi's violent elimination unquestionably had their signature written all over it. Who were these mysterious, never-before-heard-of avengers of traditional values?

Unlike in Peter Egger's case, where his closest friends rose up impassionately to protect his reputation, here the move appeared unrelated to Takeo's admirers and coming from nowhere.

But, like in Peter's case, the initiative was fruitless, for it was too late. The cautious detective had already sent the DNA test results to the Pittsburgh police, who in turn forwarded the documentation to the Kyoto investigators.

Those results, splattered all over the American and Japanese press, obtained the opposite effect intended by the "Samurais for Honor and Honesty." Takeo Shirieda, the timid and bashful priest, who always managed to divert public curiosity from himself, instantly became the center of attention and what is worse, the focus of derision and ridicule.

He had never felt so embarrassed in his life for something that happened so many years earlier, something he thought completely dead and buried.

The tragedy in all of this was the timing. When he was about to soar above the crowd and make a name for himself, when he was at the pinnacle of his career, his persona became a mockery for people in general and a total disappointment and embarrassment for his superiors.

They were completely taken aback by the serious accusations moved against two outstanding clergymen, both with a sure promotion and a brilliant future.

For the Vatican, speed and secrecy were of the essence in order to avoid more damage to an already tarnished reputation.

Takeo received a wire from the Secretary of State with a peremptory summons. He had 24 hours to collect his belongings and report to Rome.

When the *Kyoto Morning Newspaper* disseminated the news of a well-respected priest with an allegedly scandalous past, the population was gripped by feelings of panic and fear. Consternation and dismay spread like wildfire. A mysterious disease seemed to have paralyzed the city's daily routine.

Takeo's family was in total shock, ashamed to step out of the door. The member most affected by that violent media hype was a female cousin by the name of Asuka. The same age as Takeo, she grew up in awe and admiration of her cousin. He was the best emblem of his family and its past. Asuka was so proud of him that she refused to believe the news. She was convinced there was a satanic conspiracy against him.

Someone, jealous of Takeo's success and bright future, was fiercely intent upon destroying his reputation. How could anyone be so cruel as to deliberately besmirch his good name and ruin his future?

Without a second thought, the distressed Asuka confided in her husband, wishing somebody would stop the slanderer and put an end to that tragedy. She never thought her husband would take it upon himself to remedy the situation.

Whatever he did or intended to do did not help one iota. The proud family had to bow deeply to that cruel destiny and weather the storm stoically. Only time and patience would alleviate the sufferings of that unfortunate house, without ever erasing the opprobrium and discredit that had befallen it.

While Peter Egger waited in Salzburg for his sentence, Takeo Shirieda flew to Rome to receive his.

Chapter 10

"Man's mind is so formed that it is far more susceptible to **falsehood** *than to truth."*
- Desiderius Erasmus

The Pittsburgh police, after a brilliant surveillance operation followed by a flash-like arrest of Castor's girlfriend's murderer, Rudy, and his accomplice, Stavros, experienced a new stagnation period in the primary investigation.

The clues related to Castor's brutal assassination had dried up and the chief investigator, Ken Fresco, was scrambling for something new and significant.

Adding insult to injury, his superiors and prominent politicians were breathing down his neck like mastiff hounds, thirsty for blood.

The surviving twin, Pollux, had the sensation of living in a twilight zone, where real and surreal mixed to form a grey area deprived of personal control, and marred by a vague inkling of impending disaster.

Pollux was still a suspect in his brother's death, but not a viable one. At the same time, he was not totally exonerated yet, for the many signs pointing at him. Despite all the reassurances coming from everywhere, he was unable to function normally.

His life looked like suspended animation, where breathing, heartbeat and other involuntary functions may still occur, but they can only be detected by artificial means. Pollux was surely still alive, taking part in school activities and normal daily chores, but an invisible tangled web, miles long, trapped his perception.

He could not leave the country or town and he had to report every weekend to his appointed officer, Mary Rosenthal.

She was the only human that could reach inside the imponderable bubble where Pollux was allegedly operating, and inject some fresh air of reality and optimism. Not even Pollux's mother, with her frequent phone calls, could break the invisible barriers of a superimposed world.

Everything was eerie and scary for the poor Japanese student, deprived by fate of his normal existence. How long would he last in that merciless state? Was any reprieve in sight?

Did he have in his heart enough courage and strength for a prolonged battle? Like the mythological Pollux, he showed superhuman strength. He did not bend or break under the enormous weight of misfortune, but his mood and modus operandi had changed considerably.

His natural, normal self – optimistic, confident and innovative – was no longer there. A cautious, somber and routinary young man had emerged with no sparkle in his eyes and no smile on his face.

For better or worse, events and circumstances mold people in ways impossible to predict. Pollux was no exception.

Even Ken Fresco, Mary Rosenthal and others were victims of a long, dry spell, with no new clues, findings or theories. In Pittsburgh, the sky was becoming increasingly greyer and the mood darker.

All that changed one day. A brown envelope with Japanese postage had reached Ken's desk. Inside, the detective found DNA tests revealing Pollux and Castor's biological fathers.

To say the surprise was enormous when the results were revealed would be the understatement of the year. How could it be even imaginable for twins to have different biological fathers? But those tests did not lie. Pollux was the son of a prominent Austrian clergyman named Peter Egger, and Castor had for a father a distinguished Japanese priest, born into an old samurai family. His name was Takeo Shirieda.

The Pittsburgh detective, Fresco, enjoyed sinking his teeth into difficult cases, but this was much more than he had ever bargained for. This was beyond belief and expectations. This was completely wacko.

However bizarre the situation turned out to be, the surprises did not end there. A few days later, Jinpachi Nemoto's mysterious death added more intrigue to the already entangled hotchpotch.

Without proof of a conspiracy behind that alleged assassination, it would be naïve not to see powerful forces plotting to eliminate undesirable witnesses and embarrassing tests.

Suddenly, all seemed clear. The powerful churchmen for themselves, or through others, would use any means at their disposal to erase from the face of the earth a highly explosive reality.

A hired assassin from inside the country or abroad could explain Castor's bloody murder. However, the more this theory appeared plausible, the more questions remained without an answer.

What was the purpose of killing only one twin, or the reason for so much cruelty and brutality?

After racking their brains, the Pittsburgh detectives found it difficult, if not impossible, to tie their particular crime with an international plot.

Sifting carefully through theories and hypotheses, painstakingly reexamining clues and evidence, nothing appeared solid or certain. The field of investigation had been extended to Europe and the Far East and only the last one offered some very remote connection. There was no doubt that a possible crime was perpetrated in Kyoto that had everything to do with the paternity tests.

In the old continent, even if the motives were equally cogent, there was no serious infraction of the law, just a threatening letter to Jinpachi. The probabilities of a hired killer coming from Japan were potentially higher.

The Pittsburgh detectives focused their attention on this possibility and kept a privileged channel of communication with the Kyoto investigators, exchanging sensitive information.

The two law enforcement agencies were determined to shed some light on two crimes so far apart in time and space yet so connected in motives and victims.

While in Kyoto some promising leads were giving hopes of a speedy conclusion, in Pittsburgh Ken Fresco and Mary Rosenthal were wrestling with the thorny question of how to disclose to Pollux who his real father was. Mary, being closer to the surviving twin, was the natural conveyor of the truth. That did not make it any easier for her to break the news. Any reaction was possible from that young man, already tried and tested so hard by adverse circumstances. The range of emotions could go from denial to hatred, incredulity and surprise to desperation, from an emotional breakdown to a total hermetic shutdown of any interaction with the external world.

For Mary, just thinking about these possibilities was scary and disturbing. Be that as it may, Pollux was entitled to the truth. His fantasy world, so comforting, was about to collapse and his mother, adored and revered, was at the center of it. She was the one ultimately responsible for that impending cataclysm.

Pollux had already lost his twin brother, whose turn was it now?

The night before her meeting with the troubled student, Mary could barely sleep a couple of hours. In her mind, she was playing out every possible scenario and every imaginable way of wording her revelation. No one appeared correct or viable, no one looked humane and reasonable, and no one made any sense at all.

Probably only her heartfelt empathy could somehow soften the cruel reality. Only the sweetness of her femininity could make the hard-to-swallow pill less bitter. Pollux was following his routine back and forth from the university to his apartment, with a religious fixation. For Mary it was quite simple to monitor the student who had transformed himself into a creature of habit.

That memorable day, it was three in the afternoon. Back from campus, he met Mary standing at the door of his residence. At first glance, he noticed she did not look glad to see him as usual. Moreover, she showed some signs of being uncomfortable. They greeted each other without the customary warmth.

The detective opened the conversation. "Pollux, I need to talk to you about something very important."

"I hope it is some good news about my legal status," he replied.

"I wish it was," said Mary, with a sad undertone in her voice. After a deep sigh, "Let us go in," she continued. They sat down and Mary started her much-rehearsed little chat.

"What I am about to say is not easy or pleasant. It may upset you and cloud your judgment. Rest assured it is not our department's intention to alter or damage your spiritual and emotional well-being."

After each word, Pollux became increasingly unsettled, not knowing in which direction she was going.

"From Kyoto," she continued, "we received a manila envelope containing two DNA tests. The private investigator, Jinpachi Nemoto, whom you know, went through serious difficulties in order to obtain them. One pertains to your deceased twin, Castor, the other to you. They are paternity tests. And here is the irrefutable truth. Your biological father is not Hiro Kimura, but a prominent clergyman from Austria, by the name of Peter Egger. But what is most disturbing and incomprehensible is that your twin brother has a different biological father, who is neither Hiro Kimura nor Peter Egger, but a Japanese priest called Takeo Shirieda. I cannot explain how this might be possible or even thinkable."

As she spoke, she tried to capture every little facial expression on her listener. What an enormous surprise when she realized Pollux did not exhibit any manifestation of the dreaded reactions she had anticipated. On the contrary, he appeared relieved, as if an unbearable weight had been lifted from his shoulders.

Had he really understood the implications of that monstrous reality that could pulverize anybody's confidence and mental balance?

Intrigued, Mary asked, "Aren't you baffled by such a revelation?"

"Obviously," he said calmly, "I am perplexed, but not shocked. My lifetime suspicions have been confirmed. My physical appearance has always questioned my origins. I could hardly reconcile my bone structure with my Japanese lineage. During my primary education, my schoolmates teased me, calling me names. When I was twelve, I asked my mother the name of the doctor who delivered me. Without her knowing, I visited him and asked about my birth. My physical features, so different from my twin brother, were mesmerizing to the obstetrician. However, he assured me we had the same mother and that we were born a few minutes apart. That put an end to my crazy speculations, but deep down in my heart there was always a vexing doubt that would not go away, in spite of the many reassurances coming from my family and birth certificate.

Now I am in possession of a partial truth. I hope that in the future I will come across the whole truth. Thank you for your help."

In an unprecedented move, he looked tenderly at the detective, and with a fresh spontaneity hugged her. That unsolicited gesture sent shivers down Mary's spine. In a very pensive mood, she left Pollux and returned to the police station, unsure of what had just happened and how real it was.

She informed her superior, Ken Fresco, and resumed her duties with something new in her mind and in her heart.

Pollux too was faced with a complete new reality. His initial reaction, considered unexpected by Mary, did not last very long. With an inquisitive mind and a troubled soul, he started reexamining his entire childhood and youth in search of revealing clues.

The web of deception woven by his family – mainly his mother – was disheartening. He felt sick to his stomach and a wave of hatred slowly took hold of his spirit. His visual memory instinctively brought up to the surface of his conscience the picture of his mother with the two smiley students. That picture, to which she felt so attached, occupied a special place in the living room. The two alleged friends, one Caucasian and the other Asian, were indeed her lovers. Now he could see some light. However, the end of that tunnel was still dark and mysterious. How could anybody explain dual paternity in a set of twins?

A great curiosity to know his biological father was added to the mix of feelings and emotions that kept him hostage. With such heavy baggage, Pollux could hardly function as a student and as a human being.

A few days later, the disturbing news of Jinpachi's death added fuel to the burning fire. Was it an assassination, as the media suggested? Was his family involved in such a despicable crime? Obviously, the family had both motive and means.

The vision of a perfect family was unraveling mercilessly before his very eyes. In the rumbling collapse of that dynasty, was he one of the many debris, insignificant, almost vile by association?

No one could fathom a grimmer reality than that. Deceived by his mother, beguiled by his family and misled by the public's envy, his self-reputation plummeted and his image, fragmented like in a broken mirror, became a burlesque, a fake, a risible insignificance.

In subsequent meetings, when things should have reasonably simmered down, Mary found serious reasons for concern and worry. The initial reaction of relief detected in Pollux gave way to a somber attitude and an inward panic. The solid, granitic youngster who withstood the death of his brother without desperation, now appeared on the verge of a nervous breakdown, of an emotional meltdown.

How wrong Mary had been in her initial assessment! The proverbial stolid and impassive Japanese attitude was extremely difficult to penetrate and understand for a westerner. In this case, it appeared more deceptive than ever. To make things worse, Pollux repeatedly refused to open up to the only compassionate person in his life.

Mary was, without a shadow of a doubt, his last anchor of salvation. If he had lost faith in humanity, she was his last glimmer of hope, the last breath of life that could bring him back.

For how long could he refuse her helping hand, her gentle smile, and her unconditional devotion? In the raging battle of his values and visions, in the unrelenting struggle of his hormones and emotions, she stood pure like the snow on his native mountains. Offering support and understanding without asking for anything in return, she was the impersonation of a true mother.

Just as the snow melts slowly under the solar rays, the same way Pollux's heart, hardened by misfortune, started his mollifying process.

A few words here and there, accompanied by a suffused smile, signaled a reversed course. Instead of running toward the precipice, Pollux walked reluctantly but firmly in the direction of light.

Mary was there; ready to receive him, without reproach or condemnation.

The healing season could be long, laborious and probably without a happy ending.

The picture was quite different in his home country. First, the revelations by the media of Kimiko's shameful secret did not help the already fragile composition of her family. Second, the suspicion of some kind of involvement in Jinpachi's death by the same family made the situation even worse.

What had been built over many years with patience and perseverance, and jealously protected for such a long time, all of a sudden appeared to crumble like a child's sandcastle on a populated beach.

Fortune and destiny, so benevolent and accommodating in the past, had turned their backs on the Ishida family, letting the ravages of time and circumstances rage over the untouchables.

The present and future were equally bleak and seemingly hopeless. No money or prestige in the world could erase the stain of blatant adultery and the rampant suspicion of an assassination.

The so far ever-forthcoming and outspoken family had turned unexpectedly invisible and mute. No one was available for comments or explanations. Their mansion, on the outskirts of Kyoto, gave the impression of a deserted place. The windows had their shutters closed, while the door was locked. There was no movement during the day and no light flickering during the night.

The storm thundered all around and no living soul dared to raise its voice.

Pitiful as the whole scenario was, the police disregarded any call for moderation and understanding, and mounted an unprecedented investigation.

By interrogating every single member of the Ishida and Shirieda families, the detectives came up with some helpful clues.

One of them, the most promising perhaps, was the female cousin Asuka's conversation with her husband, where she vented her pain and frustration at not being able to stop the cruel gossip against her beloved Takeo.

According to her version, her husband promised to do something about it. It was widely known he had connections with the Yakuza, the notorious Japanese organized crime group.

That was more than enough for the law enforcement officers to round up a handful of notorious criminals and try to squeeze out of them some information. What they obtained was hearsay, but no solid lead or real evidence.

The crime scene offered no fingerprints, fibers or hairs. If there existed a perfect crime, that appeared to be it. Upon a second and third thorough search, the officers still came up with nothing.

It was ironic that a shrewd private detective like Jinpachi Nemoto did not live behind a clue that would lead to his killers.

The lack of any credible evidence and the absence of an informant did not deter the investigators from pursuing their investigation with tenacity and perseverance. Someday, inadvertently, they might stumble on something relevant and then the perfect crime would unravel. One loose string is all they needed. Unfortunately, the loose end never came to light and the case, after months of hard work, was put to rest.

The Ishida family, notwithstanding their powerful motives and abundant means, were as surprised and shocked as anybody else was by Jin's violent death. Not the slightest connection was ever traced back to any family member or sympathizer. This second trail, according to police estimation, was running cold even before the investigation started.

Was it a random act of senseless violence? This possibility was discarded too. However, Jinpachi's investigation on the twins' paternity created many enemies, stirring unprecedented passion and animosity. Any sensible person could see in that the source of Nemoto's demise.

The Kyoto investigators sent a report to Ken Fresco, summarizing their painstaking research. Despite failing in their attempts, they were convinced the perpetrators were Yakuza members, operating on behalf of the Shirieda family.

The threatening letter addressed to Jin, although it contained all the characteristics and style of a criminal organization, did not exhibit a single shred of credible evidence of its origin.

For this and other reasons, the Kyoto detectives suspended the investigation for the time being, giving the killers some breathing space.

In the meantime, in Pittsburgh, Taisuke Fujii, the family lawyer sent with the private investigator Nemoto by Kimiko Ishida to America, had been working hard on behalf of his client, Pollux.

Tai was in constant touch with the Deputy District Attorney handling the case, and received, as a courtesy gesture, any new development from Ken Fresco's detectives.

His diplomatic manners as a private liaison, characterized by finesse and gentleness, gained the hearts and minds of the American authorities, converting him into the ideal spokesperson for the Ishida family.

Generous in his appreciation for the splendid job being done by prosecution and police, he seemed in no particular rush. Advising his client to be confident and patient, he did not push for any quick resolution of the case. He appeared to have all the time in the world. Time and circumstances were on his side.

His philosophy was very simple. History does not need to be rushed. As in nature, things will happen in due time. Only fools believe they are in total control of their destiny.

This strategy greatly impressed his frantic counterpart, who was desperate for positive results. When the fine lawyer received the news of his friend and colleague Nemoto's death, he did not show any outburst of anger or any sign of fear for his life.

He maintained his composure and his comments were measured. Aware of how hazardous his occupation was, he did not flinch from carrying on with his mission. His open, honest activity, most of the time unassuming and unpretentious, did not create enemies. He was more a facilitator than a litigator, more a peacemaker than a troublemaker.

Like a mole, he patiently dug his tunnel out of Pollux's messy shambles. First, he convinced the Deputy District Attorney to drop the charges, since the evidence against his client was purely circumstantial. Second, he persuaded law enforcement officers to pursue other possible avenues and suspects, including Rudy Streaker and Yakuza members.

In return, he solemnly promised to share with both authorities any compromising revelations coming from Pollux, or some other source, in spite of his confidentiality obligations. On top of that, his client should not leave the country in the near future.

This last clause was of easy implementation. The Japanese student, in fact, still had five years left in his academic curriculum. However, the promise of sharing the content of private conversations with his client raised serious ethical and legal issues.

But, since this agreement was not in writing, Taisuke Fujii could sleep soundly at night without scruple.

As his deceased colleague, Jinpachi, had successfully carried out his mission, revealing the twins' paternity, the smooth operator from Tokyo had sailed the rough American legalistic sea. However, a big difference marked the two operations. The first ended in tragedy, and the protagonist had to pay with his own life, while the second achieved promotion and fame.

The Japanese media did not have enough words to praise Taisuke's achievement on foreign soil. The press converted him into a hero at home.

The Ishida family was super-thrilled when it heard the news of Pollux being cleared of any involvement in the violent death of his twin.

Kimiko, the desperate mother, could finally use some piece of good news, submerged as she was in an avalanche of mud-slinging and vicious slandering.

Pollux was the one who benefited most from Taisuke's silent but brilliant operation.

Since the shocking assassination of his brother, the unfortunate student did not have a single good day. Fear, trepidation and complete insecurity had been his constant companions. With the last security blanket – his family – demolished, he had touched rock bottom.

The blind fury of his misfortune could not get any worse or go any lower. But, according to the old adage, what goes up must come down and vice versa, the embattled twin lived to see another day. Moreover, that day had all the signs of being promising and good.

When Taisuke Fujii, the personal lawyer he never valued, graced him with his presence and offered him, along with a gentle smile, the most precious gift – his freedom – he remained speechless and astonished. Not in a million years would he ever have expected such an outcome.

All along there had been no indication of such a turn of events, nor was the most insignificant clue ever transpiring from Tai's underground work. More than unexpected, that positive conclusion had resulted in a real emotional earthquake.

Pollux, after regaining a sort of mental composure, let his emotions flood out. Tears of relief and joy welled up in his eyes and a timid "thank you" came out of his mouth.

Mary Rosenthal, who was present at the scene, held his hands and joined in the emotional outburst. Everything surrounding them was surreal and probably never captured in its entirety and intensity by any artist's canvas.

The black clouds of the storm were still visible in the distant horizon, but a brilliant sun with its insuperable luminosity was giving new life to every breathing creature. Resurrection was the proper word for that kind of experience. The rebirth of dreams and hopes, the dawn of a new day was knocking at the door, and Pollux was there to welcome them back.

Mary Rosenthal was convinced that from now on nothing but sunshine would hang over Pollux's head. Nevertheless, for the just-liberated student not all was shiny and sunny. In the midst of that invigorating catharsis, a bleeding wound pained his restless soul.

The frequent phone calls from his loving mother had dropped in number and intensity. Her usual soothing voice had turned dry and indistinct. An impenetrable wall seemed suddenly erected in their wireless communication, and a different language came from the other end.

Mistrust and hatred sounded in Pollux's voice, while shame and a frozen personality punctuated Kimiko's words. An emotional separation had begun, every passing day growing larger than their geographical distance.

The loving son had become motherless and fatherless, despite both parents still being alive. Cleared from the accusation of murdering his twin brother, and severed from his family ties, Pollux felt freer than ever. Finally, like an eagle, he could soar high in the sky and master his own destiny.

With no care in the world, he could forge a future of his own choosing. The lot was in his hands.

At this point in time, powerful and contrasting sentiments surfaced in his agitated waters. It is well known that trials and tribulations mature people and give them a new perspective on life.

Pollux was the beneficiary of such a change. The huge inheritance and the family support no longer weighed on his estimation. Instead, new tendencies and longings took central stage.

The most unusual one was an odd need to connect with his biological father. While this was getting stronger, the attachment to his mother was becoming increasingly weaker.

The most obvious and understandable was his academic future, not in great prominence before, but now on the front burner.

A new man would emerge from this transformation, where human rights and personal needs displaced national traditions and deep-rooted deference. The former submissive, stoic approach to life would give way to an assertive, well-motivated drive.

Mary Rosenthal would have difficulty recognizing the protégé she had begun idolizing in the secrecy of her being.

Another metamorphosis was taking place thousands of miles away. However, this time, it was for the worse.

The media disclosing the dual paternity of her twins had crushed Kimiko, the shrewd and capricious woman, who for so many years was able to deceive herself and the world around her.

If she was crushed, the public at large remained astounded by that revelation. It was hard to swallow such an unbelievable revelation. Many thought it a cruel hoax intended to destroy the Ishida Dynasty.

When the newspapers published the DNA test results obtained by the deceased private investigator Jinpachi Nemoto, there was no room for doubt or speculation.

That prominent family, Kimiko in particular, had been harboring a terrible secret. The disturbed mother, afflicted by bipolar disorder, saw her beautiful universe vanish in an instant. Her youthful indiscretions, where instinct and irrationality had the upper hand, could no longer remain hidden. If this was true, it was equally true that no one could ever explain that freak of nature.

In this scientific no-man's-land, she had some protection, not from gossip and rampant speculation, but from well-founded accusations.

However, this was not enough to arrest her emotional hemorrhaging. As a person, she was bleeding to death. A spell of depression, never witnessed before, made her despondent and insensitive to external stimuli. Her father, who knew her inside out, and had seen in the past so many episodes of depression, had never experienced something of this magnitude. He became extremely concerned and called a general practitioner, who in turn suggested a psychiatrist.

The diagnosis was simple and straightforward. She needed immediate hospitalization accompanied by high doses of antidepressants, individual sessions with her psychiatrist, and group therapy sessions with interactive participation.

Kimiko, well aware of the psychiatric techniques where the patient brings back the subconscious by sharing his or her most shameful secrets with others, strenuously refused any attempt at hospitalization. She was determined to reject any disclosure of her past. No one would ever violate her intimacy for any reason.

Setting this clear boundary, anything else was unacceptable. Her self-imposed seclusion, curtailing her social life, did not facilitate her recovery; on the contrary, it made her even more irritable and introverted.

Overwhelmed by feelings of guilt and shame, while at the same time sedated by powerful medication, she was running desperately through a desert of insensibility and some vague sense of dissatisfaction.

The dark moments of depression punctuated by suicidal tendencies had flattened out. Instead, a great indifference configured her psychological landscape. Amorphousness was the right word to describe her condition.

Deprived of her inner self and its eccentricities, she acted and behaved like an automaton. Even her best friends, very few in reality, cut short or eliminated their company.

Only Kimiko's father and mother stood steadfastly by her, offering support and comprehension. That famous household, so alive and bursting with activities before, now was mostly silent and deserted. No visits or phone calls, music or parties cheered the muted mansion. No roaring laughter or shrieking voices animated its many rooms. A ghostly curse appeared to be the master inhabitant. There are no words to appropriately describe such desolation and abandonment. The ruins of an ancient city would come close to the portrait of the Ishida family.

Fragments of reality, dejected people, and violent scenes populated Kimiko's mind. Castor's face inanimate and expressionless, Pollux's angry look, and two menacing students pointing the finger were a few recurrent images in her sick universe.

The whole world seemed mad, turning its back on her for some youthful prevarication. She did not mind the universal revolt against her person. What she deplored most was the physical loss of Castor, and the total alienation of Pollux. The twins had been the sunshine in her existence. Without them, she was in complete darkness. They constituted her reason for living, her only solid attachment to life.

Now she had lost the most precious thing she had ever possessed. More than twenty years back, with a daring move, she had stolen motherhood from the gods. Now, in revenge, a cruel destiny had taken it back, returning it to the irate divinities.

A strange balance had been restored by destroying a poor woman's happiness. Nature can be merciless and ruthless when it comes to its modus operandi.

Instead of the integration and socialization suggested by her doctor, Kimiko chose more isolation. The further away she moved from humankind, the safer she felt in her little upside-down world.

The family owned a beautiful cabin in the mountains near Kyoto. Rarely used, it offered the perfect retreat. Accompanied by a female helper, Kimiko packed a few belongings and after saying goodbye to her astonished parents, she left behind rumors, gossip and vicious slander.

She would protect her privacy at all costs. Hiding had never been the proper way to diffuse explosive situations. However, in this case, the embattled Kimiko, by retreating and disappearing, muffled the noise around her, and over time muted attacks from the press and malicious voices from friends and acquaintances.

Time is the best healer of wounds and Kimiko had plenty of time on her hands.

Chapter 11

*"You can **deceive** some of the people all the time, and all of the people some of the time, but you cannot **deceive** all of the people all of the time."*

Peter Egger, the alleged man of integrity, the shining jewel of the Austrian clergies, the very promising ecclesiastic to lead the Archdiocese of Salzburg, in a brief statement to the press announced his early retirement, invoking health reasons.

Surprise and incredulity gripped the city, while his order received the news with disappointment. No one could believe the justification put forward, much less his superiors, who regarded him as the perfect candidate for the job.

In their eyes, Peter had all along been a perfect model of religious life, an original thinker with orthodox views and an obedient subject, always respectful of any authority. They had never heard of physical complaints, of serious illness or somatic inadequacies.

When they received, through diplomatic channels from the Holy See, the real reason, their astonishment and dismay was indescribable.

How could he hide for so many years the existence of a son? Was he a master manipulator, a disingenuous scoundrel, or a man without conscience or morals? Perhaps he was all of the above and much more. And maybe he was nothing of the kind; he just possessed a strong natural instinct for survival.

Whatever the case, it was very hard for his superiors to picture him in a sinister, devious manner. Moreover, it was truly out of character and completely unbelievable.

Nevertheless, who could argue against a reliable DNA test and a personal confession?

No satisfactory answer was at hand for these questions and conjectures. All seemed so unreal, so nightmarish that nothing experienced before could come close to this.

Those were moments of trepidation and apprehension for Peter Egger and his superiors. While awaiting the sentence from Rome, the man with his head on the guillotine had ample time to reflect on his present and future condition.

He was acquainted with the Church's methods in similar cases. He himself had the opportunity to advocate stiff penalties for such transgressors. Evidently, it would not come as a surprise to him. There was, however, an element of surprise. This time, he was on the receiving end. He had never experienced anything more shocking than this, except for the moment of his fatal transgression so many years back.

No reflection in the world could bring him to terms with that devastating reality. Looking at himself in the mirror of his conscience, he felt repugnance and disgust. The radiant image of an irreprehensible man of God, and his well-established reputation of a spotless clergy, had fallen into the mire of orgiastic sex. No recovery or restoration to its original splendor was ever possible. It was lost forever in the eyes of the Church, the tender mother that is supposed to forgive.

However, the unfortunate Peter had not yet touched the bottom of his misery and dejection. Somebody was busying herself to make his life as miserable as possible. Susannah Brigitta Müller, his sworn enemy, would not rest until the public at large, not only the Church, knew the true nature of that presumptuous, arrogant clergyman.

Full of hatred and desire for revenge, Susannah went to the most influential paper in the city. She showed the incriminating documents to the editor. Finally, the faithful would know the real reason for Peter Egger's alleged retirement. Finally, his scandalous life would become apparent to everybody.

The excited editor had no qualms about publishing the paternity test regarding Peter Egger, accompanying it with a long article about his deviant moral conduct.

The morning the incriminatory article appeared on the city's newsstands, people held their breath in amazement and disbelief. The airwaves were suddenly bombasting the unbelievable revelation all over their programs.

The media scandal the Church authorities tried to avoid had not been prevented; on the contrary, it became juicier and more colorful because of a lack of reputable sources.

For Susannah the revenge could not have been any sweeter, while for Peter the public disgrace could not have been more humiliating.

Rome rushed to put a stop to the savage lynching by the court of public opinion. It ordered its unworthy subject to report immediately to the Vatican City. With no more than the basic necessities Peter left his enchanting town of Salzburg for a journey without return.

Searching and reinventing himself is the true essence of this new period in his life.

As soon as he arrived by train at the Stazione Termini, a low-ranking ecclesiastic accompanied him to a *pensione* for guest priests, located in Trastevere, walking distance from the Vatican.

The instructions were laconic. He had to wait patiently until summoned by Cardinal Pandolfi, the Secretary of State. There was no need to remind him of his extremely precarious position. Consequently, it was imperative to maintain irreproachable conduct.

The community that received him presented all the signs of a transient population, where everyone was taking care of his own business with no interaction or meaningful communication.

The atmosphere, figuratively speaking, was ten below zero. The superior appeared to be an alien from another planet. All seemed so impersonal and surreal that Peter felt abandoned in the antechamber of hell.

No one would talk to him or give him the time of day. Everyone kept a safe distance, as if he were the carrier of a contagious disease. Was that part of his punishment?

Poor Peter, how little he knew about Church bureaucracy! That was not even an appetizer of the main meal that would be served in due time.

Days and weeks passed without a word from the Secretary of State. Peter was losing his mind. The dream of a favorable outcome was fading away and with it, any hope of reintegration.

Just by pure coincidence, one day, in the midst of his despair, he heard gossip about a Japanese priest, lodged at a nearby religious house, waiting to answer the charges of fathering a son. He immediately recognized his former schoolmate and planned to meet secretly with him.

The meeting place could not have been more public or more sacred. It was St. Peter's Basilica, where the Prince of the Apostles is believed to have been buried.

The rendezvous place was highly symbolic. It was under the majestic statue of their founder, in the center of Christianity. As soon as they saw each other, they hugged with no particular effusion. After so many years, they could barely recognize one another, not physically but vively. The conversation was not uninhibited and fluent like in the good old days, but halted and tentative. It seemed almost impossible to find common ground or a symbiotic vibration of feelings.

The close friendship they had enjoyed during their theological training was a thing of the past. What remained now was a somber communality of a dire predicament. Even in the best days of their camaraderie, they had never talked of their heated and screwy experience with Kimiko. Painfully aware of its importune existence, they chose to bury it in the intricacies of their subconscious, convinced it did not amount to much in view of their future.

Ironically, at the present time it was the only thing that counted and the only thing that brought them together. Neither knew of the existence of a son. When the news was made public both experienced the shock of their lives.

The reality hit Takeo Shirieda much harder than his friend because the existence of a son came after his assassination. That unexpected double-punch left him numb and with no desire to live.

Had he not been Catholic and a priest, he would have committed *seppuku*, the traditional Japanese ritual suicide by disembowelment. Since his religion prohibited such an action, he embraced the closest form of Christian *seppuku* he could fathom, i.e. a total disembowelment of volitions and emotions, converting himself into the walking dead.

The Church and his superiors could do nothing with his ambulant corpse. Any humiliation, any punishment, any obliteration of his being, would add nothing to his already destroyed persona.

For Takeo the Church was still a tender, loving mother, concerned with his eternal salvation, while for Peter it was the opposite. The Church was becoming for him a cruel stepmother, intent solely on his complete elimination.

He still had much to live for. In his heart, a new crop of sentiments began germinating. A fatherly affection for the son he never knew, and a sensual attraction toward the woman he had fecundated.

The dialogue between Peter and Takeo did not flow smoothly. Anybody would have thought that after so many years the two best friends would interrupt each other, talking incessantly. The sad reality was that time and different experiences had created a divide that could not be bridged.

From the inflection of their voice and the difficulty in finding words, they sensed an arctic cold had come down over their warm friendship, paralyzing any spontaneity and sincerity.

The conversation was still breaking ground, when Peter abruptly asked, "How long have you been waiting?"

"Four weeks and one day," replied Takeo. "Do you have any idea," continued the Japanese clergy after a long, meditative pause, "why such a long wait?"

"I suspect this is their way of showing us their rabid displeasure," answered Peter. "Moreover, it is like a precursor of future punishment."

"Any inkling which direction it will take?"

"Keeping in mind past measures in similar cases, there is no doubt it will certainly be a life of banishment in some obscure convent."

A weird pause ensued, after which Peter continued, "Make no mistake, my dear friend Takeo, this is the end of the line for us. There will be no regeneration or reintegration, just a slow death."

A second long pause preceded Takeo's brief statement. "I deserve whatever punishment they deem appropriate. I will accept the sacrifice of my existence without reservations."

Peter had a different take on what he deserved and which direction he was about to embrace. Up to this moment, he had been a model of obedience and submission. From now on, everything would change.

"Whatever the gravity of my sin, I am not ready to mortgage my future, giving them the right to own my life and dispose of me as if I were an object. If they abandon me, I will abandon them and start my own life."

A sharp contrast marked the two positions, acceptance and submission on one side, rejection and rebellion on the other.

Between the two old friends, there was no longer a meeting of the minds, or empathy beyond ideologies. The same vocation that united them in the past with common goals and ideals now constituted an insurmountable obstacle.

The acceptance of a religious life based on the renunciation of personal will, sexual drive and material possessions was becoming intolerable and insane for Peter Egger. His last statement had become a battle cry for insubordination and rebellion.

Takeo's gut feeling of an inexplicable transformation in his friend received its unequivocal confirmation in those ominous words. Their friendship ended right there.

To cover that irreparable rift, so painful and hurtful, they desperately steered their conversation away from the delicate subject at hand.

Peter, always resourceful and in charge, said, "Do you mind me asking about Kimiko's health? How is she coping with Castor's assassination and all the family's tragedies?"

"Not well," answered Takeo. "She is in a scary psychological and physical slump. With the exception of her parents, no one seems willing or able to help. Given my predicament, I am unable to offer any support or encouragement. She chose total isolation and solitude, cutting off any ties with the world around her. It appears to be a desperate move to avoid further embarrassment. God have mercy on her soul."

Peter felt great compassion and pity for the woman who had changed his destiny. Moved, confused and unexpected, he asked Takeo to kneel down and say a prayer for the three of them. They needed all the help they could get. They whispered *The Lord's Prayer*. When they reached "and forgive us our trespasses as we forgive those who trespass against us," they raised their voices, as a desperate appeal to God and his representatives on earth, their superiors.

Would anybody in heaven or earth listen to their pleas for mercy? A short meditation followed. Finally, they got up, said farewell and without a hug or a handshake, left. They had come together as friends and departed as strangers, moreover as adversaries.

Both felt a desperate emptiness in their hearts and both looked back at their past with regret and nostalgia. Unfortunately, there was no turning back for either of them. The magic spell of a beautiful friendship had been broken, and no prayer in the world would make it whole again.

Life has its ups and downs and unforeseeable turns, but this bizarre happening had broken with any reasonable expectation and with any rule of human conduct. It was beyond comprehension, a complete mystery.

Takeo returned to his religious guesthouse bitter and disappointed. Not only had he lost his reputation and ruined his career, he also saw the last good thing in his life – his friendship with Peter – vanishing forever.

Peter, on the other hand, looked down on his friend, considering him a coward, unwilling to fight back and take the reins of his destiny into his own hands.

What happened next had all the characteristics not only of a low blow but also of a humiliating insult added to injuries.

The day after their historical meeting in St. Peter's Basilica, both received not a low-ranking official from the Secretary of State and Propaganda Fide respectively, but an obscure employee from their order, delivering a sealed document.

The religious emissary uttered not a word of explanation or introduction, just a polite greeting and then the handover of an envelope. All was so prosaic and impersonal, so cold and bureaucratic, that Takeo and Peter felt abandoned by their order and the Church.

The authorities of the two organizations had come together and planned their actions down to the last detail. And that had been the result. They wanted to send a strong signal of disgust and displeasure. The two provident, caring mothers had become heartless judges and cruel executioners.

Takeo, with trembling hands, opened the envelope and slowly read his obedience, which was a life sentence, with no appeal or recourse.

He had to report immediately to a convent in a remote region of Sardinia. The local superior would know what to do with him. Superfluous to say that his conduct should be above reproach when there.

Takeo's reaction was neither rebellious nor arrogant. Stoically and with some sense of relief, he packed his belongings and flew to his destination. Deep down in his heart, he felt the punishment fit the crime and he deserved to be in some kind of isolationism, far from people and places he knew and loved. He suppressed any type of emotion, only allowing himself to look back for an instant at his struggles during the last days of his novitiate. As he had then felt not up to the awesome task of the three vows, despite his Master's assurances, the same way he now felt unworthy of the religious life. He felt like a fake, a terrible failure. He deserved whatever was coming to him. He hoped only for one thing – God's pardon and mercy.

Takeo was better than his words and feelings; he was a good, honest man, very rare even among religious people. Bad circumstances and a cruel destiny had swept him away from a normal existence, making of him a bad element, an undesirable person.

Paradoxically, exiled and with his wings clipped, he felt freer than ever, soaring high above human miseries and reaching incredible heights of dignity, humility and moral stature.

His discarded and punished existence converted him into a true martyr of silence and abandonment. In his disabling misfortune, he showed character and real Christian virtues.

It is useless to say his family, at the news of his humiliating confinement, remained heartbroken and extremely pained. How could his relatives accept and explain that a direct descendent from a noble samurai and an intrepid Catholic martyr disgraced himself by breaking the vow of chastity in such a shameless, impudent way? How can anybody fall any lower than that?

People, including the Church and the order, are quick to judge and condemn. Their measurements and scale of values are geared more toward their preservation than the sinners' redemption. Looking good is more important than being good. Appearance over substance and deception over reality is the guiding light of organizations and institutions.

Virtually buried in a remote region of Sardinia, Takeo underwent an invisible transformation, giving origin to a new delicate flower.

A totally different transformation occurred within his friend Peter.

As soon as he opened the letter and read the contents, in a furious rage he crumpled the paper up into a ball and threw it violently into the wastebasket.

He would never accept the harsh punishment of being relegated to an insignificant role of confessor in a remote region of the Argentinean pampas. His predictions had been right on the mark, even if his secret expectations were of some leniency. Faced with the alternatives of accepting or rebelling, Peter chose the latter.

The champion of orthodoxy, the paladin of righteousness, the noble knight with the shining armor of morality was ready to jump ship and become a deserter, a renegade, a defrocked cleric. For the Church he loved and served, and the order for which he sacrificed the best of his years, he had nothing but animosity and disgust.

The order to leave immediately for his new destination was peremptory. That dictatorial tone touched the last sensitive nerve in his body and the fragile crystal of his humanity, overflowing with spitefulness and repudiation, burst forth violently.

The superimposed humility, for which he had worked so hard during his novitiate, flew out the window. His obedience, in which he had trained so long, lost its relevance and ceased to exist.

Arrogance and injustice have their ways of mutating normal, decent people into rebels and sworn adversaries. Rulers should never underestimate the hidden power of unfairness and oppression. There is a limit to the abuse of power, whether political, religious or otherwise.

Peter, who had been part of that power system that now banned him to a remote corner of Patagonia, suddenly discovered its ugly face. That ugliness shook him deeply. He felt ashamed and irate. He vowed to fight against it with all his strength.

To accept his superiors' decision would have meant to perpetuate the oppressive system; to reject it would have implied self-marginalization and the loss of influence. Either way he would lose the battle. Faced with this defeatist proposition, he felt powerless, almost insignificant. What an autocratic and ruthless organization he was living in! In the Church and his order, there was no room for legalized opposition or constructive criticism. It was their way or no way.

Perfectly aware of this hopeless predicament, Peter could not hide from his conscience. It was to this silent witness that he had to answer. No one, in fact, can escape this always-vigilant interpellator.

He calmed himself down and collected his thoughts. It was not easy. Rage and revenge clouded his judgment. He had plenty of ammunition in his gun. Unfortunately, they lacked firepower. Every single bullet he could use in his writing would ricochet off the target and come back to hit him.

Nevertheless, the soon-to-become rebel and traitor would not abandon the trenches without addressing his superiors for the last time. It was the honorable thing to do. If he had to die, he would face the firing squad with no blindfold over his eyes.

He grabbed a piece of paper and wrote a few paragraphs to the authorities of his order.

"I would be happy to oblige and report immediately to my future destination. But my conscience, the ultimate criterion of morality, is pushing me in the opposite direction.

I have been a faithful servant of the rules and regulations of the order, and no one knows better than this writer how painful it is to go against the Sacred Vows, mainly the vow of obedience. However, I am left with no other choice.

Therefore, I formally request dispensation from all my religious obligations and permission to return to a secular life.

I beg forgiveness for any scandal I may have caused and put myself at the mercy of God."

The second letter, addressed to the Cardinal Secretary of State, expressed basically the same concepts.

However, in one of those moments of soul-searching, Peter put down something new and startling.

Here are some excerpts from the document. "Your Eminence, I raise my voice neither for clemency nor understanding. I know the game is over, and whatever plea I formulate will go unheard. Nevertheless, for the love of God we both share and mainly for clarity's sake, I deem necessary some clarifications on what happened many years ago. Far from me to put forward these explanations as justifications or mitigating factors. They are just integral parts of a puzzle that caused me infinite pain and regret. Could I go back to that ruinous, shameful moment in time, how gladly and swiftly I would steer in the opposite direction and run for my life.

It all happened in the middle of my second year of theology, two-and-a-half years prior to my priestly ordination. During that unfortunate period, my best friend and schoolmate, Takeo Shirieda, invited me to a gala night, celebrating Carnival. A young, powerful Japanese woman, whom we had met before, requested our presence and company. Needless to say, we were reluctant. However, at the insistence of our superior, we accepted.

The ingestion of sake, the exotic oriental atmosphere, and the presence of the tempting and alluring young woman obscured my judgment and paralyzed my willpower. I am not quite sure what happened next. After the fact, two things seemed incontrovertible. First, there was no solicitation or provocation on my part. Second, the aftermath feelings were terrible. I felt dirty and destroyed. Never in my life had I gone through such a degrading experience.

The following day, overwhelmed by pangs of guilt, I sought my confessor's advice. He calmed me down, assured me God's forgiveness and encouraged me not to abandon my vocation.

With extreme reluctance, I followed his counsel. If I am guilty of anything, it is of being obedient. After that horrible event, I never saw or spoke to that Japanese woman again.

Moreover, I never knew I had fathered a son until the media broke the news. This was as devastating for me as for your Eminence and the whole Church.

Honest to God, these are the circumstances surrounding my fall.

I am well aware none of what I just said will alter your judgment and modify your decision.

I repeat, I wish I could go back and redo everything. However, that is impossible.

Obviously, in your estimation the Church's reputation must come before my personal salvation. It is for this reason I see no other alternative but to follow my conscience and leave the priesthood, where there is no room for people like me.

Every organization, including the Church, has its own internal dynamics. It is pointless to try to oppose them. With the utmost respect, I solemnly implore you to relieve me of my priestly obligations, granting me complete legal secularization.

Assuring you my constant prayers to the Almighty for your well-being, I bid you farewell."

The polite form and mild tone of both documents did not reflect Peter's true sentiments. Fuming with indignation on the inside and uneasy, almost incoherent, on the outside, he was about to step out of his comfort zone. The jump into the unknown was practically unthinkable a few weeks earlier.

The soon-to-be-consecrated Bishop of Salzburg had overnight become a rebel and a defector. However, his implicit plea for clemency fell on deaf ears. In view of this, would he lead part of his flock astray? This was the Vatican's main concern besides the obvious scandal.

Peter was not interested in forming a new Church. One was more than enough for him. It did not make any sense to perpetuate – with a new organization – the same arrogant structure he was criticizing. It is a common mistake among the reformers of all time to burden the faithful with new impositions. Different names but the same substance, domestication and exploitation.

Peter was intelligent enough to stay away from a similar pitfall and rearrange his life in a different direction.

He wrote to his family members not to worry about his future. As soon as he settled down, he would notify them.

Meanwhile, in his heart a new family was taking shape, where Kimiko and Pollux were the main components. Was that feasible, or was it beyond the realm of possibility? It was certainly a journey he wanted to undertake, a new world he had a great desire to explore.

Courage, determination and a grand in his pocket was all he had in his possession.

The expedition he was about to embark on had all the characteristics of prehistoric man trying to cross the majestic Alps. The odds of succeeding were heavily stacked against him. In fact, with little or no knowledge of the weather and terrain, with scarce provisions and ill-equipped for such a treacherous enterprise, it was a crazy proposition.

A blistering snowstorm, a dangerous avalanche, a hidden crevasse in the glacier or a wild animal could put an end at any moment to such a daring project.

However, youthful inexperience accompanied by an unquenchable thirst for new adventure would inject dynamite under his feet, making him run with obstinacy while disregarding perilous situations and mortal danger.

Like the prehistoric adventurer, Peter would feel irresistibly attracted by a life he never knew and dangers he had never prepared for.

Trusting only his gut feelings, he was ready for the journey of his life.

Chapter 12

"*Who had **deceived** thee as often as thyself?*" – William Shakespeare

Kimiko was born into a family of power, riches and prestige. Every little whim of hers received immediate attention.

No expense was ever too big or extravagant for that delicate flower. She was the apple of her parents' eyes and the true sunshine in their lives.

They could not imagine one day of their existence without that bundle of joy. Since her birth, she had them wrapped around her little finger.

Her infancy was unremarkable, except for some frequent tantrums, so common in small children.

Her nanny, a sweet Filipino woman, had a real hard time managing those difficult moments. Slowly she became used to the child's irrational behavior, considering it normal.

The happy moments of that special child were very rewarding. Her smile was enchanting, her mimicking the adults hilarious, and the sounds of words on her lips melodious.

When she attempted her first steps, it was a day of celebration in the Ishida family. Asserting her independence of movement, nobody was able to stop her from running around and discovering every single corner of the huge mansion.

Infinite stories and curious anecdotes marked that period of true innocence and infantile unawareness.

Cascading laughter and shrieks of crying brought the silent mansion to life.

As long as the little princess was around, no dull moment was possible or even conceivable. No attention, care or money was ever spared when it came to Kimiko. "To spoil" took on a new meaning with the Ishida family.

As the first and only child, heiress to an immense fortune, she received the best education available. From personal tutors to specialized trainers, highly qualified teachers and instructors to sensitive motivators, Kimiko had all the help she needed.

From the early age of four, piano, tennis, swimming and other artistic and physical activities were part of her daily routine. Twice a week she received lessons in German, French and Italian, with a view to later attending a famous private boarding school in Switzerland.

Nothing was spared to prepare her for the sensitive position of running the family business.

Some days, at the tender age of five and six, the adorable little girl showed an intensity of concentration truly unusual while taking lessons or exercising.

Other days, she gave the impression of pursuing some daydream far removed from the activities at hand.

There were several facets to her personality, two of them predominant. Moodiness was the most apparent. Kimiko, one day would be happy, excited and willing to take on the world; another, she would exhibit clear signs of sluggishness, a somber attitude, and lack of concentration. Her cheery smile and high tone of voice would disappear. Muteness and depression would ensue.

The second distinct facet was her mental acuity, with a surprising intuition and penetration into difficult subjects, like grammar, syntax and math. A sparkle of genius lit up her eyes.

Naturally smart, the girl who inherited everything and did not lack anything had a huge drawback in her education.

Being the only child, she did not have siblings to compete with or measure up to. The same happened with her home schooling. Without schoolmates to engage with, she lacked competition.

No one, in fact, should underestimate the benefits of a healthy rivalry in daily challenges. The world runs on competition. Without it, life would be dull, boring and uneventful.

Kimiko's loving parents, intent upon providing her with the best in life, unconsciously eliminated from her little world an essential element that could have converted her into a born competitor and a super achiever.

With her wings clipped, for lack of competition, she would never become an eagle. Unable to soar high in the sky, her stage for action would be the earthly ground, where mud and dirt make their home.

Happiness and sadness, elation and depression, cheerfulness and melancholy, geniality and dullness alternated like clockwork.

Kimiko grew up with the conviction that her persona was the center of the universe, and everything revolved around her.

Wrapped up in her own ego, the parents remained blind in the presence of the little monster they had created.

Their awakening was rude and painful. It happened during the birthday celebration of a female cousin of the same age.

The party, despite the scarce means of the family, was fabulous. All the members, from the oldest to the youngest, were hospitable and gracious.

Kimiko, the invitee, realized she was not the center of attention. Jealous in the extreme, she started acting out and misbehaving badly.

Her rudeness and bad manners toward her cousin and the other children became too apparent to be overlooked. Her mother, surprised and displeased, took her aside and told her clearly to be nice and friendly.

Everything the mother said to the spoiled Kimiko went in one ear and out the other. She kept pushing people around during games and competitions; she purposefully spilt drinks on the floor and disobeyed any command or directions coming from adults.

She seemed to enjoy her atrocious behavior, while everybody else remained dumbfounded. She added her finishing touch during the cake-cutting ceremony.

Her cousin was about to blow out the candles and make a wish when Kimiko, in an act of envious rage, forestalled her by blowing first.

What happened next is difficult to put into words. The birthday girl burst into tears, and the other children stopped their cheers and applauses. An ominous silence fell over the gathering and everybody held their breath.

Kimiko's parents apologized profusely and grabbed their little antisocial monster, fleeing the scene in embarrassment and humiliation.

On their way out, Kimiko pulled down the sign that read: "Happy birthday, Midori." The only thing left out from her barrage of displeasure and jealousy was the throwing of a piece of cake in her cousin's face.

No one had ever witnessed, in a polite society like the Japanese, such outrageous behavior.

Kimiko's parents were mortified, to say the least. What was supposed to be a happy occasion turned out to be a social disaster.

However, there is no evil without some positive consequence. It is in the nature of things to offer some anchor of salvation on the brink of tragedy.

Finally, the always-condescending parents had to face the results of their own ill-conceived education. In Kimiko's case, as the only child of wealthy parents, lacking for nothing meant social skills depravation, interaction deficiency and tantrum-throwing behavior.

Was it too late to remedy such a deplorable situation, or was there still time to reverse the ruinous course of their daughter?

In a secret family meeting with a psychologist present, they concluded the immediate insertion of their child into a public school would produce positive results and overturn the destructive spiral of egoism and jealousy.

The plan seemed perfect and easy to carry out. However, an important element was missing from that equation – the approval and acceptance of the subject under discussion.

The morning Kimiko was made aware of the new imposition of attending a public school, she became unglued. Her peaceful universe suffered a devastating tsunami.

Her attitude was easy to read. Total refusal was her answer. Only force prevailed against her stubbornness.

Force and imposition are hardly the right means in any human endeavor, particularly in the rearing of a child.

Kimiko, smart enough to understand her parents' predicament, used all her tricks, from absolute silence to non-participation in school activities, to render her parents' measures ineffective.

Only under heavy pressure made of promises and bribes, did the rebellious child cave in to compliance, showing some participation and interaction.

In her clever, little scheme, all was supposed to be temporary. However, time, teachers and therapy produced something remarkable.

Kimiko embraced, although still with some reluctance, the new lifestyle. In a short period, she modified her behavioral patterns, adjusting to the new rules of peaceful coexistence.

Nobody was more astonished than her parents and relatives, who had already given up on that hopeless girl. The spoiled child did not become a sensation of good manners, selflessness and sharing overnight. She still had a long way to go. The fundamental features of her character and psychological makeup remained the same, but her response to internal and external stimuli were different, more adjusted to accepted behavior.

Competing with her schoolmates was the soothing balsam that converted her aggressiveness into productive energy. Even at that tender age, she realized she had enough natural talents and physical beauty to stand out among the crowd and be noticed.

Adults and youngsters alike could not hide their admiration for her academic achievements and social integration.

Her alternating spells of cheery times and gloomy moments added more allure to her personality. Adorable and endearing would be the right words for the transformed Kimiko.

The repellent, repulsive child had become lovable and attractive, and would remain that way for the time being.

However, she was not out of the woods yet, as her dad was concerned. His dream was to send her to a private elite school in Switzerland.

Was she ready socially for such a challenge? Failure from a disciplinary point of view would have been devastating for the Ishida family. That was a huge responsibility for both parents and student.

Preparation and planning was of paramount importance.

Toward the end of her grammar school, mom, dad and daughter made a surprising trip to Surval Mont-Fleuri, an international boarding school for young ladies in Montreux, Switzerland.

The place and the building were breathtaking. The school, a haven of peace and tranquility, was perched upon a cliff overlooking the spectacular view of Lake Geneva.

The building, impressive in its structure of seven floors, had the combined features of a castle and Swiss hotel.

Retaining all its original old-world charm, it had been renovated and constantly updated to keep pace with the latest modern trends.

The principal, along with the teaching staff and students, left a lasting impression on the three visitors. Courteousness and affability were the most visible traits of that educational establishment.

A young woman by the name of Roxanne took them on a tour of the premises, explaining the programs and rules. Kimiko had to wait another three years before being able to start 9th grade as a freshman. The official language was French, but many classes were taught in English.

The courses for the first year were Mathematics (Basic Mathematics, Pre-Algebra, and Algebra), General Science, Social Studies, English and French. Among the electives were Foreign Languages, Business and Fine Arts.

The basic rules were no alcohol or drugs and no smoking. Students were expected to be neat, clean and appropriately dressed at all times.

After this informative tour, they had a brief interview with the principal. Lady Clarisse had an aristocratic air and possessed a rare charisma. She seemed to read the minds of her interlocutors. Looking into Kimiko's eyes, and reassuring her, along with her parents, she said, "Do not worry. You will do fine, I assure you."

With that lovely introduction, everybody felt comfortable and at ease. The conversation, albeit short, contained a priceless piece of knowledge of Swiss culture that would help the young student immensely.

"Westerners," she said, "tend to verbalize their feelings and tell their life story to perfect strangers, while Japanese people are more reserved, rarely manifesting their true sentiments. Kimiko, if you learn to open up and be frank, you will find no cultural barriers."

The perceptive girl, despite her tender age, understood clearly what the principal tried to convey.

After touching on different topics, Clarisse concluded by inviting the parents to fill out an application form. The waiting list was long, and it was imperative to apply well in advance. The parents complied gladly. Finally, with a smile and a handshake, they took leave of the building.

Kimiko and her parents left that beautiful place with warm feelings in their heart and many hopes of a bright future.

Back in Kyoto, the future boarding school student could hardly wait to tell everybody her great experience. Now she had something very important to look forward to. Moreover, the principal made a lasting impression on her, and she strived to emulate her in every possible way.

She was so eager to get ready that she implored her parents to provide her with an English tutor. Kimiko certainly already had her hands full with languages. First German, French and Italian, now English.

It is difficult to understand how she could handle such a burden, but the trip to Switzerland gave her wings. Nothing was out of reach and everything appeared possible.

The seasons alternated quickly and the time flew irreparably.

The former tantrum-throwing child was becoming a young lady before her parents' very eyes.

However, a serious accident perturbed the peaceful march toward the much-desired goal.

One day, while exercising on the parallel bars, she attempted to do a double somersault landing. Unfortunately, she miscalculated her timing and energy level. The fall was nasty and extremely painful, breaking her right leg.

A dark cloud covered her horizon and her future seemed in serious doubt. During her moments of solitude, when nobody could see her, she silently vented her frustrations by shedding many tears.

Being in a cast for months was not pleasant. However, the frequent visits from friends, and schoolmates writing get well wishes on the white plaster of her leg, made it easier and almost enjoyable. She had not been the center of such caring attention in quite a while.

After several months of forced inaction, Kimiko was able to resume the use of her restored limb, walking normally. With great gusto, she went back to her scholastic routine, as if nothing had happened.

The prolonged period in bed was somehow beneficial. In fact, she intensified her English classes, becoming proficient in that language. She could carry on a basic conversation with no difficulty.

Tutor and parents were very pleased with such an unexpected outcome.

The three years of middle school were over before she even realized it.

Kimiko's mom dreaded the moment of separation, while her dad couldn't wait any longer to see his daughter off to an exciting future.

Both parents had a different outlook, yet the same deep feelings of love and great expectations.

Nobody could blame either one, because both, in a different way, wanted the best for their daughter.

Finally, on a nostalgic day in September, accompanied only by her father, Kimiko was off to Switzerland, the land of beautiful dreams and generous promises.

Clarisse, the same principal she had met previously and whom she idolized, was there to receive them with open arms. Only when her father said the final goodbye and disappeared did she feel her stomach knot with strong emotions.

Definitely, she had left her comfortable nest. Flying away from all familiar faces and places had been courageous. There was no turning back, no regrets, unless she wanted to compromise her future.

The first-year students were in the same position of anxiety, novelty and curiosity. Coming from different cultures and different corners of the world, they had to find common ground and adapt quickly to a lifestyle quite different from their own.

Since the very beginning, there was an underground scrambling for secret alliances and open friendships.

Only a few girls showed no interest in such natural tendencies, preferring to run their lives independent from any attachment.

Kimiko, mindful of Clarisse's piece of advice three years earlier, wanted to form close ties with some congenial students. That way, she could come out of her shell and share feelings and experiences, fears and hopes, dreams and achievements.

Abigail, a girl from Detroit, Michigan, and Courtney from Johannesburg, South Africa, became her best friends. The first was the daughter of an executive in the automobile industry, while the second was the only offspring of a famous South African politician.

For some strange reason and for some unknown affinity, they formed an indivisible trio, complementing and supporting each other.

Abigail and Courtney would help Kimiko with languages, mainly English and French, while Kimiko offered them invaluable support in science.

With the passing of time, their friendship grew stronger. Sharing their most intimate experiences, they felt and behaved like sisters. They were jokingly nicknamed 'The Three Musketeers.'

They did not mind that kind of teasing. Stimulated by the needs of their schoolmates, they developed one of their most endearing characteristics. They put their abilities at the service of others. Instead of forming an exclusive circle, they were open to anyone in need.

Obviously, that was welcome by the school authorities, who publicly praised their positive influence within the community.

By comparison, Kimiko possessed greater mental talent than either Abigail or Courtney. But these two were far superior in relational skills and physical abilities.

These great talents, accompanied by a keen desire to help others, propelled them into an array of social activities.

Excelling academically and busying themselves in philanthropic endeavors was their distinguishing mark.

Even during social events, like dances, parties and outings they never lost their focus. How many people among the staff and villagers benefited from their helping hands!

More than musketeers, they deserved the title of angels, sent by some mysterious divinity. An extraordinary golden period dawned on Surval Mont-Fleuri, never seen before or after. Those three girls were a breed apart, so uncharacteristic they made people think of some exoteric indoctrination by a secret society. The phenomenon defied human tendencies and teenagers' usual conduct.

The rare conjunction of beneficial energies emanating from the three little stars spurred other students into action, creating a flourishing movement of significant proportions.

However, that golden season did not last long. As often happens, things and conditions do not remain stable, let alone immutable.

Terribly sad news reached the Swiss boarding school. What made it worse was the timing. The great festivities of Christmas and New Year were around the corner. The death of Courtney's father, brutally murdered by an apartheid fanatic, fell like an avalanche, blanketing feelings, burying initiatives and paralyzing the unfortunate girl.

Despite the enormous outpouring of sympathy, Courtney's heart and spirit were crushed, bleeding profusely. Against her will, she had to leave that happy place and return to her native country. The financially struggling family needed her presence and help.

Even assurances by the other two girls' families of substantial economic assistance could not stop the grieving girl from leaving the school.

Courtney's departure signaled the decline of the movement that had aroused so much interest and created so many expectations.

Kimiko and Abigail, deeply touched by that cruel event, lost all enthusiasm. The previous spontaneity, mixed with ingenuity and inventiveness, had left their minds and soul. No persuasive reasoning, no rational argument, no encouragement from friends and teachers could bring it back to life.

It appeared like a one-time gift from above. Once gone, it was gone forever.

Incredibly, Kimiko was the most affected. Like a fresh branch under the fury of a storm, she bent to the point of breaking. Her natural propensity toward spells of exaltation and depression contributed to the inward movement of narcissistic tendencies and withdrawal from the external world.

The radiant girl of yesterday had crossed an invisible threshold, leaving behind the land of plenty and entering the arid terrain of a moonlike landscape.

Even her mother, during her frequent visits, could not breathe into her a puff of vivifying spirit, a breath of renewed optimism.

Kimiko smiled, played and went about her daily activities with no conviction or confidence whatsoever.

She remained close friends with Abigail, but the previous solidarity that propelled them into notoriety, slowly dried up.

That winter of misfortune and sorrow marked them for life.

This notwithstanding both miraculously kept up their academic concentration and intensiveness, at the end of their first year reaping the highest honors and awards.

Life had been good at Surval Mont-Fleuri but extremely trying. What was in store for them in the second year?

Returning from her vacation in Japan, Kimiko had to face another unpleasant surprise. Her dear friend Abigail had not returned from the States. Without any warning, her parents had decided to transfer her to a prestigious school in California.

Abigail wrote a sweet letter to her friend, telling her how much she missed her company. Regrettably, she could not persuade her parents to revoke their decision and change their minds.

Kimiko, made stronger by the first blow, did not falter this time. Stoically and impassibly, she took control of her emotions and steered her ship toward the stormy sea ahead.

One lesson emerged clearly from that murky reality – survival is the lot of the fittest.

Kimiko threw herself body and soul into physical activities and scholastic challenges, never forgetting to extend a helping hand to the most needy. In the process, she made several friends, without getting too close to anybody, for fear of losing them.

The curriculum included some elective courses and Business was one of them. After the high school diploma, Surval Mont-Fleuri offered a three-year bachelor's degree in Business Administration. Kimiko concentrated all her efforts toward this goal.

The future CEO of her father's company could barely wait to sink her teeth into that coveted program. Obviously, her life at the boarding school was not all work and no fun. There were parties, dances and outings in which she took part, although her eagerness for this kind of entertainment was not overwhelming at first.

Inadvertently, she came to love them, mainly after the unusual encounter with a young student from the town's higher education institute. His name was Jean-Paul. Blonde hair, blue eyes, average height and complexion, he possessed a certain magnetism. He was not a rock star that drives teenagers crazy, but rather a silent movie actor with a dreamy look and a great presence.

In one of those social gatherings, he politely insisted on dancing with her. Reluctant at first, Kimiko gave in, accepting the invitation. Although a little insecure, the elegant, good-looking man gave the impression of being interested in her.

Other similar social encounters followed. Inevitably, the conversation became more personal and the physical attraction deeper and stronger. His laugh was contagious and his warmth soothing.

For the first time, Kimiko found herself romantically involved with a member of the opposite sex. Was it a teenager crush, intense but volatile, or true love, honest, sincere and long lasting?

In the midst of this whirlwind romance, the attractive oriental could not separate the wheat from the chaff, the mere sexual from the pure affection. Infatuation and longing, passion and yearning, lust and fondness were coming together, melting in a powerful and uncontrollable drive.

Even a cool machine, like a brain scanner, able to map out with infallible precision intentions and feelings, would have had difficulty in discerning and reading that incandescent and raw human magma.

The handsome hunk, so enigmatic and intriguing, was he the real thing or just a creation of her ebullient passion? It is not uncommon for people in love to project on the object of their affection qualities and attributes that are not there, or if they exist to aggrandize them in a disproportionate fashion.

Was Kimiko a victim of these frequent lovers' pitfalls? All seemed too beautiful to be true.

Before going any further on her conquest march, before caressing impossible dreams of an everlasting union, before facing a ruinous and deceptive abandonment, she took a moment to reflect and investigate.

She wanted to know more about his family, relations and habits from people that knew him best. What she found out was not to her liking. Moreover, it was highly disturbing.

According to well-informed sources, the irresistible Jean-Paul had a girlfriend to whom he was engaged.

Did Kimiko have enough courage to confront him, or was it more in her style to silently bury the ashes of an ill-fated love affair?

The pain of such a finding was so intense that during the night she shed bitter tears of disappointment and desperation.

Her credulity and naivety remained crippled for life. She did not believe or accept any of Jean-Paul's explanations. He had the nerve to justify his behavior by saying he intended to break up the engagement and leave his girlfriend.

For the straightforward, simple Japanese student he had been a two-faced liar, a master manipulator, a diabolic deceiver.

The more she found out about her Casanova, the deeper her heart-wound became. Many girls before her had fallen for the same trick, and very likely, others would follow.

Abigail, her best friend in whom she confided and with whom she kept in touch through mail, persuaded her not to dwell on her mistakes and to move on. The past was the past and better things were ahead.

On top of that, precious words of wisdom came from the principal, Clarisse, who had so much invested in the talented student.

Kimiko's admiration for her superior would not allow any deviation from the suggested path. She would embrace even the most insignificant advice with devotion and religiosity.

The saying "What does not kill you makes you stronger" rang true for the unfortunate Kimiko. From this experience, she acquired a new outlook.

She stopped chasing after shiny things. "Not all that glitters is gold." She would no longer take things at face value.

She had matured rapidly. In the future, her trademark would be more cautiousness and less naïveté.

No other significant episode marks the rest of her stay in that artificial Garden of Eden.

The roaring days of her first year, where notoriety and instant superstardom had propelled her into an unintended visibility full of admiration, faded away.

Alone and with a failed romantic affair behind her, Kimiko concentrated her energies on her scholastic program and extracurricular activities. Excellence surrounded by anonymity would be the guiding light of her last three years, wherein she obtained her bachelor's degree in Business Administration.

She would go back to her family and native country as an accomplished young lady, fluent in foreign languages, academically prepared for the world of business, and psychologically equipped for life's onslaughts.

School authorities and her parents beamed with pride and satisfaction, sure that a brilliant future was in store for the promising student.

Would Kimiko be successful, adding splendid accomplishments to her family name? Or, contrary to any expectation, would she fall prey to mysterious forces beyond her control?

In concluding this chapter, it is only fair to say destiny had something special reserved for her. No one could have ever predicted or foreseen such a bizarre turn of events.

Chapter 13

*"All **deception** in the course of life is indeed nothing else but a lie reduced to practice, and falsehood passing from words into things."* – Robert Southey

To rebel against Church authorities has never been easy or pain free. More often than not, the consequences of such an action are dire. In the old days of the Inquisition, various forms of punishment were used when dealing with people rejecting some doctrines, religious authority or ecclesiastical laws – from being burnt at the stake to imprisonment, torture to complete isolationism, excommunication to destitution, to name a few.

In modern times, rebellious clerics have to face an uphill battle when struggling to free themselves from the shackles of a strict religious upbringing. Besides the Church's hostility, they have to face society's prejudice with its scornful, contemptuous treatment.

Peter Egger was no exception. However, his struggle was more an internal one, a matter of conscience, than an abusive external one.

His dear friend's example of humbly accepting the Vatican's decision added more pressure, resurrecting doubts and fogging his judgment.

The moment of liberation had arrived, but with no exhilaration or satisfaction. Instead, fear and scruples would agitate his tormented soul for a long time to come.

Two powerful sentiments pulled him in opposite directions – longing for the woman who had seduced him in a moment of weakness, and love for a son he never knew.

Who would win – the sexual allure or the paternal affection, the sweet woman in need of a shoulder to cry on, or the boy in search of a new direction in his life?

Who would have benefited most from his presence? Conversely, who would suffer more from seeing a perfect stranger with parental claims?

The dilemma was real and the outcome of a family members' reunification uncertain and double-edged.

Love and hatred, anger and joy, disappointment and satisfaction were both possible.

For Peter to leave a priestly past behind had been trying. Now, to choose the future would be terrifying in the extreme.

In the glorious days of his religious fervor, Peter used to kneel down and pray to God before embarking on any risky endeavor. Now, not only did he have serious doubts about the efficacy of prayer, he was also unsure on which side God stood. Was the Almighty with the Church and against him, as faith would dictate, or with him and against the Church, as his hope was inclined to believe?

At this stage of his radical transformation, religiosity no longer made much sense to him. Secular categories replaced the previous pious ones, opening frightening sinkholes along his path. Reasserting himself as an independent thinker and operator would imply some stumbles here and there. Nothing Peter Egger couldn't handle.

Returning to his basic dilemma of whether to meet first with his son, Pollux, or Kimiko, the lovely temptress, his painful decision was in favor of the boy he had never known.

The need to see his son, before anything happened to him, superseded any other need or reason. As an overdue act of justice, he badly wanted to explain what had happened between him and his mother. Pollux deserved at least an explanation and a sincere apology.

Peter had not abandoned him; he was unaware of his existence. This was the painful truth. Once he cleared this initial hurdle, perhaps some sentimental connection could be possible.

The prodigal father was not expecting any miracle, just an explanatory apology and some kind of reconciliation. This was not the right word because he had never broken any ties, but it was good enough for lack of a better one.

After putting some order in the tangle of his confused ideas and sentiments, it was time to spring into action.

He obtained a tourist visa from the American consulate and a one-way ticket to Pittsburgh from a travel agency.

The departure from Rome was like cutting his umbilical cord with the Church.

Once in the air, among the hissing noise of the engines and the chitchatting of the passengers, he experienced a silent vacuum in his heart. As scary as it was, for lack of contrasting emotions and ideas, Peter went through an indescribable emptiness and a severe famine for affection.

All this became more dramatic when he contemplated, in the distant horizon, the majestic symbol of Christianity – St. Peter's Basilica – disappearing in an ocean of red during a memorable Roman sunset. Nothing could be more emblematic than that.

The old life, cut short by the stroke of a perverse genius, rendered its last dying breath while a dark night wrapped every living creature in its obscure mantle.

Peter was afraid of dozing off for fear of never waking up. What kind of existence awaited him? What continent would be his final destination – America, Australia or Asia?

A young woman was sitting next to him, reading a magazine and giving him a bewildered stare from time to time. Apparently, she could not figure him out, because of his out-of-the-ordinary demeanor.

He did not bother to reassure her or show any sign of friendliness. The world surrounding him was unimportant. He kept to himself during the whole flight, undisturbed by what was happening in the immediate vicinity.

Tired out by the unusual day and lulled into a sense of security by the constant hissing of the plane, he closed his eyes on the old world.

When he woke up, the new world loomed on the distant horizon. At New York's La Guardia, Peter Egger, along with other passengers, took another plane bound for Pittsburgh.

The flight was relatively short and uneventful. After landing, he looked for accommodation with some apprehension.

He called up a priest, a former theology schoolmate from his formation years in Torino. Father Thomas was surprised to hear his voice, and even more surprised to listen to his story.

The initial warmth of the welcome gave way to an uncustomary coldness in his voice and an open refusal to Peter's request for hospitality.

Hurt but not discouraged, Peter checked into a cheap hotel with a bitter taste in his mouth. That was a pale reflection of things to come. Church and society members would not look kindly upon a renegade priest.

No humiliation or rejection was big enough to prevent him from meeting his biological son. Anything was a small price to pay, no matter the pain and difficulties involved.

His next move was to contact the nearest police station and reveal his identity. Surely, somebody would know about Pollux's case and be forthcoming with information.

Peter's assumption was correct. A police officer gave him the name and address of the investigator handling the case.

For Ken Fresco to meet face to face with Pollux's father was a real shocker. He would never have dreamt of such a possibility.

He had hit an impenetrable wall in his investigation. Now a great opportunity to shed some light had presented itself. He would not hesitate to grab it and exploit it to his advantage.

Reenergized by the prospect of something positive, he hurriedly assembled his team. Mary Rosenthal appeared elated at the news. She could barely wait to see that mysterious man who had been with Kimiko, the talk of the precinct.

In a brainstorming session, Ken came up with a strategy, based on tempestivity and improvisation.

He had a valuable piece of the puzzle in his hands. Peter, as a witness, possessed a virgin mind, pure and uncontaminated. If handled with care, he could be a source of precious information.

Rejecting any notion of a formal interrogation, Ken would sit down in front of a cup of coffee and have a friendly conversation, showing interest in his predicament and offering any reasonable help.

That informal meeting should take place immediately, before Peter had a chance to talk to his son, and his lawyer Taisuke Fujii.

Since Peter did not have a complete command of the English language, the smart detective got an interpreter.

The place chosen was a cozy bar not far from the police station. Ken, Peter and Mary Rosenthal, the interpreter, sat in a quiet corner and, sipping steamy cappuccinos, set in motion a friendly conversation.

From Peter's own account, two things appeared clear and uncontroversial. First, Peter Egger only discovered he had a son after Castor's murder. Second, a possible connection between Castor's assassins and a European secret organization linked to the Austrian priest should be discarded as improbable, if not impossible, from a chronological standpoint.

In his streamlined narration of the events, Peter showed a rare sincerity and a touching interest for his son. In Ken's estimation, a dishonest person would never possess those qualities.

Satisfied with the results, they concluded their meeting and wished each other a successful conclusion.

The following day, Mary Rosenthal, the ideal interpreter, would accompany the searching father to the son's residence. She was probably the best person to carry out such a delicate mission. In fact, besides her German roots, her feminine touch and knowledge of Pollux were unparalleled.

Before going home, she took the liberty of filling Peter in on his son. Without elaborating extensively, she mentioned the rough time he went through after his brother's assassination, the falling out with his mother for lying to him, and the hope of someday meeting his biological father.

This last revelation touched Peter deeply, although he did not know what it meant exactly. He was afraid of going in with too much confidence and at the end being disappointed.

It is no secret these types of meetings entail a high level of volatility. Any gesture or phrase may trigger a negative reaction. The accumulated resentment and abandonment might explode at any turn. Nothing is a given or a sure thing.

Question after question popped up in his mind without a clear answer. The two more frequent were certainly: will some connection be established, and if so would it last?

Peter's intentions were undoubtedly honest and sincere. He wanted to reconstitute the family he never had. The problem was at the other end. The family was already constituted, even if it had crumbled at the revelation of the scandal. Would it be willing to substitute the old formation with a new one and run the risk of a repeated failure?

No one would be so hasty and blind at the same time. Personal desires were one thing, and somebody else's experience a very different reality.

The quiet conversation with Mary Rosenthal had been informative and stimulating. However, it compounded previous fears and future hopes.

After that, she got hold of Pollux. In their brief phone conversation, she asked him to meet with her the following day. Without giving away any details, she promised a big surprise.

Exhausted, Peter went to bed, dreading the upcoming encounter with his son. Pollux was not a child, easily swayed into acceptance or compliance. He had his life with traumatic events that had matured him rapidly, and he was certainly set in his ways.

Was he prepared for an unexpected twist with the many imponderables attached to it? Pollux was surely brave and adventurous, but before taking any decision or making any commitment, he would want to test the waters.

Peter was open to any suggestions with no intention of forcing anything on anybody. If the worst came to the worst, he was ready for rejection too, however painful that might be.

At this point, a good sleep was surely more beneficial than uselessly racking his brain. It took some doing before he dissolved softly into the arms of Morpheus. Finally, when he did, it was smooth sailing until morning.

The day of reckoning had arrived. Well rested and in a positive mood, Peter got together with Mary. There was no need to strategize. Both understood the importance of that meeting and both were extremely anxious.

The word "anxious" did not even describe half of the feelings Peter was experiencing. During his many years as a student, he had taken numerous exams. However, nothing could be compared to this. Here, preparation and knowledge did not count. As strange as it might sound, the examiner was his son. His whole future was riding on this one. Failure could have been catastrophic.

Panic was settling in, while Mary drove him to the designated place. It was a park, quiet and with secular trees, far from crowds and the noises of the city. She parked the car at the entrance. In silence, they proceeded to the nearest bench, sat down, and waited for Pollux.

The weather was mild for that time of year and the leaves were falling from the trees. Nature was getting ready for the dormant season. The birds seemed to chirp a happy tune and the squirrels were busy hiding their nuts.

The unlikely couple carefully scrutinized any person entering the park. Ten minutes had passed, when a tall youngster in casual clothes made his entrance with a firm gait.

Unaware of the great surprise awaiting him, he kept walking normally without a care in the world. As soon as he approached the bench, Mary stood up and greeted him with a smile. An awkward moment followed. Without being introduced, he was unsure whether to greet the stranger, or wait for Mary to do the proper introductions.

During those seconds of confusion and embarrassment, the man stared at the newly arrived with intense curiosity and fascination. Pollux too concentrated his gaze directly on Peter. What a magic moment it was!

Pollux remained frozen, when by some primeval instinct he recognized some of his facial features in the man who was looking at him, almost in disbelief. The same striking and unmistakable characteristics – eyes, nose and hair – had impacted Peter.

Pollux was overcome by a sudden epiphany. The stranger was himself with a few years more on his shoulders. Was he his biological father? Was it a vision or the real thing?

He did not have to wait long for the answer, because Mary in a sweet tone of voice said, "Pollux, this is Peter Egger, your father." His heart and instinct had discovered him first. Mary's acknowledgment and validation did not add anything new.

Deeply touched by that overwhelming reality, Pollux was not sure what to do. His state of inaction seemed to prolong Peter's agony. In fact, he was dying for a spontaneous reaction, which never materialized.

Mary broke the impasse. With the greatest simplicity in the world, she said, "Don't you think a hug is well overdue?"

Peter did not need any translation. Both hugged each other, first hesitantly, then with great emotional charge. The intense moment originated by that gesture remained indelible on their memories. Finally, father and son had been reunited. Finally, a stream of love flowed freely between the two, as nature had intended.

The fleeting moment was too precious to be marred by pessimistic fears.

Silent tears welled up in Peter's eyes, while Pollux fought back a few of his own. Mary, the perfect intermediary, savored every instant of that dramatic scene.

High above in the skies, a peregrine falcon flew in circles, seemingly celebrating the human reunification down below.

A blanket of multicolored leaves, detached from the branches by a gentle autumn breeze, danced softly in the air expressing their ephemeral joy.

What a moment and what an experience! For a second, animate and inanimate beings forgot their conflicts and inhaled a fresh air of love and reconciliation.

All too soon, the magical time was over. Father and son recovered their composure and stared at each other. Peter broke the silence first. Mary translated word for word faithfully.

Still with an ill-disguised emotion in his voice, he said, "My son, I stand before you overwhelmed by unusual feelings. I never knew I had a son, until recently.

Had I known before, my life would have been different. I apologize profusely for what happened.

Since I was not part of your past, I would very much like to be part of your present and future. However, it is totally in your hands whether you will open the door and let me in. Whatever space you will allot to me in your heart will be fine with me.

From what I said, you should not infer, not even for a second, that your mother is to blame for what happened.

Her costumes, traditions, cultural heritage, beliefs, position, and responsibilities, all conspired against her being forthcoming with what happened. It was a freak accident of nature, an unfortunate tragedy. No one should fault her on any account. She is as much a victim as you and me.

I love you, Pollux, with all my heart and I shall do the impossible to be the father I never was. Again, forgive me, and accept me as I am."

With a strange sensation of chills and shivers all over his body, the son scrambled for words. He was afraid of saying the wrong thing and ruining the cozy atmosphere of the encounter.

At last, taking his courage in both hands, he managed to say, "Father, this is a very touching moment. I admire your decision to leave everything behind in order to meet me. Thank you for your love. However, at this moment, I have difficulty discerning what is genuine and spurious inside me. One thing is certain. I experience some resentment against my mother. I adored her all my life, but when the revelation of my biological father was made public, all crumbled, and with it my love, affection and respect. Now, here I am, scared and with bad feelings."

"I understand," said Peter, "let time heal the wounds."

After observing the scene and listening to the two confessions, Mary was left with no choice other than to admire their sincerity. Both had poured out their hearts and both needed reassurance and support. And she provided just that.

With a tremendous sense of togetherness, never felt before, they left the idyllic spot in the park, mute witness to an emotionally charged encounter and joyfully walked to a nearby restaurant.

Over a warm meal, Pollux lost all inhibitions and spoke freely about his studies, his future and his disintegrated family. His presumed father had left his mother. Kimiko, already tried by the brutal murder of her son Castor, suffered a severe bout of depression, making people doubt her mental stability. Only her parents stood by her, helping and comforting her in the darkest moments of her life.

He loved his studies and had a special fascination for the experiments conducted in the university lab. Research in brain tumors was his specialty. After his degree, in five years time, he would return to Japan and work for some prestigious pharmaceutical company.

Apparently, in his plan there was no room for his father's physical presence. It was neither rejected openly, nor mentioned expressly, just left to the listener's interpretation.

Peter's heart missed a beat, believing his son would have him in the forefront of his mind, the same way Peter had him and his mother.

Recovering from the sinking feelings, with a bewildered look on his face, he went to great lengths to present his future moves.

Obviously, he would pay a visit to Kimiko and, from the result of that encounter, would plan the rest of his life. He did not spell out word for word the main objective – reunification of the family – but anybody could have read it between the lines.

Mary, the facilitator of that rapprochement, could foresee the directions each of them was projecting. More than convergent, they were parallel, running ad infinitum without ever meeting.

Maybe intervening factors would make them converge, but at the moment they would run separately, and Mary did not have much to say or do about that.

In the midst of that cryptic uncertainty, one positive note emerged when Pollux assured his father he would call his family and let them know of his arrival.

That was a good occasion to reconnect with his mother and break a long, hostile silence.

The three left the restaurant, certainly not in an exuberant mood, but with some expectations. Mary returned to the precinct, while Pollux took his father to his apartment.

The conversation was kept to an elementary level, since Peter's knowledge of English was rudimentary. Despite the awkwardness of the situation, all seemed conducive to a relaxed atmosphere. Father and son were finally alone together. Peter could not remember an instance in his past with a similar gratifying sensation. Just by looking at his son, he felt an irrepressible joy and happiness.

Pollux too, for the first time since his brother's death, experienced a sense of security and companionship. He had his father with him and language barriers notwithstanding, he could communicate even silently, because there was love.

After a restoring shower and a cool drink, Pollux grabbed the phone and dialed home.

Grandmother answered, "Mushi, mushi."

"Hi, obachan, it is me, Pollux. How are you?"

"I am fine. How about you? We haven't heard from you in a long time."

"I am sorry, Grandma. I was disappointed with my mom. Can I talk to her?"

"She is not available at this moment. Can you leave a message?"

"I hope she is not ill. Anyway, tell her my biological father, Peter Egger, the one in the picture in the living room, is here with me. He plans to travel to Kyoto and visit her. I miss you, Grandma, and I miss Grandpa. Love you."

The content of the conversation, conducted in Japanese, remained a mystery to Peter.

Pollux hung up hastily, as if the receiver were burning his hand. He looked at his father and said, "Everything is fine."

From the tone of voice and general demeanor, Peter was not convinced of his son's reassurance. Moreover, the dialogue, short and to the point, left some doubts. Nevertheless, Peter did not ask any questions. He just forced a smile on his face and thanked his son for his mediation service.

That day had been memorable, marking a real transition moment in his existence. With a mixed bag of emotions, Peter returned to the hotel, where he spent the night dreaming of a family of his own.

How sweet to be able to sit at a dinner table and share your most intimate thoughts and experiences with your beloved ones. Could that be possible in the not-too-distant future? Alternatively, was it a mere dream, impossible to materialize?

Anyhow, the mere idea of it was sufficient to fuel hopes and rekindle passions.

Over the following days, Peter spent precious hours with his son, at the same time preparing for his trip to Japan.

The land of contradictory realities, where atavic traditions coexisted with modern technologies, was a total mystery for the former clergy. Honestly, he did not know what to expect from his surprising visit, unthinkable weeks earlier.

Did he really love the woman that produced his son during highly unusual circumstances? More importantly, did she still love him? So many years had passed and so many things had changed that any flame might be totally extinguished and non-existent.

Was the old flame a real one or just a figment of his imagination, a whim of the moment that disappears like morning dew under the sun's rays?

Peter could barely wait to find out whether under the ashes there were still red embers. Was it possible to reignite the fire of a romantic passion with a visit agreed upon only by one side?

The improvised globetrotter always got the jitters before initiating something important. However, this time, unlike any other time before, he experienced fear, panic and stomach cramps. Was that an omen of things to come?

Determined as he was, Peter did not pay much attention to those signs. He was beyond speculation and presages.

Before departing for New York, he had a sincere talk with Pollux. With Mary's help, he left him his final assurances and recommendations. Should anything happen to him, Pollux should never have any doubts about his father's love and availability. He would always be there for him.

This was his last testament to his son, a testament full of caring and affection.

It was a very emotional goodbye. With a sinking feeling, Peter marched to Pittsburgh's airport.

Conceivably, that had been the hardest thing Peter had ever done in his life – leaving a son he never knew until a few days before, with no certainty of ever seeing him again. That was heartbreaking.

The flight was uneventful. From New York, he flew straight to Narita, Tokyo.

On the plane, a Japanese carrier, he had time to collect his thoughts and put them in some sort of order. One basic conviction, which had held true before, had to be reassessed.

The former clergyman, Peter Egger, with a brilliant future in front of him, was now a private citizen with no country and no ties to any religion.

Before, he had been the moral compass of his community. He always possessed the right word and the right advice. Now, he was nobody's moral compass, and that included himself.

What a traumatic change! The dogmatic truths, the firm moral convictions, the clear visions, all had gone out the window.

The eternal order, preordained by God and manifested in nature, in which he believed, had lost consistency. Diluted in a pantheistic reality, it had assumed complex, multifaceted forms where truth and rightness were relative to space and time.

A revolutionary vision that had put man and changes as measurements of all things was not exactly what he had in mind at the outset of his journey. His new ideological leaning was not a fruit of a preconceived idea, but the result of his life's dramatic changes.

God, Church and vocation were no longer the primary and direct objects of his love and work. Pollux and Kimiko had taken their place. Powerful human attachment, not abstract devotion, was the new guiding light, the new compass, the new object.

How could a man with sound principles and sound mind turn his entire value system upside down? How could Peter, the respected ecclesiastic, abandon in such a short time his dogmatic path and embrace a dangerous trajectory of uncertainty and relativism?

Wasn't he afraid of provoking the wrath of God, who did not look kindly on people betraying Him by breaking their sacred vows?

How many stories had he heard during his formation years of priests enduring a life of misery, shame and punishment after abandoning the Church?

Still aware of the dire consequences awaiting him, Peter did not mind going down the alleged road of damnation and facing a supposedly vengeful Judge on his deathbed.

For him the torments of a rebellious soul were nothing compared to the joys and satisfaction of a free spirit. His motto was to be true to himself.

His reality was perception, while negation of reality was deception. Both perception and deception were deeply human. However, the first was giving life, while the second was taking it away. One was vivifying, the other mortifying.

The initial order in which he wanted to put his thoughts did not work out as he planned. His efforts seemed lost in a quagmire of possibilities.

Looking through the window of the plane, he could not distinguish any defining horizon, any set limitation. It was a pure vastness of space, immense and infinite latitude. The same way, peeking through the meanders of his soul, he discovered an ocean of possibilities and a firmament of unanswered questions.

All rumors big or small, all confusions real or imaginary, all fears religious or profane, faded into insignificance compared to the struggle for survival that awaited him as soon as he stepped off the plane.

Lost in his thoughts and exhausted by the highly charged day, Peter Egger dozed off among the noise of the engines and the chatting of the passengers.

When he awoke, the plane was nearing Narita Airport. It did not take very long to land on Japanese soil.

The movement of travelers was impressive. From there, Peter flew to Kyoto. The closer he got to his destination, the higher his anxiety level rose. In the ancient imperial capital, he used the services of a taxi driver. The man, in his spotless uniform, seemed familiar with the address. He smiled politely and navigated without difficulty through the busy streets. On the outskirts of the city on a gentle slope, an enormous mansion towered over the rest of the dwellings.

A solid wall protected the property. At the entrance gate, the driver rang the bell. The gate opened and they proceeded to the main entrance.

At this point, the taxi left, while a young housekeeper introduced the guest. Peter did not have to wait very long. An elderly lady, in her early seventies, appeared. Serious and composed, she bowed slightly and with an imperceptible voice said, "I am Kimiko's mother."

Peter answered, "My name is Peter Egger. Nice meeting you."

A long pause ensued. Finally, in his broken English, Peter dared to say, "I would like to see Kimiko."

"She is very ill," her mother replied, "and I am not sure she will recognize you."

At those words, the poor man froze, not knowing what she meant.

Was that a polite way of telling him Kimiko did not want to see him? Peter became extremely nervous and embarrassed. He never wanted to impose on anybody, let alone the grandmother of his son. With no words on his lips, he waited for the lady to make the first move. After all, he was a simple guest, with no pretenses of any kind.

Kimiko's mother seemed hesitant and pensive. She looked at him, carefully scrutinizing his demeanor, and after some disturbing silence, in a maternal gesture she took his right hand, inviting him to walk along with her.

They entered a room, where the light was dim. Without uttering a sound, she invited Peter to look in one direction.

As soon as he turned his head, the poor man observed a woman sitting on the floor with a vacant stare in her eyes, disheveled and confused. Beside her, there was a nurse.

Pointing at the sitting woman, the mother said, "There is Kimiko."

That was the last thing Peter would have ever imagined. He was shocked to the core. She was not even a shadow of her old self. The pretty, vivacious, intelligent young woman he remembered with fondness was not there. To all appearances, Kimiko was nowhere at all.

Hoping against hope, Peter came closer to her and kneeling down he asked softly, "I am Peter Egger, do you remember me?"

He expected to bring her back from the abyss of insanity. He was counting on a miracle of love. However, no sign of acknowledgment came from the patient.

Kimiko started rambling incoherently. She kept staring into space. Any effort by Peter to establish some connection proved futile.

He had never felt so much impotence and frustration. The only person who could fulfill his life was not answering the call.

Delicately, he stamped a kiss on her forehead. In silence, he got up from his position, looking down at her with intense emotion and a sense of guilt. Should he bear any responsibility? How he wished to hug her and make her happy!

The undue amount of suffering had pushed the beautiful, rich Kimiko over the edge, breaking her spirit and destroying her as a human being.

Now Peter understood why the mother had said, "I am not sure she will recognize you." He understood also, why his son could not speak to his mother on the phone. Unfortunately, Pollux was unaware of Kimiko's situation.

Once more, the truth was denied to the boy and this time too with the intent of protecting him.

Back in the reception room, where the tea ceremonies were usually held, the old woman, in a voice exuding pain and suffering, explained briefly to Peter what had happened.

"A chain of devastating events, among them Castor's murder, the private investigator's mysterious death, the revelation of the paternity tests, Pollux's subtle rejection, and her angry husband's abandonment, pushed Kimiko to the limits.

Having lost all the most precious things in her life, she fell into a terrible spell of depression. From there, insensibly she slid into a catatonic trance and then the complete loss of her mind.

The doctors suggested immediate institutionalization. My husband and I rejected the idea, considering it beneath our social position. Instead, we provided the best medical care, with specialized nurses and physicians, at home.

It seems, according to he experts' opinion, that there is not much hope for a recovery."

Peter, still in shock, listened, absorbing as much as he could.

Kimiko's mother paused for a while. Resuming the conversation, she unexpectedly turned the tables on Peter, asking what his situation was and what he was going to do.

Caught by surprise, he struggled to come up with an answer. His dream of forming a family had vanished. He could not go back to his country, being a deserter from the Church. He did not wish to interfere with his son's studies and career. The only alternative left was to immigrate to some hospitable country, find a job and make a living.

Kimiko's mother understood his precarious social and financial situation. He had left a comfortable life, even if no longer glamorous, for her daughter and grandson. He deserved some assistance. She was there for him. She made sure he grasped that point.

Peter was deeply moved by her kindness and generosity. At first, he politely refused any helping hand. But at her insistence he accepted some pecuniary contribution, enough to settle down in a faraway land.

The farewell from that family and country was very emotional. Before leaving, he wanted to repeatedly kiss his love and hug her tightly. It was like kissing and hugging a rag doll. Such a heartbreaking moment would mark his future life, showing him how inconsistent, transitory and deceiving are things in life. One moment you are reaching for the stars, a moment later you are crying your eyes out.

Fighting back tears of emotion, grief and pain, Peter left the Ishida residence. With a heavy past behind and a blank future in front, he flew to an undisclosed location overseas, in search of a new life. Despite this radical decision, painful and incomprehensible at the same time, Peter will always keep close to his heart the two loves of his life, Pollux and Kimiko.

Chapter 14

*"The faculty of self-**deception** is an essential requisite for anyone wanting to guide others."* – Giuseppe Tomasi di Lampedusa

Kimiko, the brilliant graduate from a prestigious Swiss school, returned to her native country full of dreams and hopes. Her parents were beaming with pride.

Fluent in foreign languages and with a degree in Business Administration, she was a real asset to the family business. Add to this her oriental beauty and you have a perfect picture of a successful businesswoman.

Her father, who nurtured high expectations, did not miss an occasion to introduce her to his partners and rivals. She was a formidable weapon. Kimiko loved to accompany him on his trips, mainly abroad.

One city in Italy, Torino, remained particularly stuck in her mind and more specifically in her heart. The first visit to the Piedmontese metropolis did not start exactly on the right foot.

She arrived there exhausted for delays at both airports. Anything, however insignificant, appeared to annoy her, from the accommodation to the landscape. People too, like the luggage carriers and the concierge at the hotel, were getting on her nerves. The weather did not help either. It was drizzling and cold.

Everything seemed to conspire to make her life miserable. She greatly regretted having accepted her father's invitation.

The first two days of meetings and luncheons did not raise her level of satisfaction one inch. However, the last day of their stay, the Italian host threw a lavish party with famous bands, regional dishes, and original invitees.

Among these, two young men in their twenties caught her eye. One was Japanese and the other Caucasian. Their way of dressing, black suit and white collar, and their reserved manners impressed her the most. She would never forget the goose bumps and shivers down her spine when she was introduced to them. Their smiles and delicate voices melted her heart.

She understood immediately that they were somehow forbidden territory, for being clergies. However, they were not priests yet, and therefore to fantasize about them was not so sinful in her book. Their names were Takeo Shirieda and Peter Egger.

These are the three protagonists of this story — Kimiko, Takeo Shirieda and Peter Egger.

The dawn and morning of their existence had been portrayed in previous chapters as very promising, full of hopes and dreams. However, each character had a serious drawback in his arsenal of good qualities and natural endowments.

This factor, in combination with a series of unfortunate events, forged their destiny, so contrary to all expectations, which probably left the reader gasping for breath while reading the previous chapter.

Takeo, the only one with doubts about his religious vocation, kept his faith and vows, but ended up in the solitary confinement of a Sardinian convent.

Peter, the intrepid crusader and supreme preserver and defender of chastity, betrayed his sacred promises, left the Church and cursed, sought refuge in a foreign land.

Kimiko, the beautiful and sophisticated oriental, crushed by a mountain of tragic happenings, literally lost her mind and never recovered her sanity.

What a desolate and depressing sunset!

The time has come to unveil the single shameful and devastating event that led to their disastrous downfall.

And this is how it all came about.

The host's wife, Stella, thought Kimiko would feel more at home with a compatriot of her age around. In those days, there were not many Japanese in town. The only one she knew was a student of theology by the name of Takeo, with impeccable pedigree.

Since Stella and her husband were donors of the Pontifical Institute, she asked his superiors whether she could borrow him for an evening of social entertainment.

Takeo's immediate superior, the Director of the Institute, did not present any objection, even if the request was not in full accordance with the accepted religious standards of the day.

At first, Takeo was hesitant in accepting the offer made by his superior. His strict moral code saw a great incompatibility between the ways of the world and his religious vision.

However, he did not want to disappoint or indispose his Director, and thus accepted on one condition. He would go only if accompanied by his best friend, Peter Egger. That way he would feel more comfortable, almost protected.

The two students had come from different countries and different backgrounds. They had never met before their first year of theology in Torino. All seemed to divide them, from language to ethnicity and culture to costumes. However, the sincere love for their priestly vocation became a conduit for a lasting friendship.

The connection was established almost immediately. By sheer coincidence or cruel destiny, nobody will ever know, the first day of their arrival, they were assigned seats next to each other in the refectory, and, even stranger, beds next to each other in the dormitory.

That physical proximity forced them to communicate on a deeper level. Peter, who had spent three years of his formation teaching young adults, had acquired some knowledge of human behavior. During their first meal, Peter detected an embarrassing shyness in Takeo and an understandable inferiority complex.

Conceivably, he felt a moral obligation to help and protect him, as an older brother would do with his younger sibling.

This initial empathy developed over time into an indissoluble friendship, difficult to comprehend for outsiders. Peter transformed himself into a brother, tutor and guide. He helped Takeo with Italian, kept him company during free time and outings, explained difficult theological issues, and guided him through inevitable crises.

Needless to say, they felt comfortable with each other. They became so inseparable to the point of fueling doubts and suspicions in the minds of their superiors.

One day, the Director summoned them separately inquiring whether they nurtured strange, unnatural feelings toward each other.

That question not only surprised them but also hurt them deeply. With nobility and dignity, far superior to their age, they rejected the insinuation, and assured their superior that their friendship was as pure as it comes.

It would not be superfluous at this point to remind the reader how Peter Egger fought strenuously, during his junior formation, that contagious plague among the seminarians. He became the watchdog of public morality.

After that episode, difficult to characterize, no one ever brought up the unpleasant subject again. In fact, if they had lied, eventually their conduct would have betrayed them. But nothing inappropriate ever emerged from their conduct. The vicissitudes with Kimiko would prove the opposite.

Before leaving the Institute, Takeo was instructed about the high-society party and the presence of a Japanese contingent. His mission was to mingle with them and make them feel at home.

Festive parties, joyful gatherings and mundane celebrations had been things of the past for him. His religious life, which started in his early teens, had prevented him from participating in any of those traditional festivities where people indulge in questionable behavior.

Now, after so many years, he was thrown into unfamiliar territory. His apprehension appeared understandable and his asking for a companion completely justifiable. Peter provided him with the assurance and support he needed.

The dreaded time came when they were whisked off to a millionaire's mansion in a luxury car. Despite feeling somewhat out of place and inadequate for the job, they put up a valiant front, showing confidence and self-assurance.

The moment Kimiko saw them, a shiver of pure excitement went down her spine. The handsome duo not only took her breath away, but also provoked a faint smile on her face. Their fake self-confidence, mixed with their attractiveness, gave the impression of a child mimicking an adult. Nothing could be more irresistible and hilarious than that.

Where in the world could anybody find a presence so refreshing and stimulating? They were there for her and her alone to enjoy. She completely monopolized their conversation. From Japanese they switched to Italian and despite their extraneity, there was no shortage of subjects to talk about.

She showed a keen interest in their studies and activities, but above all in their vision of life. In turn, Peter and Takeo quizzed her on her views about education and business.

In a great spirit of camaraderie, they put forward their opinions in a fashion becoming to their religious status. However, after a few drinks, they let their defenses down and with it their ecclesiastic composure and restraint. They laughed, they danced, and they joked and had a jolly good time.

All too soon, the party was over. The goodbye was inevitable, yet the modality remained floating in their imagination. A handshake or a hug would have been appropriate and above suspicion, even if a spontaneous kiss would have felt more natural and sincere.

No one made the first move waiting for the other to take the initiative. Kimiko, drowning her excitement and spontaneity, bowed with irresistible grace before those two attractive students. With a nostalgic look on her face and a gentle smile on her lips, she bade them farewell.

Still trapped in her ancestral traditions she had a real hard time in giving up her company. Peter and Takeo answered in kind. They watched her leave with a sinking heart. What an unrewarding departure for such a rewarding evening!

The two students of theology experienced a human complementation never felt before. It was difficult to explain that sensation of plenitude and satisfaction as a person. Had they established a simple platonic friendship with the opposite sex, so demonized and banned by their founder, or had they stepped out of line? The truth is that their intellectual curiosity had transformed itself. Overnight it became a thirst for more contact and communication.

When they returned home, something had changed radically within their souls.

Kimiko too went back to her country with an enormous change inside. She had left her heart in that northern city, most likely the least romantic in the whole of Italy. She could not deceive herself or deny the amazing metamorphosis she had undergone in the blink of an eye, from awkward schoolgirl to mature woman.

Hard to admit, but she had an intoxicating crush on both of them. It was a strong feeling of love with a sexual undertone. It was attraction, fascination and passion all rolled into one.

During the prolonged silence of the nights in her native country, the lovely Japanese heiress kept looking up to the starry skies in search of some mysterious connection to her secret loves. Two bright stars captured her imagination, the twins, Castor and Pollux.

On earth, only Peter and Takeo came close to those celestial realities. In her estimation, they were germane souls, superior to any ordinary being she had ever known. Full of spirituality and substance, endowed by nature with intelligence, wit and beauty, who could ever compete with them or top them? They seemed unreachable, unattainable.

For the two inquisitive students of theology, intent on the discovery of God, Kimiko assumed the characteristics of a delicate flower, whose extraordinary perfume bewitched and mesmerized their intellectual vision. Two opposite entities were now the object of their intense scrutiny – the eternal essence of God, and the enchanting but ephemeral beauty of a mortal princess.

Both entities strived for supremacy. Who would be the victor? During the idle hours of the day, the struggle intensified, with no clear winner. Each of them yearned and longed for the missing part, covertly one, openly the other.

Each engaged in his or her personal battle, and each had his or her favorite fantasy to deal with. On reflection, the reaction to that unforgettable encounter was diametrically opposite.

In the students' conscience, the initial elation was superseded by a bitter taste of guilt and betrayal. How could Peter and Takeo surrender to the most common temptation in the book? What about the proven strategy of their founder of not engaging the enemy? In essence, shame and guilt were their overriding feelings.

The opposite was true for Kimiko. No regret or remorse ever troubled her soul. Instead, an intense hunger for their presence tormented her day and night. How sweet those pangs for love and companionship!

Obviously, the prolonged separation proved very trying and painful, even for the guilt-ridden conscience of the two students – trapped between the moral obligations of their career, and the irresistible sexual allure of the flesh. No one would ever know the hellish torments those inexperienced students went through, the difficulties they encountered and the terrible doubts they had to live with.

They never overstepped the boundaries between acceptable and unacceptable, virtue and sin, but they came awfully close. Would their flirtatious attitude someday get the best of them? Would it precipitate them into an abyss of endless misfortune?

Who would lead the charge, the captivating oriental princess, blind destiny or unbridled passion?

With every passing day, Kimiko became moodier, more restless and dissatisfied. In her eyes, all was tasteless without Peter and Takeo. They were the spice of her life, the sunshine of her day and the inspirational motive of her boring career.

Her father took notice of that sad state of affairs and, solicitous as usual for her emotional welfare, did the impossible to accommodate his daughter.

Meanwhile, on the old continent, thousands of miles away, a nostalgic expression was creeping up in the two unsettled students' expression. In their prayers and meditations, during classes and recreations, night and day only one image was invariably present – Kimiko's attractive smile and the sound of their names on her lips.

Whether this persistent presence was a curse or a blessing, it did not matter at all. What mattered was her pervasive influence in their lives. Imperceptibly, a material goddess had displaced Jesus and the Virgin Mary. And what is worse and unthinkable before the memorable party, both irreproachable students felt a cozy sensation, a rare spiritual warmth, an insane drive for more. Instead of quenching the flames of a raging passion, time and distance redoubled the fury of an inextinguishable inferno.

All seemed beautifully choreographed by a perverse genius and all seemed set by an invisible hand for the final explosive act.

Kimiko's father, for some reasons best known to himself, fixed a date for their trip to Torino. This news sounded as pure music to his daughter's ears, impatient to see the boys who had disquieted her peaceful universe, turning everything upside down.

Her mind raced at a thousand miles an hour, picturing provocative postures, tender scenes of love, and forbidden embraces.

Anything she was imagining, could it come true? Alternatively, was she deceiving herself with an impossible dream and a sacrilegious love?

Did she have enough courage even for a chaste kiss or a sisterly hug?

Her emotions ran high at the sight of Torino. Kimiko was on cloud nine, barely containing herself.

Reminiscing on her days at Surval Mont-Fleuri in Geneva, where a young handsome guy had taken advantage of her naïveté, she had a hard time picturing herself in the new role of seductress.

This time she was the one with a plan and a purpose. However, despite an unrestrainable elation, serious doubts nagged at her.

In human relations, there is no sure thing, only probabilities. Was she more likely to succeed or fail? No previous or future endeavor would ever come close to the one at hand. In essence, this was the mother of all battles, the defining moment of her entire existence.

With the help of hell, she was provoking heaven for a slice of happiness on earth. No obstacle was big enough; no punishment was serious enough for her determination. She would do everything in her power to achieve her coveted goal.

Her father, not completely sure, as everyone else, of what was going on inside his daughter, noticed a peculiar sparkle of excitement in her eyes and an unusual matter-of-fact attitude. Surprised but not suspicious, he would not attach too much significance to his observation. After a couple of days, he concluded his business and returned to Japan, leaving Kimiko with friends, at her request.

Now the enterprising girl could give free rein to her imagination. More importantly, she could follow any course of action she deemed appropriate without restraint.

Her father had rented a beautiful mansion, brightened up by flowers and fountains and surrounded by secular trees.

In her estimation, that was the ideal place for wild parties and out-of-the-ordinary love affairs.

The stage was set for Kimiko to put in motion her insidious and unscrupulous plan.

The summer vacation had long gone and with it, the explosive encounter. The year-end festivities, Christmas and New Year, were becoming a thing of the past. Peter and Takeo were wondering why not even a greeting card had reached them. Had Kimiko stashed them away like out-of-season clothes?

Carnival and Ash Wednesday were around the corner and the two theology students were readying themselves for an intense period of emotional purification and physical mortification.

Their hearts, still on fire over the oriental princess, needed a major overhaul and that was the perfect moment for it.

Kimiko was in complete agreement about the timing, but her agenda was outside their scope. She couldn't care less about Ash Wednesday and its profound meaning of penance and purification. Instead, she would celebrate Carnival in style.

Following a deep-rooted medieval tradition, she would indulge in the pleasures of the senses Italian style, ignoring the upcoming austerity of the Lenten season.

She planned the event down to the last detail. Peter and Takeo had made peace with themselves, when they received from the Director's hands an invitation, signed and sealed by Kimiko and delivered by a courier. The Japanese beauty was inviting them to a Carnival party in her residence.

Taken by surprise, they remained speechless. Their reaction did not differ in substance. Both experienced a moment of pleasure, since Kimiko had not forgotten them. At the same time, a crippling fear seemed to paralyze their decision. To accept or not to accept, that was the fundamental question. By accepting they could run into a very awkward situation, by refusing they might offend their gracious host and their superior.

On one hand, they were literally dying to see their earthly goddess and enjoy her company for a little while. On the other hand, they were not sure of possessing a bulletproof armor against any feminine seduction.

However, being in each other's company and not alone, they thought would constitute enough of a safeguard to keep them away from trouble.

The reasoning was without a wrinkle and made perfect sense. What could happen to a couple of seminarians, so dead set against the pleasures of the flesh and with a spotless record?

After a brief consultation, they accepted the invitation and, lacking any youthful exuberance but with an abundance of naïveté, they marched to the shocker of their life.

On their way to the residence, a bird of prey flew over their heads, emitting piercing shrieks, similar to foreboding warnings. But they paid no heed to nature screaming at them. Instead, they rushed to their fatal rendezvous.

Kimiko, with a calmly smiling countenance, was there to receive them. She looked more stunning than ever. Bowing respectfully to them, she said, "I am very glad you came. I hope you will enjoy your stay."

"Thanks for having us, we appreciate your invitation," Peter answered.

"Later on," she added, "I would like to spend some time with each of you, individually. In the meantime, enjoy the food, the music and the dance."

Peter and Takeo, mesmerized by the gracious host and the festive atmosphere, felt like small boys on a birthday party. She was so lovely they did not have words to describe her. Despite the tenderness in her demeanor, she was in charge, unlike the first time.

Sweetness and total composure, deference and authority, femininity and command formed a rare combination that could melt a rock. The two apprehensive students experienced a tremendous inner drive. They wanted to hug and kiss her. Their desire was to stay with that enchanting creature forever.

Inadvertently, the artful Kimiko was working them up in an unsuspecting way. She had everything planned out to the last detail.

The lavish Carnival party would have been the envy of any self-respected millionaire. The food was excellent and the music playful and melodious. The drinks were exquisite and abundant, as were the participants selected.

People, seemingly with not a worry in the world, were laughing and drinking. Some of them had started dancing with a partner of their choosing and treasuring the moment.

Kimiko too had picked up a handsome young lad with whom she was displaying very sensual movements. For quite a while, she kept dancing and changing partners with an admirable coolness.

She seemed to purposely be taunting Peter and Takeo, making them feel jealous and unwanted. The two had the distinct impression of belonging somewhere else, of being part of the choreography, and not of the main act. Perhaps Kimiko's heart belonged to someone else, and perhaps they were not the center of her universe.

Their male pride was deeply hurt. Moreover, it was bleeding, when none of the girls invited them to a dance. At that time, it was not proper for a female to ask a man of the cloth to dance.

Their religious convictions became blurry, their steadfast resolutions weak, and their determination almost inexistent. Embarrassment and emotional neglect were eating them up inside.

Was that Kimiko's plan, to make them feel vulnerable and exposed? Was she a wolf in sheep's clothing, cunning and diabolical? Nobody will ever know the twists and turns of a woman in love.

The noise levels and the merriment had increased considerably. Wine and liquor kept flowing in abundance, while guests began showing signs of tipsiness. Peter and Takeo, under the influence of the alcohol, felt their heads spinning and their legs shaky, in spite of their moderate consumption.

It was at that crucial moment that Kimiko decided to spring into action.

With a delicate gesture, she invited Takeo to follow her. He blushed scarlet at the thought of being alone with her. Shame and fear notwithstanding, he obeyed the invitation.

What indescribable feelings the moment he found himself face to face with his earthly goddess in her room. Without wasting any time, she kissed him gently and whispered in his ear, "Wait here, I'll be right back. Make yourself comfortable."

An obscure passion for her, which he never noticed was there, made him blind to everything around him. With that blindness came a submissive attitude and the loss of self-control.

A few minutes later, Kimiko reappeared, covered in a beautiful silky robe and emanating a delicate fragrance. The way she smiled and spoke to him was extremely seductive.

"Don't be afraid. I love you very much. If you want me, I am all yours." Having said that, she opened her robe and slid out of it. Totally naked, she invited him to take off his clothes and make love to her.

Takeo, shaking like a leaf, did not wish to cross his attractive temptress. He started hugging and kissing her with tenderness, quenching his insatiable thirst for affection. When she gently grabbed his penis and rubbed it against her vagina sheer terror took hold of his body. At the same time, a mental blockage paralyzed his brain. His attempts to penetrate her and release his semen remained ineffective.

He had an erection but he was unable to produce a proper ejaculation. Both were at a loss in that kind of business, being their very first time.

Disappointed and frustrated, Takeo apologized profusely to his idol. Doubly ashamed, for his ineptitude as a man, and his unspeakable action as a religious person, he left the room in a shambles.

During his multiple attempts, did Takeo deposit any sperm inside Kimiko? From the DNA results, it appears so.

Kimiko, stunned by what had just happened, took her courage in both hands, and invited Peter as promised. He did not have sufficient time to quiz his friend, but from his dejected look, it was not difficult to guess that he was unhappy.

What had happened? He would soon find out. With some minor variations, Kimiko recreated the same atmosphere, putting on a great display of charm and seductiveness. Peter, less inhibited and more adventurous than his friend, immediately captured the girl's intentions. Tipsy as he was, he was bursting with male hormones and an irrepressible desire. He did not have to force himself to play along. All came naturally and spontaneously. As soon as he observed Kimiko undressing with graceful fruition, he could not help but admire the divine attributes of her femininity. He too proudly showed his virility to her.

The reciprocal contemplation did not last very long, because they felt a great impulse to kiss and touch each other intimately.

That foreplay, so intense and unsophisticated, drove them to the brink of insanity. Finally, Peter inserted his turgid penis into her moistened receptacle and they became united in an embrace of intense love and sexual satisfaction. A few movements and they reached their climax, with an unimaginable explosion of pleasurable sparks. Their minds, along with their senses, were blown. Peter could not contain the sperm that kept flowing in abundance and with frantic interruptions from his member to Kimiko's womb.

She fell into an ecstatic trance, holding Peter tightly in her arms. Even when all was over, she would not let him go. She had what she desperately wanted, the precious semen that hopefully would make her pregnant.

Kimiko, the sweet, lovely girl, had just perpetrated a classic human deception.

Indubitably, love is deceptive by nature, because it obfuscates the mind and obnubilates judgment, converting people and things into something magnified or unreal. Adding to that premeditation and intent, it rises to treachery plain and simple. Let it be clear. Kimiko dearly loved those two ingenuous souls, but her ulterior motives and deceptive ways did not set her apart from the most prominent seductresses in history.

Peter, after the explosive sexual intercourse, seemed to sober up rather quickly, grasping the gravity of the situation. Without savoring the moment, as his loving partner was doing, he kissed her quickly for the last time and slipped away in silence and shame.

He rejoined his friend, who was waiting anxiously for him. Not a word, not a comment came out of their mouths. A downcast face and remorseful conscience accompanied them to their residence.

In some measure, everything had changed in those two promising students. Nothing looked the same outside them, and nothing felt the same inside them either. The playful bite at the forbidden apple had proved fatal. There was neither a turning back, a clean restart, nor a total forgiveness, just a painful experience that would mark their lives forever.

The more time passed, the bigger the enormity of their action appeared to be. A few seconds of indulgence, and all they had stood for during many years came crashing down.

If the pleasure of the flesh had been intense and exhilarating, equally intense and mortifying were the pangs of guilt. While the first lasted a few instants, the second would be permanent and excruciating.

In sum, that memorable Carnival remained just that, a farewell to the flesh for each of them, even if in a totally different way.

Kimiko, with no scruples or fear for having used two ingenuous human beings, returned radiant to her motherland. Her mission had been accomplished. However, not completely satisfied with her masterpiece, she added a touch of class to it.

Much to her father's surprise, she agreed to her previously proposed arranged marriage. Her reluctance had disappeared overnight. Within a week, she was married with pomp and ceremony to her anxious suitor.

Once more, under false pretenses of love and devotion, she had covered her tracks, proclaiming to the world her immaculate past.

Even when her mixed-race twins were born, and everyone wondered about their origin, she was ready to swear to God the only man she ever knew was her husband.

Cover-ups, deception and lies became her way of thinking, her protective armor, her lifestyle.

A victim of her own doing, eventually she would succumb under such a heavy, unbearable burden.

Beautiful, intelligent and promising, she would be wasted on the altar of a violent passion, so human and so pervasive in history that nobody would ever wonder or ask why.

Another somewhat different yet somewhat similar story is Peter's story.

The defender of morality and a paladin of orthodoxy, so quick and smart in assessing every situation, had fallen for the oldest trick in the book.

It was hard, even for himself, to understand what had just happened.

His burning passion, so jealously controlled under the cover of a strong will and strict discipline, once given the right circumstances, had erupted with unusual virulence, getting the best of him.

Well aware of the terrible predicament he was in, he felt powerless to stop the onslaught. Weakness, curiosity and sheer stupidity entrapped him in a golden cage.

Like Kimiko, he enjoyed the sinful and immoral act of copulating with a woman, which he had renounced years back with his religious profession.

Unlike Kimiko, after the fact he was not beaming with pleasure and satisfaction. On the contrary, sudden sadness, dissatisfaction and panic overtook him.

It was not a natural, normal feeling, in accordance with the Roman saying, "Post coitum omni animal triste est." (After sexual intercourse every animal is sad.) For Peter, it assumed a universal moral dimension, of guilt, moral condemnation and emotional desperation.

The guileless man had lost his innocence. By tasting the forbidden apple he had plunged himself into a rotten sewage of putrefaction and corruption. Nothing in the world could restore his innocence to its former splendor. It was gone forever.

With his mental acuity still intact, he perceived clearly the inconsistency and incompatibility of his position. He became a living contradiction that had no right to exist. It was better to abandon his priestly vocation and his religious life, and return to the filthy, immoral world, where he belonged.

The night of his shameful, despicable behavior, he was torn between remorse, despair and self-destruction. He could not close an eye. He could not remove from his mind the torments of hell awaiting him.

In the morning, still distraught and delirious, he ran to his confessor to unburden himself and cleanse his conscience.

The confessor, an old, pious man, who had intimate knowledge of human frailty, calmed him down, giving him hope and a second chance.

He had sinned against his religious vow of chastity. However, that did not mean the end of the world, much less the termination of his ecclesiastical career. The priesthood with its obligations, including chastity, was still two-and-a-half years away. He still had plenty of time to prove himself worthy of that profession. God is merciful and forgives a repentant soul, with no strings attached. He will never go back on his word and reproach a remorseful sinner for his past missteps.

This was pure balsam on Peter's bleeding wounds. His Jansenistic vision of Christian life gave way to a more Catholic one, where sinners can convert and become saints. After all, he did not have to give up the dream of his childhood.

Had his confessor followed the Vatican's strict guidelines on the formation of seminarians? Apparently not, because the last instructions on the formation of future priests made it quite clear that any candidate to the priesthood who had sexual intercourse during the first and second year of theology should excuse himself and immediately leave the house of formation.

Obviously, the confessor did not agree with those concepts, a product of Vatican bureaucrats. Was Peter aware of the official Vatican position on that matter? The answer to this question cannot be anything other than "yes." Peter was in complete cognizance of the papal requirements for a candidate to the priesthood. His Director, in fact, had a special conference on the subject, with all the students present. Hence the internal tension and doubt, despite his confessor's assurances.

After so many years of effort and hard work, he would never voluntarily renounce his vocation. Yet he felt the moral obligation of imposing a harsh corporal punishment on himself.

He made a solemn promise to the Virgin Mary never again to covet a woman and to wear a cilice as long as his body would tolerate it. This obviously was without his superiors' knowledge. The cilice is a medieval type of physical punishment that makes the wearer suffer excruciating pain at every small movement. It consists of a barbed-wire chain worn around the groin.

In this manner, Peter believed he had found an acceptable solution to his problems, giving to God what belonged to God – satisfaction – and to his flesh, what it deserved – pain.

It is extremely difficult to establish whether or not it was a good decision. However, that was the path chosen by Peter in order to ease his conscience.

Takeo's case, despite its multiple similarities with his friend's case, possesses some relevant peculiarities that set it apart.

Subsequent to the infamous act, never consummated, the poor lad not only felt terrible but also found himself on the brink of suicide.

His shame and remorse were so intense he could not see any viable way out. His ecclesiastical career was over and eternal damnation was around the corner as a well-deserved punishment.

Ironically, the less guilty of the two had the dimmest view of his predicament. The circumstances surrounding the impure act not only spelt out diminished capacity but also incomplete consent. Proof of this last assertion is the psychological barrier that prevented him from ejaculating. His natural tendencies were following a course not approved by his will. As strange as it may sound, Takeo was in such a state of confusion and disarray that any moralist would have a hard time attaching moral responsibility to his actions.

On the verge of a complete meltdown, he too rushed to his confessor. With tears in his eyes and panic in his heart, he narrated what had happened the previous evening. In his sketchy recount, he kept stressing his unworthiness to become a priest, as he had done many years before, with his Master of Novices on the eve of his religious profession.

The confessor, full of understanding and persuasion, felt compelled to point out some important theological notions. Firstly, in God's eyes no one can ever claim any type of worthiness. All that comes from God is pure gift or grace, including the priestly vocation. He does not call a person because of his merits, but because of his infinite love for him.

Secondly, God does not run his Church using angels. He runs his Church through men, prone to sin and error. Only men who had experienced human frailties can understand and empathize with sinners.

In this way, the confessor convinced Takeo not to abandon his vocation and to make amends of his faults.

Being an obedient man, he did not give up his priesthood, even if he was unconvinced.

However, he was in complete agreement with his confessor regarding the second part. He would make amends for his sins in a radical manner.

According to the cultural traditions of his country, the only way to make amends would have been with a ritual suicide or *seppuku*.

Since this was out of the question for a Christian, the next best thing was a surgical castration. Without his superiors' knowledge and during his summer vacation in Japan, he secretly made all the arrangements for the unusual operation.

The procedure was carried out with success and nobody ever knew of its existence.

Takeo deemed it necessary to pay this price for his sexual misconduct. His conscience regained some tranquility, but the memory and remorse of his thoughtless action remained with him for the rest of his life.

Conclusion

*"To live is to **deceive**; to **deceive** is to live."*

The unfortunate story of Castor and Pollux and their progenitors Peter, Takeo and Kimiko is as real as the stars in the sky, the birds in the air and the fish in the ocean. However, the names of characters and places are fictitious.

Nothing is more compelling than an impossible love affair, three desperate lovers, dual paternity twins and a disastrous ending.

All started with a random act of cruel violence, in which a young man met his premature death. Neither the insane perpetrator nor the victim's unfortunate family ever suspected the chain of events put in motion by such a criminal action.

The isolated incident, not uncommon in urban areas, brought back to the surface a shameful reality that was supposed to remain buried for all eternity.

The pieces of the wreckage that emerged from the murky waters of a never-written chronicle had a name and a story.

Their names are Kimiko, Peter and Takeo and their story has just been narrated. What is missing is the framework in which the three protagonists operated.

Even if repeatedly mentioned, it needs to be sketched out with a few finishing touches.

All of them, including Rudy Streaker, convicted in the murder of Castor's girlfriend, at a certain point in their lives and coerced by circumstances, underwent a radical transformation.

From a normal, transparent existence, full of joy and pain, they stepped into a dark tunnel, made of lies, cover-ups and deceit.

Deception became the common denominator configuring their frame of mind and their activities. In order to survive, every one of them had to think and act in a deceptive way.

For all of them "to live equals to deceive" became painfully true.

The moment they thought their cover was perfect, the unthinkable happened, and all came unraveled.

Incontrovertible evidence revealed the ugly face of their deception. Their innocence was no longer sustainable and their life could not feed on more lies.

Up to that diacritical event, deception had adopted multifarious forms. Deception, in fact, comes in different shapes and sizes. Everyone manufactures his own model adjusted to his needs. However, one thing remains the same, the essence, which is the survival instinct. Like breathing and eating are vital and indispensable to life, the same way deception seems connatural and inherent to human nature.

As inescapable as it is, how did each protagonist adjust to it?

Kimiko is the highest exponent of that deceptive form of living. The very promising young lady, with a great future in front of her, felt an irresistible attraction toward two theology students, already consecrated to God by the three religious vows.

However, a powerful passion – a mixture of love, sexuality and infatuation – drove her to commit the unspeakable, through sheer deception.

She set the perfect stage with the clear intent of seducing them. Deception in her case became an art form. It was not just an animal instinct, or a moment of human frailty; it was a rational, calculated plan, carried out with the highest degree of precision and coolness.

She never felt remorse for what she did. Neither did she ever apologize for her actions. She believed herself to be entitled to such conduct.

Under false pretenses of pure love and admiration, she used her feminine charm to deceive two gullible students of theology. Her next victims were her parents, who believed her mendacious desire to accept an arranged marriage. Her husband too fell into that deadly trap of deception, along with the twins Castor and Pollux.

When the DNA evidence revealed the terrible fraud of her motherhood and marriage, she kept denying and hiding the truth.

Only when she found herself abandoned by everybody, except her disconsolate parents, did she seem to come to her senses. However, it was too late. Tragedy and desperation, anger and impotence broke her spirit, and her embodied soul started living in an unconscious state of insanity.

She would never recover and come back to sanity. By wanting everything her own way, she lost it all, including herself. Natural instincts are not always the right solution to personal needs.

Peter Egger, the righteous and clever man, who had promised solemnly and officially to God and to himself to be pure and chaste, let his guard down.

The moment he engaged in the illicit sexual intercourse, he was perfectly aware of his actions. His excitement, tipsiness and stupidity are not excuses.

They might rest capacity to his judgment in that particular instance, but they will never be enough to prove his innocence.

He knew what he was doing, but did it anyway, muting the voices of his conscience.

On his way home, he was too stunned to speak. Slowly, the effects of the alcohol subsided. Far away from the electrifying atmosphere of the Carnival party, with no music, company or buzz, he began recapacitating and assessing the damage. The desolate landscape, full of debris and remains, brought him back to his senses.

Feelings of unworthiness, guilt and desperation transformed him into an emotional cripple. The possibility, not so remote, of having fathered a child terrified him. That would have meant the end of his dreams and the drastic termination of his ecclesiastical career.

Panic and remorse would torment him for days and years to come, despite his confessor's assurances.

He would do anything to deny what happened. His only recourse was to lie and cover it up.

Peter's overriding concern was not his serious offense to God and the breaking of his vow, but the fear of being caught. When he thought everything was buried and forgotten, his past came back to haunt him, and it happened at the worst moment of his life, just when he was about to be nominated Bishop of Salzburg.

He and his collaborators put in motion an elaborate scheme to suppress evidence and eliminate obstacles. Unfortunately, it was too late.

Deception was no longer an option. He had to confess and suffer the consequences. It was at this point that he rebelled to his authorities, taking off his mask and revealing his true self.

From that moment on, he solemnly swore to be sincere and transparent, even at the cost of his life.

He lived in obscurity and by the sweat of his brow.

Takeo Shirieda, honest, hard working and with not an unkind bone in his body, had a very modest opinion of himself. Attracted to a life of abnegation and sacrifice, he came to an early realization of being unworthy of it.

He would have gladly abandoned his vocation if it had not been for the insistence of his Master of Novices. The same with the priesthood, had it not been for his confessor.

The lack of a strong personality and the sense of duty and submission explain most of his adult life's decisions.

He couldn't resist the allure of a beautiful woman. Physically he accepted the invitation and surrendered, but psychologically he experienced an insurmountable barrier that prevented him from a complete copulation.

Only at his confessor's strong suggestion, would he hide his shameful sin and put on a deceitful mask.

However, his deceit and hypocrisy is only skin-deep, because deep down Takeo is a guileless, truthful man.

At the news of having fathered a son, his honesty does not allow him to suppress the evidence or, even worse, eliminate the source. The fall from grace and the temptation of fame and power does not obcaecate him.

Moreover, in spite of being spiritually destroyed, with no future or hope, he does not rebel against authority, institutions or rules.

He humbly accepts his punishment, convinced that he deserves it. He is happy to be alive, and spend the rest of his life in a convent, making amends for his immoral transgression.

Clearly, for Takeo deception is a forced-upon suit that does not agree with his moral stature. He is the only protagonist in whom deception does not go hand-in-hand with his nature.

In this parade of characters, Rudy Streaker represents something original in the area of deception.

Unlike Takeo, Rudy is a hardcore criminal. Born and bred in a world without laws or moral restraints, he exuded deception from every pore.

Violence and murder were the answer to his problems. He rarely dirtied his hands with blood. His henchmen, Stavros Kalidopulous and others, were in charge of carrying out murders and intimidations.

He knew how to cover his back and present an irreproachable front. However, his luck ended with the murder of his ex-girlfriend, Susan Bajouke. Put on trial, along with his right hand, Stavros, both were found guilty and both ended up in jail.

The days of confinement and solitude seemed to have softened his rough conscience and brought to the surface of his twisted nature some semblance of sincerity.

Serving a life sentence, he was heedless of the consequences. Every passing day, his tongue was getting looser and the need to unburden himself bigger.

It wasn't his conscience that propelled him into confessing the most heinous crime of his criminal career, but a natural psychological urge to share with his inmates and the world the treasures of his resourceful past. Confession in this case meant showing off, not contrition and purification.

One day, in front of an ecstatic audience, he recounted down to the last detail the murder of Castor Ishida.

The moment he heard his girlfriend Susan Bajouke had left him for the Japanese student, he flew into an irrepressible rage and hired a professional killer. He gave him clear instructions to massacre Castor, without leaving a clue. That was executed to the letter. Among sarcastic comments and deriding the inept investigators, he explained that the alleged capital X, splattered on the wall, was just a freak happening, with no meaning attached to it.

Anybody can imagine Ken Fresco's reaction to the startling revelation. For him and his dedicated team it amounted to the ultimate humiliation.

Rudy Streaker, the poster child for criminal behavior, had struck again from his jail cell, ridiculing police officers and investigators.

Unlike Kimiko who never acknowledged her deceptive behavior, Rudy publicly admitted his deceptions. Unlike Kimiko who always kept everything bottled up inside, Rudy uncorked himself, letting out no remorse, just arrogance and defiance.

Deception comes in many forms and shapes. Human nature is never tired of reforming and reshaping this powerful tool of survival.

Just take a moment to reflect on what is at the basis of our high-tech, fast-evolving society. Marketing, advertising, broadcasting, politics, religion, education, etc. all have something in common. They portray their products not according to facts but according to impact. We love to be impacted. If we are not impacted we are not attracted. In simpler words, we not only admit deception, we love it. It has been humankind's favorite tool of survival since time immemorial.

In conclusion, it is fair to say man and society are deceptive by nature, even if in varying degrees and measures.

Publications by the same author

1. - **Dario Lisiero**, *People Ideology, People Theology*, Exposition Press, New York 1980.

2. - **Dario Lisiero**, *My First Life*, Trafford, Victoria (Canada) 2004.

3. - Dario **Lisiero**, *Angelica*, Lulu, New York 2006

4. - **Dario Lisiero**, *José Benito Lamas, I. Reconstrucción histórica del gobierno eclesiástico en 1852-1857*, Editorial Dunken, Buenos Aires 2003.

5. - **Dario Lisiero**, *José Benito Lamas*, II. *Relectura del pensamiento y de la acción de José Benito Lamas*, Editorial Dunken, Buenos Aires 2004.

6. - Dario **Lisiero**, *Uruguayana*, Lulu, New York 2006.

7. - **Dario Lisiero**, *El Vicario Apostólico Jacinto Vera, Lustro Definitorio en la Historia del Uruguay, Primera Parte*, Lulu, New York 2006.

8. - **Dario Lisiero**, *El Vicario Apostólico Jacinto Vera, Lustro Difinitorio en la Historia del Uruguay, Segunda Parte*, Lulu, New York 2006.

9. - **Dario Lisiero**, *El Vicario de Montevideo*, Lulu, New York 2007.

10.- **Dario Lisiero**, *Justice Unfinished*, Lulu, New York, 2008.

11.- **Dario Lisiero**, *American Doctrine*, Lulu, New York, 2008.